# MURDER IN MANOLOS

A Heidi Hart Novel

# MURDER IN MANOLOS

Linsey Mastin

TATE PUBLISHING & *Enterprises*

*Murder in Manolos*
Copyright © 2011 by Linsey Mastin. All rights reserved.

---

No part of this publication may be reproduced, stored in a retrieval system or transmitted in any way by any means, electronic, mechanical, photocopy, recording or otherwise without the prior permission of the author except as provided by USA copyright law.

This novel is a work of fiction. Names, descriptions, entities, and incidents included in the story are products of the author's imagination. Any resemblance to actual persons, events, and entities is entirely coincidental.

The opinions expressed by the author are not necessarily those of Tate Publishing, LLC.

---

Published by Tate Publishing & Enterprises, LLC
127 E. Trade Center Terrace | Mustang, Oklahoma 73064 USA
1.888.361.9473 | www.tatepublishing.com

Tate Publishing is committed to excellence in the publishing industry. The company reflects the philosophy established by the founders, based on Psalm 68:11,
*"The Lord gave the word and great was the company of those who published it."*

Book design copyright © 2011 by Tate Publishing, LLC. All rights reserved.
*Cover design by Kristen Verser*
*Interior design by Joel Uber*

---

Published in the United States of America

ISBN: 978-1-61739-910-7
1. Fiction; Contemporary Women
2. Fiction; Mystery & Detective, Women Sleuths
11.01.05

# DEDICATION

This book is dedicated to Sarah, for teaching me how to be a friend, and to the Bryants, for teaching me how to be a nanny.

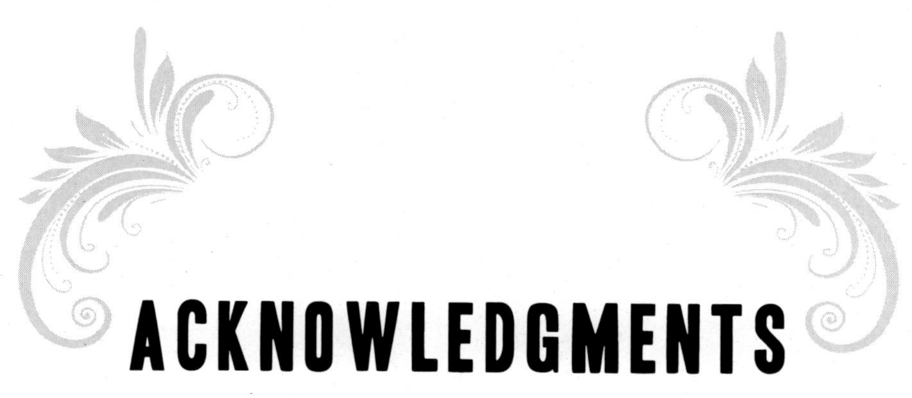

# ACKNOWLEDGMENTS


With much love and many thanks to:

...my Lord, Jesus Christ, who gave me the desire to write and blessed me with the ability to do so.

...my family for their love and support, and for all the times we caused a scene in a restaurant and laughed so hard we were crying.

...my Cheesecake Sisters, for being simply stunning. I heart you.

...my very first readers, otherwise known as my focus group. Lydia, you made me a better writer; Kim and Emily, you motivated me to write more and faster; Megan, Anne, Cari, Michelle, Rachael, Brent, Dan, Nikki, and so many others, you not only gave me great feedback, you helped fill my characters with personalities.

...my church, Draper Lake, for being my extended family and teaching me what "unconditional" means.

...Joe and Michelle for fixing my computer and saving my manuscript...and my life.

...Meg Cabot and Amy Sherman-Palladino for writing the way I want to write, and for being all about the girl power. Thanks for making me laugh, cry, and think.

# CHAPTER 1

*Sometimes you shouldn't believe the job description.*

I walked into my neighborhood's Starbucks with a feeling of dread.

*Probably not the feeling you generally associate with seeing your two best friends for the first time in ten weeks,* I thought to myself bitterly.

Despite the fact that I could clearly see my two friends were already there—that particular shade of fake blonde hair reflected even the smallest hint of light, resulting in a Prada-wearing beacon—I went and ordered the biggest calorie-loaded drink Starbucks had. My friends may be three sizes smaller than me, but at least I was happy.

Well, happier. Although, not at this moment in my life. I watched the coffee boy flip the lever to add espresso to my drink with a glum outlook on my life. I was nearly broke; the twenty-seven dollars in my bank account wasn't going to land me on any Fortune 500 list.

I picked up my drink and walked to the table where Rachel Mayer-Farthington and Jennifer Donnelly-Pierce were sitting, each holding a diet iced tea in their well-manicured hands.

"Heidi! Darling!" Rachel cried, throwing her arms around me. "Look at you! Look at you," she repeated, her voice becoming concerned.

I fought to keep the smile on my face. So I'd gained ten—fine, fifteen—pounds since I'd last seen them. And I'd let my perfect fake blonde hair go back to the natural mousy brown color. I secretly thought it was more flattering anyway, but it was still a shock even for me to look at in the morning. Surely Rachel and Jen wouldn't point it out to me; although, I knew for a fact that they would discuss it after I left.

"Oh, it's been a long summer, that's all," I said lightly, sipping on my coffee as if it were a lifeline.

*It really is at this point,* I thought in my most pitying tone.

Rachel and Jennifer looked at me as if they didn't know what to say to me. I knew they thought I was a failure according to the rules of our social set; I had managed to make it to twenty-three without marrying a young, rich businessman. It didn't necessarily have to be any certain businessman; it just had to be someone who would make a suitable first husband.

Both of my best friends had married just that—men that made plenty of money and could support their insatiable need to decorate homes and small children. That had been my plan since birth, but I had never embraced it the way my friends or my sisters did.

Rachel grinned at us, clearly ready to move on to a different topic, and she had one in mind.

"Well, I was going to wait a little longer to tell you guys, but I just have to say something or I'll burst. Donald and I are having a baby! I'm due in March!"

Jennifer let out a startled shriek and said, "No way! Oh, Rach, Kevin and I are due in March too!"

They hugged and screamed, and I tried to keep a smile on my face. Jennifer and Kevin, I could understand—Kevin Pierce was one of the nicest, smartest, best-looking people I had ever met, and one who would make a great dad—but Donald and Rachel was a hard idea to wrap my head around. Donald Farthington was very full of himself and not the most handsome guy in the world—stomach paunch from drinking, constant coffee and cigar aroma around him, white blonde hair that was slightly balding—and Rachel was beautiful. Besides his five million in the bank, I couldn't see anything that Rachel would be attracted to there. And for Rachel to be having a baby with him? To be risking the chance of giving the world another Donald? I didn't understand that. Even at thirty-five, Donald wasn't much to brag about; with his genes and Rachel's kind but dim mind, this kid didn't have a shot.

They were deep into a conversation about Gucci baby clothes and Versace maternity wear when they realized I was still there. I could see the "poor, husband-less, non-pregnant Heidi" look go through their eyes, but before they could remind me that it wasn't too late and that I still had plenty of time left to find a suitable husband, I perkily suggested, "Why don't you two go get some ideas on your nurseries? I mean, it could take you months to find the perfect crib sheets." Knowing them, maybe more. Jennifer spent ten months deciding between two wedding dresses. Rachel spent seven debating red roses or pink roses for her bouquet.

I wondered if they would actually leave, or if they would stay and try and convince me my life wasn't over. But I needn't have worried. In a flurry of hugs and kisses and well wishes, Rachel and Jennifer flew out of the coffee shop, gabbing a mile a minute.

I stood, stretched, and tossed my cup to the trashcan. The cup missed the hole. I sighed, closing my eyes.

"Seriously?" I muttered, stooping to pick it up. I theatrically flung my arm back to dunk the cup in the hole and felt my elbow connect with something very solid.

"*Oof!*"

I whirled around and gasped. A man had been standing behind me and had taken the full brunt of my elbow.

"Oh, my gosh! Oh, sir, I am so sorry! Are you okay?"

The man grinned and rubbed his jaw, the point of impact for my rogue elbow.

"I'm fine. A little jarred, but fine."

"No, really, I'm so sorry! Are you sore? Is there a bruise? Oh, man, if there's a bruise…" I realized I probably sounded like I was on crack, but instead of calming me that thought made me even more hyper-actively remorseful.

"I don't think there's a bruise. Yet. I mean, it could bruise, but it's okay if it does. Really."

"Can I buy you a cup of coffee? Or a bag of ice?" I asked, wringing my hands.

The man laughed, and I did a quick inventory of my victim. He was dressed impeccably, in a very nice suit, and was tall, blond, and very good-looking. Of course. He should be good looking. I never had the opportunity to slug any of the creepy people that I met in my daily life. I realized he was talking and tried to pay attention to his words and not debate whether or not his teeth were that straight and white on their own or if they had orthodontic assistance.

"I'm okay, thanks."

Horrified but unable to stop my arm from doing so, I reached out and touched his cheek.

"Oh, crap, your jaw is turning purple! Purple! How can that not hurt? Oh my gosh. You should just sue me! Except, please don't sue me. I have no money."

He laughed again.

"I'm not going to sue you. And it's okay about the bruise. I'll have a cool new war wound. The guys at the office will think I got it from some act of heroics."

"Still," I pushed, praying I hadn't made someone very powerful very injured. "Are you sure I can't buy you a cup of coffee? Or ice? Or something?"

"I'm okay, thank you. Thanks for your concern. I need to get my tea; I'm going to be late for work."

"Tea?" I asked skeptically. I didn't think anyone who was under the age of forty and wasn't British drank tea anymore. Maybe tea was in again.

The guy quickly explained, "I can't do coffee. I'm kind of anti-caffeine…as much as I can be."

"Wow. That's very…sixteenth century of you."

The guy paused. "I don't even know what to say to that."

"That's okay. In case you haven't noticed, I'm kind of strange… and a little quirky."

"I always enjoy quirk."

I shifted awkwardly. "Well…enjoy your tea."

The guy grinned at me and gave a sort of parting bow. "Enjoy your day. Don't beat up any other innocent bystanders."

"No promises, but I'll try," I joked. I waited until he had walked away before hitting myself in the head and muttering, "And, scene. Man, I'm graceful. Maybe tomorrow I'll accidentally brain Tom Cruise. Not that at this part of his career he doesn't need it, but…I am an idiot."

I pushed the door open and left Starbucks. I wandered aimlessly for a while, but my thoughts were racing. I needed a job. I needed a place to live, considering my lease on the apartment my father had rented for me was up in six days. I needed money and security and to know that my four years in business school hadn't been a waste of time. True, my father, the great Maxwell Hart, had offered me a six-figure job at his firm with the possibility of a promotion within the year, but who wanted to spend their entire life under Daddy's wing? Or so I had thought to myself boldly ten weeks ago, when I had graduated. Now I was missing the shade of that great big wing, not to mention the paycheck and the health benefits.

I bought a newspaper from the man on the corner and flipped to the classifieds. Not a lot of options. A broker position, but I'd have to lie my butt off about my qualifications, and, considering the physical pain I had just caused a stranger, I wasn't sure how many more hits my immortal soul could take.

A receptionist was needed for a well-respected law firm, but I couldn't see myself doing that. Besides, my social skills tended to fly out the window while I was on the phone. For some reason, as soon as I got a receiver next to my mouth, I became a caveman, totally unaware of any cordial way to conduct business or even a conversation that wasn't filled with grunts and awkward pauses. That, and my father sometimes dealt with that law firm, and there was no way I was going to explain to my father that after whining about being independent for so long, I was going to take a job jotting down messages and making coffee.

The last thing that looked even remotely like there might be a chance I could do it made me shudder: a nanny position. I had loathed all the nannies my siblings and I had gone through in our childhood. True, Max—my brother—had been horrible to each and every one of them ("So like his father," our mother used to say bitterly whenever Max would throw a fit, to which I always thought, *Well, maybe you shouldn't have named him Max. Maybe Shakespeare was wrong, and there is something in a name*), but the nannies had been pretty horrible in return. Diana and

Leslie, my sisters, had always gotten on well with the nanny, but I couldn't for the life of me think of a single one they had actually liked. Could I really have a job where the kids hated me?

I stopped and read the rest of the ad. "Excellent pay," it read, "with benefits and perks. A one-child household."

I considered this. Maybe I could use all of my negative experiences with my nannies to be a good one. I had a sudden vision of a little girl, freckled, pigtailed, looking up at me with missing teeth and telling me how fun I was to play with. I looked back down at the ad and sighed. I dialed the contact number and prepared to sell myself.

A pleasant sounding woman answered. "George Dayton's office, Emily speaking, how may I help you?"

"Hi, my name is Heidi Hart, and I wanted to see about the nanny job?" I blurted out, trying to sound perky.

"Right, well, Miss Hart, I have an interview time open at three o'clock this afternoon, would you like to come then?" Emily said easily.

*Now this was someone who could talk on the phone well,* I thought.

"Three is fine. What's the address? Oh, never mind, I have it right here in the ad! Sorry!" I closed my eyes in disgust at my utter lack of suave phone skills.

Emily, ever the professional secretary, simply said, "I'll inform Mr. Dayton of your appointment. Have a nice morning."

I returned to my apartment and dug out a nice black pantsuit. I had all of my belongings packed up as best I could so I could leave as soon as I found another place to live. I wondered if the nanny job was live-in or not. I probably should have asked.

At a quarter to three, I walked into George Dayton's office and froze. My father was standing in the lobby, flipping through some folders.

"Heidi," he said, surprised. "What brings you to the offices of George Dayton? Not getting a divorce; you'd have to be married to do that."

"Funny, Dad. And no. I'm here for an interview," I said, clasping my hands.

"Really? You mean you might work for George Dayton?"

Judging from the impressed look on my father's face, I assumed he knew nothing of the nanny position. Fine by me.

"Yes. I might."

"Well, I'll pass that on to your mother. Good luck, Heidi."

As Maxwell Hart left the room, I felt like a balloon deflating. Four years in business school to take a nanny position? Was I serious? I should hold out, see if I could find a decent marketing job. One that I hadn't already applied for, that is. Although there was a good chance that such a job didn't exist anymore.

Emily, the receptionist, stood and pointed toward a closed door. "Mr. Dayton will see you now."

I nodded at her and walked as confidently as I could manage into a very nice office. I gave a quick thought to how much nicer this man's office was than my apartment before concentrating my attentions on the man himself. George Dayton was in his early sixties, with white hair and tan skin, and was still a very handsome man. A picture of a beautiful woman sat in a gold frame on his desk. A picture of a little girl with blonde hair was in another frame, and, finally, one of three kids—two boys in their late twenties and a teenage girl.

"Hello, Heidi," he said warmly. He stood and shook my hand. "Let me tell you a little bit about the job. You'd get your own suite—a room, a bathroom, and a sitting room—and a weekly budget for activities conducted with Lauren—"

"Lauren is your daughter?" I asked.

"Yes. Anyway, let's see, suite, budget…oh, yes. A car of your choice, a phone with whatever kind of plan you need, Sundays off, and a starting salary of…" George trailed off, scribbling a number on a post-it note and sliding it toward me. I looked at it, refrained from fainting, and nodded my approval.

"Your responsibilities would be making sure Lauren is on time to school, picking her up from school, and making sure she is happy. She has piano lessons and dance lessons, and you'd need to make sure she gets to those on time. It's a fairly simple job, to be honest."

I cleared my throat and said, "Sounds like it."

"Do you have any questions?"

"Uh…what is Lauren like?"

"Lauren is a sweet girl who needs someone to look after her. She'd do really well with a big sister, but that didn't happen. She was stuck with two brothers, although don't get me wrong, they dote upon her with ridiculous abandon," George joked.

I smiled. "I wish I had an older brother like that. Max, my brother, wasn't all that supportive of anything I did, let alone dote in any way, shape, or form."

"Have you ever been a nanny before?" George asked.

"Um, no. But I have a three-year-old nephew named Maxie. He's Max's son, Maxwell Hemmingway Hart the Third. I've kept him before, so your daughter shouldn't be that different, right?" I said, trying to sound like I was sure of what I was saying.

"Well, Lauren isn't exactly a toddler. She's fifteen."

I blinked. "Fifteen? And she needs a nanny?"

"I believe she needs someone to look after her. Her mother was…spirited. I don't want Lauren to be quite so devil-may-care with her life."

"Was?"

"Excuse me?"

"You said she was spirited?"

"Yes. Lauren's mother died ten years ago. We never speak of it."

"Oh," I mumbled, feeling bad for having brought it up. "Well, uh, do you have any other questions for me?"

"Did you bring in a résumé?"

I handed him the sheet of paper with all my college information on it, plus my internships and a few other tidbits I had added, hoping to make it look more impressive than it really was.

George read it carefully, moving his mouth with the words and occasionally nodding or highlighting something. Finally, he looked up, took his glasses off, and said simply, "Would you like to start today?"

"Really?" I gasped. "I got the job? Just like that?"

"You're bright and personable, and that's what I was looking for in a companion for Lauren. Here's our address"—George paused to scribble something on another post-it note—"and I'll call around the company car to take you. I will also let Alexis, my wife, know you're coming. Lauren won't be home for another hour or so, so Alexis will show you around the house, and Tom, the butler, will help you with any bags you have. You can bring in your things whenever is convenient for you. Alexis will also help you with keys, passwords to the security systems, and so on. I'll have some papers for you to sign when I get home, and I hope this will be the beginning of a very successful partnership."

I grinned. "Me too!"

George showed me out of his office, and I walked down to the garage to meet Greg, the chauffer. From there, Greg (a forty-year-old, married father of two little girls, he informed me proudly) took me to my apartment and helped me carry and load all of my boxes. I left the key with the landlord and signed out of my apartment. On the drive over to "the house" as Greg referred to it, I was suddenly struck by the enormity of my situation. I had a job. A job I had no idea how to do. A job that required me to take care of—no, sorry, be a companion to—a teenage girl I had never met, that was "spirited" like her deceased mother. Just as I was starting to talk myself out of the job, Greg tapped on the window and called, "Home!"

I looked up at the most impressive apartment building I had ever seen, even for Manhattan. My parents lived in a lovely, historical building. My siblings had very modern, hip digs, but this was a building of architectural dreams. We pulled into the garage and rode the elevator to the penthouse.

First off, I had never seen a penthouse that was two stories high. That was definitely a new experience. And I had never seen someone as pretty as the woman walking around the front hall of the penthouse, either.

"Hi! Are you Heidi?" the woman asked, rushing toward me.

"Yes," I said, staring dumbly and taking a small step back. I offered her what I hoped was a big smile, but I was afraid it came out more like scared grimace.

"Oh, wonderful! My name is Alexis Dayton, and I hope you feel comfortable here. Let me show you your rooms!"

*Rooms. Huh. So George hadn't been kidding,* I thought to myself. *I will actually have rooms to myself. They are probably small. Better not get my hopes up.*

Then the other shoe fell. This woman that was showing me around was maybe a decade older than me; I'd put her age around thirty-four. Yet she said she was Alexis Dayton, George's wife? She was almost half his age!

I suddenly had new respect for George.

Alexis walked up the stairs, and, as I followed her, I got a good look at her. She had shoulder-length, soft brown hair that curled under, ivory skin, and big brown eyes that crinkled prettily when she smiled. She was wearing a cute little dress and heels that were the exact same color of royal blue and a headband in her hair. She was a few inches shorter than me, and definitely twenty pounds lighter, but she didn't look overly skinny at all. She looked, in a word, perfect. And the weird thing was, it looked natural. And I actually liked her. She seemed genuinely nice.

I wonder how she got to be a New Yorker.

I pulled two of my bags along with me, looking around as we went. This place was definitely impressive. There were two wings; one that was done in soft gold tones and the other in richer violet and lilac. That, Alexis told me, was Lauren's side of the house.

"You and Lauren will have the east wing to yourselves," Alexis said, smiling warmly at me. "George and I have the west wing. The bedroom suites downstairs are for when the boys stay over, which isn't frequently, but we keep them ready because George loves it when all the kids are here."

"He has…two sons?" I asked, remembering the pictures in his office. I hadn't been able to see the faces of any of the kids, but I could tell they were male and older than the girl standing between them.

"Yes, Lance and Lucas," Alexis said, her smile softening. "They are such sweet boys."

"And they don't live here? Are they away at school?" I asked.

She laughed. "No, no, Lance is thirty, and Lucas is twenty-six. In fact, Lance is married and has a four-year-old daughter."

I nearly swallowed my tongue. This woman, who looked like she was in her early thirties, had a stepson that was just a few years younger than her? And she was someone's step-grandma? If someone told me the mayor was sending everyone in New York from north Albany on up to live in Maine, I'd have been less surprised.

"You're a grandma?" I blurted out.

Alexis shrugged but didn't look upset. "Well, technically. Isobel just calls me Alexis. We don't want to confuse her with the two grandma thing."

"But I thought George's first wife died? His kids' mother?" I asked, thoroughly confused.

Alexis sighed and opened a door to a sitting room decorated in blues and greens. She motioned for me to sit down and sat down across from me.

"Maureen Dayton is Lance and Lucas's mother. She and George divorced about twenty years ago. Daniella Dayton was Lauren's mother. She died about ten years ago. George doesn't like for anyone to talk about it, though, because it still hurts Lauren. George and I got married a little over two years ago."

I nodded to show I was following, but I still had a hundred questions.

"Lance is married to Julie, and they have a four-year-old daughter named Isobel Ella Dayton. He works with George at the investment house. Lucas is…" Alexis trailed off as she tried to find the right words. "Lucas is finding himself right now. He has a job at a PR company, but we don't think he likes it very much. He wants to do something else with his life; he just doesn't know what yet."

I knew how he felt.

"Lauren is fifteen, as you probably know, and George is just worried that she's lonely. This big old house gets kind of empty sometimes, and we think it would be better for her if someone could be here as her companion. She's very sweet and not a bit of trouble, but George is worried she'll be like her mother," Alexis said, laughing nervously and slipping a piece of hair behind her ear.

"Why would that be bad, exactly?" I asked, frowning. "Was Daniella—"

"Oh," Alexis said, blushing. "No, she was a lovely woman, or so I'm told. She just…marched to the beat of her own drum. Her own orchestra, some would say."

"How did she die?" I asked, feeling morbid.

"She drowned in a boating accident," Alexis said immediately, as if she had said it a hundred times. I blinked. Her phrasing made me think of a book I had read years before, but I couldn't put my finger on which book. That was going to bother me.

"I'm so sorry to hear that," I said politely, and suddenly we heard a door shut and someone's feet running up the stairs.

"Lauren must be home," Alexis said, looking relieved to be done with our conversation.

A teenager burst into the room just then and froze when she saw us. She was wearing a short plaid skirt, an un-tucked white Oxford, an open navy blazer, and a red tie. Between the outfit and her pretty, round face, she looked like she'd just stepped out of that old Britney Spears video. She looked at me and then at her stepmother and asked, "Who is this?"

"Lauren, your father has hired someone to live with us to be a companion to you when we aren't here or when you don't want to hang out with your parents," Alexis explained. She stood, straightened her skirt, and pointed to me. "This is Heidi Hart. She's going to be moving in to your guest room."

*Her* guest room? Jeez.

Lauren looked at her stepmother in horror, her face slowly turning red. "He hired someone to be my friend?" she asked, her voice breaking. She dropped her backpack and ran out of the room, and a few seconds later we heard a door slam.

# CHAPTER 2

Alexis sighed. "I probably could have handled that introduction better," she said ruefully, and I was inclined to agree.

"I'll go talk to her," I offered, trying to convince myself that I wasn't the completely wrong person for this job.

"Thanks," Alexis said gratefully. "I'm going to go give the cook the dinner menu. You eat meat, right?"

"That I do," I said absently, staring after Lauren.

She excused herself, and I went to the door that Lauren had slammed. I knocked on it. "Lauren? It's Heidi. I totally understand if you don't want to talk to me right now, but can you open up just for a second? I want to get a better look at your shoes."

She opened the door frowning. "My shoes?" she repeated, looking at me as if I were demented.

"Are they really Chanel?" I asked, raising my eyebrows.

"Yeah." She pointed one of her feet toward me so I could admire them. "Sarah Jessica Parker has the same pair."

"Oh, I love her," I sighed, smiling. "I think she and Matthew Broderick are the cutest couple in the world."

"I know, right?" Lauren grinned. "Who wouldn't want Ferris Bueller to end up with Carrie Bradshaw?"

We both laughed at that, and she studied me for a minute, the wariness waning from her blue eyes.

"You can come in if you want to," she said, and I followed her into her room. Her bedroom was beautifully decorated in purple and blue, with stack after stack of fashion magazines on the floor and desk and a huge bouquet of irises, tulips, lilacs, violets, and hydrangeas next to her bed.

"Beautiful flowers," I said, leaning over to smell them.

"They're from Lance," Lauren said, smiling. "He likes to send me flowers every once in a while to brighten my day."

"Nice brother," I said, wondering if my brother had ever sent anyone flowers. Maybe his wife, but I doubted it.

"I like them," Lauren said, meaning the flowers, "but Lucas brings me these."

She opened the drawer to her bedside table, and I peered inside. Thousands of tiny knick-knacks filled the drawer—everything from small, smooth rocks in every shade and hue to miniature doll furniture to little glass figurines. Everything in the drawer was one of a kind and could fit in my palm.

"Do you collect miniatures or something?"

"Ever since I was little. Lucas got me started. When my mom died, Daddy gave me one of her pearl necklaces, and I accidentally broke it. Instead of telling on me, Lucas took all the beads except one to the jewelry store and had them restrung. He took the leftover one and told me that I could collect these little bitty things and that it would be like I was collecting them for my mom."

My heart melted. "That was very sweet of him."

"Yeah, that's Lucas. He's like that. I realize now he was just trying to cheer up a sad little kid, but he really made me feel better about my mom dying. So I can't complain too much," Lauren said, reaching into the drawer. She pulled out a pearl. "See? Isn't it pretty?"

"Very," I said, smiling at her.

*Lauren doesn't miss much,* I thought to myself as she replaced the pearl and closed the drawer. She slipped off her blazer, got a hanger out of her closet, and hung up the coat. She turned to me, her sun-kissed face slightly pink, and said, "Are you really here to be my friend? I mean, are you getting paid to be my friend?"

I shook my head. "I don't know why I'm here," I said honestly, shrugging my shoulders. "I saw the ad and answered it because I needed a job. Your dad said I'm just supposed to be here for you. I may not be qualified to do much else, but I could be on the Olympic 'being there' team."

She smiled a little and said, "You don't have to be my friend."

"No," I agreed, sitting down on her bed. "But I think I'll end up being your friend anyway."

She grinned at me, a real grin, and said, "What did you think of Alexis?"

"I've never met anyone that pretty. Or uncomfortable."

Lauren laughed, tilting her head back as she did so. She really was a very pretty girl. "Alexis is one of the nicest people in the entire world. She has her own charity foundation, did you know that? The Alexis Dayton Foundation against Children's Hunger. She started it two years ago, right after she married my dad. She does all sorts of charity stuff, so she's gone a lot. Daddy says she's making the world a better place."

"Does your dad do charity work too?"

"Sometimes Alexis makes him come to banquets and balls and stuff, but mostly he just writes checks. She's the one who'll get down and dirty building houses and distributing clothes."

I nodded. That was kind of like my parents. My father did all the work, earning the money that kept my family filthy rich, and my mother's job was to wear the wealth well. She did it splendidly.

I heard a melodic buzzing go off. Lauren reached into her purse (Gucci, and it was making me salivate) and answered a small purple phone.

"Hey, Lucas," she said cheerfully after checking caller ID. "It was good…I got an A on that English paper you helped me with…No, just a B. I don't care about biology." She laughed at something he said and responded, "Very funny…Well, when I got home, Daddy had hired someone to come live with us as my companion, so that was different…No, I'm not kidding…No, it's not that big of a deal. I like her."

She sent me a smile since she knew that I could obviously hear every word she was saying.

"Yeah…Well, you don't have to, but I wouldn't mind seeing you…Okay. I'll tell Alexis…What did you do today?"

She listened quietly for a moment, moving efficiently around the room to tidy up her desk and the top of her bureau.

"You're kidding!" she said suddenly, laughing. "Are you okay?"

Her eyes were wide, and her mouth was partially open. I wondered what in the world could have happened that made her that interested.

"Well, I'll give Alexis a heads up about that so she won't freak out. I'll see you tonight, then, okay? I love you."

She hung up and giggled. "Someone punched my brother in the face today."

I raised an eyebrow. "On purpose?"

"He said it was some loon on the street. They were probably trying to mug him or something," Lauren said absently, rifling through one of her drawers. She pulled out a pair of jeans and said, "I'm going to change before dinner. Did Alexis show you which room was yours?"

"Uh, yeah," I said, moving to the door.

"Heidi?"

"Yeah?"

Lauren looked at me for a long moment and then said with a small smile, "I think I'm going to like having you here. It will be like having a sister."

I smiled at her, thinking about my sisters and hoping it wasn't anything like having a sister. I opened the door to my new room and was pretty impressed: queen-sized bed, large bureau, walk-in closet, spacious bathroom, ancient oak night table. Everything in this room was done in silvers and pale blues, and it looked like it shone. I dropped my bags on the bed and realized that someone had brought up the rest of my stuff. I spent about an hour putting things away until there was a knock at the door. I looked up and Lauren stood there, barefoot in jeans and a pink baby doll shirt.

"I think dinner's about ready," she said, looking around the room. "Are you hungry?"

"Am I…um…supposed to eat with you guys?" I asked awkwardly. "I mean, technically, I'm the staff."

Lauren rolled her eyes. "No, technically, you're my friend, and I am inviting you to dinner."

I smiled and said, "Let's go."

I followed her down the stairs and wondered again why George thought this girl needed watching. She was clearly self-sufficient, self-confident, and mature enough to take care of herself. So far she hadn't said anything that made me think she was remotely wild. I vowed to ask him as soon as I could to remind me why I was here.

We entered the dining room in time to hear Alexis exclaim, "Oh, what happened to your face?"

Lauren winced. "Lucas must be here. I forgot to warn Alexis."

We followed the voices until they led us to the den. George was sitting in an armchair with a decanter of brandy, looking amused at something. Alexis had both hands pressed to her hips and was looking disapprovingly up at someone much taller than she was.

"Heidi," George said in a rumbling voice upon noticing our entrance to the room, "this is my son, Lucas. Lucas, this is Heidi Hart, Lauren's new companion."

Among Lauren's complaints about the term "companion," Lucas turned to face me and all the color drained out of his face.

Probably going to mine, considering my face flushed dark red. Because, of course, in a city of two million people, I would have to get a job working for the father of the man I had elbowed in the face just a few hours ago.

My mouth dropped open, and Lucas said, "You?" with an insulting amount of incredulity.

"Am I being punked?" I muttered before plastering a fake smile on my face. "It's nice to meet you, Lucas. I'm sorry to hear...I mean, I'm sorry to see...Sorry about your face."

"I think you apologized enough this morning," he said, his voice lifting to a level of amusement.

"This morning?" Lauren asked, looking intrigued. "Do you two know each other?"

"Heidi gave me this," Lucas said affably, pointing to his purple jaw.

Three sets of eyebrows rose at once, and I frowned at him. "Not on purpose," I said, feeling the blush coming back on. "He sort of ran into my elbow."

Lauren let out a short burst of laughter, and George smiled. Alexis remained surprised. "Small world," she said lightly, obviously not sure what to say.

Lucas hadn't stopped looking at me like he wanted to burst out laughing, and I got the impression that he would be laughing at me, not with me. I turned stiffly to Lauren and said, "You mentioned something about dinner?"

"Oh, yes," Alexis said suddenly, snapping out of her surprised reverie. She gestured toward the door and said, "Go ahead to the table."

George shook his head as he walked past me, still smiling. Lucas followed his father out, grinning at me as he walked by, obviously enjoying the turn of events. Lauren linked her arm through mine and said, "Did you really slug my brother?"

"Elbowed. Accidentally," I repeated through clenched teeth.

"Huh," Lauren said, and she sent me a sly grin. She shook her head and pulled me to the dining room.

We sat down in chairs across from Lucas, with George and Alexis on either end of the table. I was tempted to mock the traditional family dinners, but I kind of thought it was cute. My family had never sat down to meals together. My father had never been home from work on time, my mother usually ate out with friends, my sisters were usually on some sort of a diet that prohibited regular dining anyway, and my brother was no one I would have wanted to sit and spend time with.

A maid came out with plates of salad. I fought the urge to pick the mandarin oranges out of my salad and waited for everyone else to be served. No one else seemed bothered by the fruit in their salads, so I just ate around them. I was an adult. I could refrain from commenting that mandarin oranges reminded me of obese worms.

I had a mouthful of cucumber when Lucas asked, "Have you ever been a…what did you call it…companion before, Heidi?"

I swallowed and looked up at him from my plate. He had a smug grin on his face as if he were enjoying something immensely.

"No," I said, wiping my mouth.

"It's so funny that you found this job, then. What were you doing?" Lucas inquired, sipping his water.

I tried not to glare at him. *I should set a good example for Lauren,* I reminded myself. "I graduated in May with a degree in business, and I was having some…difficulties finding a position."

"Really? You look like someone that would get hired quickly. Good for overall company image," Lucas said, taking a bite of salad but not breaking eye contact with me.

I heard Lauren giggle softly under her breath as I bristled. I realized that while his comment hadn't been derogatory—he had, I suppose, just called me pretty in some strange way—it still rubbed me the wrong way.

"I guess the businesses of downtown New York have already filled their…company image quota for the year," I said stiffly, and this time I heard George chuckle.

Oh great. This man was taking his revenge for the bruise I had given him that morning by making me look like an idiot in front of his family, also known as my new employers. I nearly cried with relief when at that moment, the maid came back in with the main course—lamb chops, string beans, and new potatoes. I shoved my salad bowl at her and accepted my plate with a gratitude that made her frown at me as if she was wondering at my sanity.

I was wondering about my sanity. What was I doing here? I was horrible with kids, and I knew nothing about teenagers, not having been around one since I was one. Even if this was a high paying job with perks that were pretty darn perky, and even with George's assurance this would be easy and Lauren turning out to be pretty cool, what in the world had convinced me I could do this?

I opened my mouth to say that I had made a mistake, that I was sorry about the trouble, but I had better go now, not knowing where in the world I would go, when George said, "Lauren, have you picked out something to wear to that class yet?"

Lauren grinned at her father with an eyebrow raised. He had changed subjects so quickly that Alexis looked like she might have whiplash, and Lucas looked disappointed that I wasn't in the hot seat anymore.

"If by class you mean ballroom dancing, and if by something to wear you mean my formal gown, then, no. I haven't had time to shop for one yet."

"Heidi can take you tomorrow," George said, spearing a potato with his fork. "Just charge whatever you want to my card and go have lunch or something. Get to know each other."

Lauren perked up at the word *charge* and grinned at me.

"Let's go to the Tavern on the Green," she said excitedly, forgetting her food completely. "And then we can go to Bloomingdales and Saks and Bendel's and—"

"Stop her now, Dad, before she shops you out of house and home," Lucas teased, and Lauren shot him a look. They were very comfortable together, I realized. I had initially assumed that Lucas and Lance would treat Lauren like a baby since they were so much older than she was, but Lucas, at least, treated her like a friend. That was, so far, his only redeeming quality—the fact that he was so good to his little half-sister.

He turned his expression to me and added, "Do you like shopping, Heidi?"

I shrugged. "When I have something to shop for, I like it. I don't like just going out and spending money and window shopping."

"But it's so much fun!" Alexis said, grinning. "At least, if you're good at it. Haven't you seen *Breakfast at Tiffany's*? It's the ultimate window shopper's movie."

"I've seen it," I said, swirling the water in my glass, "but I liked *Roman Holiday* better."

Lucas grinned approvingly as Lauren and Alexis gasped. Apparently the entire Dayton family loved old movies and was very opinionated about them. They discussed their favorites—and least favorites—with rapid-fire commentary until dessert came when they called a truce, and we all ate chocolate cake that I could have married if it were legal to wed a baked good.

I was licking the icing off of my fork when Lucas started looking at me again. It was subtle at first; I would see him out of the corner of my eye. Then when I turned to see what he wanted, he would turn away. Eventually he stopped turning away and started sending me grins. I couldn't figure out why he was doing that, so I kept checking my chin for stray food, never finding anything.

As dinner and dessert plates were being cleared from the table, Lauren said, "I'm going to go work on homework. You'll come up soon, right, Heidi?"

I smiled at her and nodded. Alexis left the table too to fill out some thank you cards. When it became very clear to me that Lucas wasn't leaving the table anytime soon, I sighed and turned to George.

"Mr. Dayton," I said, as politely as I could, "I don't mean to sound ungrateful for this job or that I'm doubting your judgment in anyway, but to be perfectly honest I still don't understand why I'm here. Lauren is a wonderful girl. I really like her, but I haven't seen anything to make me think that she needs someone to watch her."

George looked at me for a long time, and I could see Lucas out of my peripheral vision glancing back and forth between us. Finally George said, in a voice a great deal gentler than I would have thought possible, "Daniella, Lauren's mother, she had some problems. She suffered from depression, and she got lonely easily. Even when the kids were all here, sometimes she still felt very alone. It broke my heart that I couldn't make her happier in that aspect. Lauren doesn't have many friends at school. Most kids know about the scandal her mother caused many years ago, and

I couldn't let her go through the same things that Daniella went through. I just want her to be happy, and I think she would be happier if someone was there for her to go to and talk to about her day or her problems."

I nodded, feeling slightly better. I wasn't supposed to tame some wild child. I was truly here to be her friend, to make her teenage existence a little easier. Still a tall order, but I could handle that.

Then I realized I was basically getting paid to listen to a teenager whine.

"Still, Mr. Dayton, I don't think Lauren truly needs someone to entertain her," I said truthfully.

George looked at me for a long moment and finally said, "If you don't want this job, you can always quit. Lauren seems very taken with you, but she'll get over it. All you have to do is say the word."

I pursed my lips. The man was going to make me choose between having a job and having a small shred of dignity.

"Of course I still want this job," I said, sitting back.

Dignity doesn't make chocolate cake as delicious as the Daytons' chef.

"Very good. And please, Heidi, call me George. We're all going to be living together; we should be on a first-name basis."

I nodded and stood mutely. I contemplated saying something more and ended up saying, "I'm going to go finish unpacking. I'll see you...well, later I guess."

I turned and walked out of the room feeling like an idiot.

A hand on my elbow stopped me halfway up the stairs. I turned and was eye to eye with Lucas, who was two steps below me.

"What?" I asked uncomfortably, as he still had hold of my elbow.

He looked troubled. "Can I talk to you in private for a minute?"

I looked around. "We are in private. Everyone is somewhere else. That's pretty private."

He gave me a withering glare and jerked his head up. "Come on. Which room is yours?"

"Oh, no," I said with a chuckle. "We aren't talking in my bedroom. That's the last thing I need today, my new boss seeing his son coming out of the help's room."

Lucas threw me a small smile and said, "He'd probably understand actually, but I see what you mean. Lauren might be upset."

We were standing on the upstairs landing by that point, and he grabbed my upper arm and pulled me into a linen closet the size of my old apartment's bathroom.

"Look, I'm not saying that you being here is bad in anyway," Lucas started, and I couldn't help but laugh.

"This sounds promising," I said, crossing my arms and leaning against a shelf with chenille blankets stacked on it.

"But there's a few things you should probably know before spending time with this family," he continued as if I hadn't spoken at all.

"Wow, you must hate bringing girls home," I teased, and that did catch his attention.

"Maybe you could call this conversation a preemptive strike," he said wryly, and I nearly fell off the shelf ledge. He grinned at my surprise and went on, "My mother and my father divorced over twenty years ago, but because they have two children and a grandchild together, they are still friendly. We often get together. However, my mother doesn't really care for Alexis, so we try to keep them apart."

"How can anyone not like Alexis?" I asked. "It's like not liking puppies."

Lucas shook his head and looked a little amused. "Well, when your ex-husband marries someone that's just a few years older than his oldest child, it makes you a little insecure, I guess."

I crinkled my nose. "Gotcha."

"My mom didn't like Daniella either, but she adores Lauren. I think it's the whole she never had a daughter thing. Daniella, well, Mom kind of blamed, or really blames Daniella for breaking up her marriage. Which isn't possible, by the way, since Dad and Daniella didn't meet until my parents had been divorced for over two years. I think my mom had some weird idea that they were going to get back together eventually. Mom didn't exactly mourn when Daniella died," Lucas admitted, looking upset for the first time in this conversation.

I didn't know what to say. Here he was spilling the family secrets to me in a linen closet, and, for the life of me, I had no words.

"Daniella's death nearly killed my father. He really loved her. He was happier in the eight years he was with Daniella than I've ever seen him. The only two times I have ever seen my father cry in my whole life was when Lauren was born and when he got the news that Daniella had drowned."

Without explanation, I felt a lump forming in my own throat. I couldn't imagine what it must have been like for this family to get that awful news. I suddenly wanted to give each and every one of them—even George, even Lucas—a great big hug, especially Lauren.

Lucas continued, drawing a breath. "Daniella was one of those people you couldn't help but like, but she had her faults. Like Dad said, she was depressed. She was a society girl before she got married, and she was used to the life of cameras and bright lights and attention. Getting married and having a baby put a big damper on all that fun. You know how beautiful Lauren is?"

I nodded.

"She's all Daniella. Looks just like her, except for her ears maybe. Looking at her is like looking at a ghost."

I shivered. Poor Lauren. All this stuff going around behind her back.

"Did…was Lauren with Daniella when she died?"

Lucas's jaw tightened, and I could see a muscle jump there. "No," he said finally, his hand clenching one of the chenille blankets on the shelf. "Daniella was at a party on a yacht. She left Lauren with my dad and went off for a party with her friends. She had too much wine and fell overboard, and by the time her fellow drunks could get to her, she had drowned."

My heart broke for Lauren, for Daniella, and for the whole ordeal.

"Oh, I…" I trailed off, not knowing what to say.

Lucas nodded once. "Yeah, I know. It kills me sometimes to look at her and know that she knows how her mother died. Her behavior wasn't exactly a highlight that night."

"Lucas?"

"Yeah?"

"Why exactly are you telling me this? I mean, I'm grateful because, to be honest, I was pretty curious, but why do you think I need to know?" I asked, my eyes searching his face.

He looked down at me for a long moment before saying, "I just wanted you to know what you're getting into. We have a lot of skeletons in the closet. Wow, that sounded incredibly morbid. What I meant was, the Daytons are kind of known for their drama. I just didn't want you to get overwhelmed and quit."

I grinned. "So I guess I really am forgiven for clocking you this morning?"

Lucas smiled at me. "It's completely forgotten. Actually that's a lie. I'll probably tease you mercilessly about it, but you won't have to worry about me returning the favor, if that's what you're asking."

I assumed the conversation was over, so I put my hand on the doorknob to leave. He apparently had the same idea, and his hand covered mine for a nanosecond. I glanced up at him to make a joke about it, but he was slightly pink and avoiding eye contact. So I kept my mouth shut. This really was a weird family.

He reached out again, cautiously this time, and opened the door, saying, "After you."

I was almost to my bedroom door when he called my name very softly. I turned to look at him over my shoulder and he said, "Night."

I gave him an amused smile and said it back, escaping to my room. It was still a disaster area, with boxes and clothes everywhere. Plus something I didn't pack: a fifteen-year-old blonde girl sitting in my armchair reading from a big textbook.

Lauren glanced up when she heard the door click closed and gave me an appraising look. "That took a while. What were you doing?"

"Just…chatting with your family," I said nonchalantly, grabbing some hangers and starting in on the pile of clothes at the foot of my bed.

"Including Lucas?" Lauren asked, her eyes back on the textbook, her smile bordering on smug.

"Yes," I said, raising an eyebrow.

"Huh," she said, and this time she was really working to keep her smile under control. Her lips fairly twitched with unexpressed amusement. "What about?"

I narrowed my eyes. "How nosy you are," I said, throwing a pillow at her.

Lauren laughed and said, "I'm sorry. I'll behave. Tell me about yourself. Do you have any siblings?"

I nodded, stacking belts onto one particularly sturdy hanger. "I have an older brother named Max and two sisters, Diana and Leslie. They're all married, but Max is the only one that has any children. His son is three, and his name is Maxie. Actually it's really kind of funny because both my sisters and my sister-in-law are all pregnant right now. They're all due within the next month. And my two best friends are pregnant too, but they aren't due until next spring."

Lauren raised her eyebrows. "Does that make you want to have kids?"

"Not really," I said honestly, pausing to look at her. "I'm only twenty-three. It frustrates me that society's expectations haven't changed that much in the last two hundred years. I mean, have you ever read any Jane Austen?"

"Yes," Lauren answered immediately.

"Well, the heroines in her books—and really girls in general in that time period—their main concern was to marry well and marry soon. Those are the kind of girls I was raised around. Both my best friends are only twenty-three too, and they've been married for less than a year. They assume after you get married you're supposed to have kids, so that's what they did. My brother and his wife did that too. My sisters were a little slower. Diana has been married for six years, and she and Barry are just now having a baby. Leslie and Brady have been married for three years."

"My mom and dad had been married for a year when they had me," Lauren offered. She shrugged. "Daddy says they wanted to have a baby right away."

"See, and I get that," I said, shaking a hanger toward her. "If you truly want a kid, have one! But most of the people I know just have kids because they think they need to, not because they want to. And that's what bothers me."

"So what you're saying is that you want to have kids, but not until you're good and ready?"

I paused in my unpacking and said, "I guess so."

"And you aren't good and ready because you think you're too young?"

"No," I said, sighing. "I'm just saying I'm not ready because I'm just not ready. That and the significant lack of a man in my life," I added as an afterthought.

"So you don't have a boyfriend?" Lauren clarified, looking very interested.

"No. My college boyfriend and I broke up in April. Since then I've been...picky," I said, wondering how much of my personal life to share with her.

Lauren closed her textbook and looked at me with a suspicious amount of nonchalance. "So was it a scarring breakup that left you embittered concerning all men?"

"No. He wanted to get married, and I didn't want to. I guess I kind of ended it."

"So you'd date again if you met someone that interested you?" Lauren pressed, leaning forward eagerly.

I fixed her with a glare. "I do not like to be set up, Lauren Dayton, so move that pretty little head of yours back to biology and stop digging for information."

Lauren smiled at me comfortably. For someone I had just met a few hours ago, she was already completely at ease to say whatever she thought around me.

"It's not digging for information when it's two friends chatting about boys. Say, a particular boy. For instance...the available male heir to the Dayton fortune?"

I dropped the sweater I was holding. "*What?*"

Lauren grinned at me even wider. "Huh. It didn't occur to you at dinner?"

"What didn't occur to me at dinner?" I asked warily, narrowing my eyes at her.

"Seriously?" Lauren asked, looking amused. "You couldn't tell that Lucas is interested in you?"

I rolled my eyes. "I probably gave him a concussion. You should check his pupils for dilation."

"He'd probably like it more if you did it," Lauren giggled, covering her mouth.

I tried not to smile but did anyway. "I think he was just enjoying making me uncomfortable, Lauren. I'm pretty sure that was where that thought train stopped."

She shrugged, looking far too smug and knowing for a teenager. "We'll see."

I shook my head, laughing and hanging my last sweater in the closet. "New topic. What's this class your dad was talking about?"

Her upper lip curled in distaste, but she said, "I'm doing a cotillion in a few weeks, and I have to take ballroom dancing lessons. I have to pick out a fancy dress, get new shoes, have an escort, and, except for the shoes, it's pretty much a forced march."

I smiled and asked, "Why are you doing it if you don't want to?"

Lauren shrugged. "Don't we all do things for our parents we don't want to? My dad said it's important to him, but I think Alexis is the one who really wants me to do this. It's a small price to pay to see them happy."

That comment floored me. I couldn't remember ever, in the last ten years at least, caring if I made my parents happy because they didn't seem to care. My mother gave birth, my father set up the trust fund, and after that my brother and sisters and I were promptly handed to a nanny. As far as I was concerned, my parents and I had a business arrangement kind of relationship, no maternal/paternal bonds to speak of. For the umpteenth time today, I felt jealous of the girl sitting in my armchair. Her mother may have died ten years ago, but she had more love, affection, attention, and kindness than most kids could ever hope for. Lauren smiled and looked back down at her biology book, and I realized that in the few hours I had known her, I had unconsciously added myself to the "taking care of Lauren" bandwagon.

I knew without a doubt that I would do anything I could to make this girl happy, to keep her content and safe, and that was a new feeling for me. I had never felt that way about my brother or my sisters; I had never felt that way about my nephew, my best friends, or any of my boyfriends.

I don't know what triggered it. One minute I was giggling with a new friend, the next minute I was having an epiphany that ended with the conclusion that this girl could be the sister, the best friend, the confidant I'd never had in my life. Getting this job was the luckiest thing that had ever happened to me.

Before I could grasp this fully, my phone rang. I jumped and reached down to pick it up. "Hello?"

"Heidi," my mother's voice said, resonating her trademark absentness. She never gave you the feeling that she was actually listening to you, much less paying attention to what she was saying to you. It was as if my mother had a permanent "out to lunch" note stuck to her forehead—only, knowing my mother, the note would have been diamond encrusted and over a hundred grand.

"Hi, Mom," I said, rolling my eyes toward Lauren, who smiled.

"Leslie wanted me to call you and inform you that you have another nephew," Mom said, and I was pretty sure she was either reading or watching something because she sounded very distracted.

"Oh, that's great," I said; although, in all honesty, I wasn't that excited about it. Leslie and Brady lived upstate and would rarely be around, anyway. "What did she name him?"

"Um, hold on. Let me check. I just got Brady's fax, and I don't remember what he said."

I wondered if Chanel made "World's Greatest Grandma" shirts.

"Oh, here it is. Isaac Maxwell Brady Walden. Kind of long, I suppose."

I shook my head. "Well, thanks for calling. I'll call to congratulate Leslie in a few days. Any word on when Diana and Susan are due?"

"I don't know. Soon. I'll call you when they call me. I have to go, honey. I'm waiting for Ginger Lowery to call me back about the opera for next week, talk to you later!"

She hung up before I said good-bye, and I tossed my phone to my bed. I gave Lauren a wry look and said, "Sometimes I just don't know what I'd do without those little talks of ours."

She giggled and went back to her biology.

A little while later, when Lauren had said good night and gone to bed, I lay in the huge bed of my new room thinking about the bizarre-ness of this whole situation. I rolled over and buried my face in my pillow. *Don't think about it,* I told myself, closing my eyes and willing myself to sleep. *Thinking about it will only end badly.*

# CHAPTER 3

The next morning, a Saturday morning, the pounding at my door woke me up. Quarter to eight. *You have got to be kidding me,* I thought as I dragged myself out of bed and toward the door. Near the armchair I almost lost motivation, but I made it after all. I opened it, trying to keep the blurriness out of my eyes and to reduce the size of my tongue, as it was still stuck to the roof of my mouth.

"Hey," Alexis said, smiling brightly. "Little miss sleepy head, good morning! You about ready for breakfast? Lauren's up."

I nodded and tried not to think bad thoughts about one of my bosses. Hard. So hard. I shut the door and pulled on a red blouse and dark jeans with black flats and ran a brush through my hair. I washed my face, added moisturizer and lip gloss, and thudded downstairs, trying to keep my eyes open and look sweet and happy to be awake at 8:07 a.m. On a Saturday morning.

George had the paper open and was sipping coffee and reading the international business section from his place at the table. Alexis was now sitting at her place, making a to-do list, wearing a pantsuit that would have made a first lady proud, her hair pulled into a neat French twist. She had tea and a half a grapefruit in front of her.

Lauren was wearing jeans and another baby doll top, this time green. She was eating cereal and looking pretty sleepy herself. I plopped down next to her and the maid promptly brought me a cup of coffee.

"What would you like for breakfast, Miss Hart?" Eliza—that's what Lauren said the maid's name was—asked me politely.

I blanked. I literally couldn't think of a breakfast food. I cast an embarrassed look over to Lauren, who frowned at my bout of tongue-tied idiocy, and said, "She makes a great egg white omelet."

"Perfect," I managed to say, smiling. I took a long, comforting draw from my coffee cup.

"Morning," came a voice from right behind me, and I choked on the coffee and inhaled a great deal of it. Alexis gave me an odd look, as if she didn't quite know what to think of me, and Lauren giggled and handed me a napkin.

"Jumpy in the morning, huh?" Lucas asked, going around to the other side of the table and sitting down. He looked up into Eliza's adoring eyes and said, "Egg white omelet."

As Eliza hurried off into the kitchen, George lowered his paper. "Stayed the night, huh?" He asked his son gruffly, looking over him with suspicion in his eyes. "You haven't done that in a while."

Lauren started humming something that sounded vaguely familiar, smiling to herself as she stared into her cereal bowl, swirling through her milk with her spoon. I frowned at her. It didn't take an idiot—or, more to the point, a fully awake normal person—to get at what she was smiling and humming about. She thought Lucas stayed because of me. I sank lower in my chair and nearly rejoiced when my omelet showed up.

"Good choice," Lucas said, smiling at me from across the table as he noticed my breakfast. "Egg white omelets are my favorite."

I eyed his half-sister with ire. "You don't say?" I said dryly, and Lauren blinked at me, the picture of innocence.

"It was just a suggestion. You didn't have to take it," she said, sipping her orange juice out of a champagne flute. I hadn't even noticed the flute until then. I guess I was finally waking up.

I dug into my egg white omelet and closed my eyes, savoring the taste. Oh my gosh. Just one of the best things I had ever had in my mouth, second only to the delectable chocolate cake from the night before. I sighed happily and opened my eyes to cut another piece when I noticed the whole family looking at me oddly.

"What?" I asked, suddenly self-conscious.

"You just…you look like you really like that omelet," Alexis supplied primly. I noticed Lucas putting his hand over his mouth as if to hide a smile out of my peripheral vision.

"I like to eat. Good food is one of the last true pleasures of this world," I said simply, shrugging off their fascination and cutting another piece off my omelet.

"You aren't worried you'll get fat?" Lauren asked, looking impressed.

I frowned. "As long as I'm healthy, who cares if I have more skin than a super model? Besides, most of them don't know how to smile anymore because they're so starved. I, however, am an avid smiler."

Lauren and Alexis were both looking at me with varying levels of respect. George shook his fork at Lauren and said, "See? You can eat whatever you want. I'm so tired of these endless conversations at dinner that begin and end with the recitation of the calorie content of every course. Look at Heidi. She eats whatever she wants and she's…decently sized."

Lucas couldn't hold back a snort at that, which I heard despite the hand still covering his face.

"Yes?" I asked him, raising an eyebrow.

"What?" he asked, trying to keep a straight face.

"You snorted. Would you like to weigh in on the subject?" I asked, enjoying my turn to embarrass him in front of his family.

I needed to remember my tendency to prematurely gloat. He grinned at me, folded his arms on the edge of the table, and asked, very reasonably, as if he were requesting I hand him the salt, "I'd love to. What would you like me to say about your body in front of my father, stepmother, and sister?"

I had no words. I glared at him from across the table, trying to keep the smile on my face, even as Lauren laughed hysterically, albeit quietly, into her linen napkin. Alexis gave Lucas a reproving look, and George shook his head in amusement.

With as much dignity as I could muster—which wasn't a lot, considering the stream of never ending blows my dignity was taking this week—I turned to Lauren and asked stiffly, "Are you ready to go?"

"Shopping? Yeah, hold on, I'll grab my purse," Lauren said, scrambling from the table and out of the dining room.

There was silence for a few minutes while we waited for her to come back. I stared at the gold pattern on the dishes as if my life depended on it. When Lauren came back in, I jumped up and grabbed her arm, fully intending to drag her out of there at the speed of light, but George cleared his throat. We were forced to delay our escape.

"Here's my credit card," he said, digging it out of his wallet. "Like I said, go to lunch, get your dress, your shoes, whatever you need. Greg is on-call the entire day to take you wherever you need to go."

Lauren bent down, kissed her father on the cheek, and said, "We'll be back tonight, Daddy. Have fun today. And try not to work too long. It's Saturday, you need to have some fun."

George made a noise that can only be described as a *harrumph.* "Yeah, yeah, yeah," he said, hiding his smile from her.

We left without further interruptions, thankfully. We gave Greg a cheerful hello and told him where we wanted to start shopping. Lauren wanted to look at dresses first, so we were headed to Bloomingdales, her favorite store apparently. We talked about the cotillion a little bit—what she would have to do, what color gown would be appropriate, whether or not she would die dancing in stilettos—and we talked about who she really wanted her escort to be.

"It's completely stupid, and it would never happen, but Dad and Lance have this intern working for them. And he's so beautiful," Lauren admitted, smiling tightly, obviously embarrassed.

"Why is it stupid?" I asked diplomatically.

"He's twenty-two and a senior in college. So it would not only be stupid, but illegal." Lauren laughed, tipping her head back to rest against the backseat cushion.

I smiled thoughtfully. "A little illegal, yes," I said, popping my knuckles. "But that doesn't mean it's wrong for you to think he's cute. You just need to find someone cute in your age bracket."

"Well, apparently Connor Whitson wants me to ask him, but the Whitson family is so dramatic, it would be like we were announcing our engagement and not simply a long evening of toile, roasted duck, boring music, and canapés."

"Well, I'm sure it won't be—Canapés? Really?" I asked sitting up straighter, and Lauren laughed.

"Yes, they have really good canapés at these things. You're going to come, right?" Lauren asked, looking at me in what I thought might be panic.

"I guess so. If you want me to be there," I said.

"I do. Want you to be there, I mean. Oh, Heidi, that means we have to find a dress for you too!" Lauren squealed, her eyes lighting up.

*Goody*. "Um, we really don't. I'm sure I have something I can wear."

"Nope. We are doing what I say today, and I say a new dress is in order. I swear I won't make you get one that matches mine, if that's what you're worried about," Lauren said slyly, giggling.

I grinned at her. "Fine. Whatever you say."

We didn't find anything we liked at Bloomingdales or Neiman Marcus or Nordstrom. We took a break and ate lunch at a ritzy little restaurant on Fifth before diving back into the search. Lauren finally found a floor-length purple halter dress at a dress boutique I had never heard of, and since it was on sale, she splurged and bought a pair of Gucci heels that were a true work of art. A pair of faux purple diamond earrings and a large purple cocktail ring later, Lauren was feeling pretty happy about the cotillion—or at least, what she was wearing to the cotillion—and she was ready to focus on me. She made me try on literally dozens of dresses, and when I came out of the dressing room in a knee-length pale pink Chanel dress, she insisted it was the one.

I argued with her for half an hour that it was too expensive, and before I could stop her, she had her father on the phone telling me to just go along with her and that if buying this dress for me was going to make her happy, I was to let her buy the dress. I reluctantly let her buy it—okay, maybe not completely reluctantly, because let's face it, it's Chanel, and Chanel is the one thing in the whole world that makes me feel like a princess—but I drew the line at shoes. I told her I had a pair of pumps that would match the dress perfectly and that I didn't need jewelry, which she pouted about, but eventually I wore her down.

We celebrated our finds with mocha lattes and a stroll through Central Park. While we were walking through the petting zoo—something we both used to do when we were little, we discovered, though Lauren went with her parents, and I went with whatever nanny hadn't quit yet—I noticed him. This guy was staring at us with the oddest expression on his face. I didn't want to stare back because hello, how rude. But I didn't like how he was looking at us, specifically Lauren. I really wanted to shout, "She's fifteen, you sleaze," but I thought that might draw unneeded attention to us. I kept my mouth shut.

Until he approached us, that is. When he was within three feet of us and I was certain he meant to talk to us, I turned to him and placed myself between Lauren and The Creeper.

"Can we help you?" I asked, trying to keep my voice pleasant.

The man—who was six inches taller than me and about eighty pounds heavier—continued staring at Lauren while beginning to speak to me. "My name is Claude Keller. I was wondering…I mean, I thought…you are Daniella Dayton's daughter, are you not?"

Claude had a look on his face like he didn't know which answer would hurt him more. He was attractive—darkly skinned, jet-black hair, black eyes, black jeans, gray sweater. He looked like a slightly-over-the-hill male model.

Lauren glanced at me and said, "Yes, I am."

Claude closed his eyes and put his hand over his heart. "Oh my," he said brokenly, shaking his head. He opened his eyes and looked at Lauren with such intensity that it completely freaked me out. "My dear child. I was your mother's closest friend before she died."

Lauren frowned. "I've never heard of you before," she said skeptically.

"She did not want your father to know about me, my dear child. George was an incredibly defensive, jealous husband, and he did not give my Daniella what was so deservedly hers," Claude said in the air of one in deep mourning.

I nearly swallowed my tongue at his implications, but Lauren immediately bristled. “My mother and father were in love,” she said hotly, her eyes glittering dangerously. “He gave her everything she could ever want, and she would never have cheated on him.”

“I did not mean to upset you, dear child,” he said, and I swore that if he dear child-ed her one more time, I was going to deck him. “I thought by now, surely by now, you would have known. I was with her the night she died. We had a fight, and she was so angry. She didn’t notice how close to the edge she was.”

Lauren made a choking noise, and I slid my arm around her shoulders and positioned her behind me again. I turned to glare at Claude, who looked very mournful indeed by now, but something struck me as odd about his whole conversation. He had known how Daniella had died? He had recognized Lauren. He had taken it upon himself to inform a fifteen-year-old that her mother was supposedly unfaithful to her husband before she died tragically a decade ago.

No matter how mournful he was, for that last part, he was going down.

“Listen, Claude,” I said evenly, coldly, and I saw his eyes tighten as if he was wary about something. I doubted the authenticity of his sorrow immediately. “You are leaving now. If you aren’t out of my sight in thirty seconds, I will call the police. Or better yet, I’ll just start screaming bloody murder and see how fast all these people react when they see the big, tall man and the two tiny, screaming women. That might be fun. However, I can assure you that if you don’t leave this instant that I will be the least of your problems. George Dayton—not to mention his sons—will be all over you like bargain shoppers on Black Friday, and believe me, pal, you can’t imagine what a man like George Dayton could do to you with his power, prestige, and pocketbook.”

I watched as Claude debated this in his head and decided to do the smart thing, the non-suicidal thing, and began to walk away. I turned to comfort Lauren as he jogged away from us, glancing over his shoulder as he ran, glaring at me—or maybe he was glaring at Lauren. I couldn't tell.

"Let's go home," I whispered, tightening my hug and stroking her hair.

"He was lying, Heidi," Lauren whimpered, her fingers furiously pushing tears off her cheeks. "My mother would never have cheated on my father. She loved him."

"I believe you," I said, and I did. Something wasn't quite right about Claude's story, least of all that he was telling it ten years after Daniella's death, and I intended to get to the bottom of it. I had no idea how I was going to do it, but I was.

I led Lauren back to where Greg was waiting with the car and told him to take us back to the house. Lauren had tears running down her face, and I wasn't sure if she was crying because she was mad, upset, or just sad at all the talk of her mother. I wasn't sure what to say to her. I mean, even if she didn't believe Claude's story, it had to have brought up some bad memories and horrible thoughts. I didn't particularly care for either of my parents, but if someone had told me my mother had cheated on my father, I'd be, to say the least, sick to my stomach. I wouldn't want to talk about it. But I wasn't a fifteen-year-old whose mother died when I was a little girl and whose father clearly adored her more than any other thing on the planet.

"Lauren," I started, though I had no idea what I was going to say.

"Why would anyone say that?" she asked, her voice breaking. "How could anyone think saying something like that would be a good idea?"

"I don't know," I said honestly. "It was uncalled for and cruel. Don't worry about it, though. We will get to the bottom of this, and, I swear, everything is going to be okay."

She nodded and looked at me with an intense interest. "You'd really do that?"

I nodded, but then paused. "Wait. Do what, exactly?"

"Help me find out the truth about my mom's death."

"Oh. Well, Lauren, I mean…" I was going to try to convince her that a business grad failure and a fifteen-year-old had about as much of a chance to figure that out as Madonna had of becoming queen of the United States. I really was. But she was looking at me with this look that said, so clearly, that her curiosity had finally won out after all these years, and she was afraid to look into things by herself. I sighed and ran a hand through my hair, pretty sure this was a great way to get fired, but I said, "Sure. I'll help you."

She smiled at me, almost a real smile, and we got into the car. I gave Greg a warning glance when he saw the tears so he would keep his mouth shut, and we drove home in silence. When we got back to the penthouse, Lauren grabbed my arm and said, "Are you going to tell Dad what happened at the park?"

"Yes," I said, raising an eyebrow. "This may not be the ideal job for me, but I like it and I like you. I'd like to make it past two days of employment before I withhold information from my boss."

Lauren nodded. "Can I be upstairs before you say something to him? I just…I want to avoid the 'are you okay' speech."

"Sure," I said, rubbing her arm as we got out of the car.

"And you'll tell me what he says? Everything he says, you won't leave anything out?" Lauren asked, her eyes and tone serious as could be.

"I promise," I said, hoping it was one I could keep.

We walked through the front door, and Lauren hurried to her room, ignoring Lucas's wave hello.

He frowned and looked at me. "What's wrong with her?" He leaned against the railing of the stairs that Lauren had just run up, dressed in gray slacks and a black sweater. His blond hair had no product in it, but it still looked perfect. I hate that guys don't have to do anything to their hair to make it look good. It's so unfair.

"We had an…incident in the park today," I said, still looking at his hair. Did he just comb it? Did he just wake up that way?

"Goat?" he asked sympathetically, and I frowned.

"What?"

"Was it a goat? At the petting zoo?" he pressed, crossing his arms.

"No," I said slowly, smiling. "Why would it be a goat?"

Lucas shook his head. "The last time Lauren had an 'incident' at the park it was because a goat at the petting zoo ate part of her jacket. Of course, that was eight years ago."

I nodded as if I understood, which I didn't, and said, "Right. Of course. Well, it was something a lot worse this time. Is your dad around?"

"He's in his study. I'll show you where. What happened?" Lucas asked, leading me off toward the east wing of the first floor.

I shook my head. "Some creep at the park upset Lauren, and I figured I should tell George about it."

"Upset Lauren?" Lucas repeated, frowning fiercely. "What did he do?"

"Um, you mean besides tell her that he was her mother's lover? Creeped me out, mostly," I said, and then I had to stop walking because Lucas abruptly grabbed my arm.

"Excuse me?" he said angrily.

I raised an eyebrow and looked down at where his fingers were cutting off my circulation.

"Hey, I know you're upset, but I'd like to have feeling left in my arm when you let go," I said pointedly, tapping my foot.

Lucas immediately released his grip and looked slightly remorseful, but mostly he still looked ticked off. "Come on," he muttered, marching angrily toward a door at the end of the hallway.

Lucas threw the door open, and George looked up in surprise. I could tell he wasn't used to being disturbed in his study, let alone from his younger son and the quasi-nanny.

"What's going on here?" he demanded, looking at us over his glasses.

Lucas looked pointedly at me, and I sighed. I hadn't expected an audience. Stupid me.

"Lauren and I went to Central Park today after we finished shopping," I started, and Lucas began to make "hurry up" movements with his hands. I frowned at him and continued, "And we went to the petting zoo. While we were there, a man came up to us and introduced himself as Claude Keller."

George shrugged his shoulders. "Should I know who that is?"

"He told us he was…well, not in so many words, but he very strongly implied that he was…Daniella's lover," I said quickly, swallowing. If Lucas had reacted the way he did, how would George take the news of his deceased wife's supposed affair? The phrase "kill the messenger" flashed through my head ominously.

His reaction was, if anything, anticlimactic. He frowned, but it was in concern, not anger. "What did Lauren say?" he asked, sounding worried.

Lucas looked at him in disbelief, and I stammered. "She… she didn't believe him. She told him so. She said that her parents loved each other and that her mother would never cheat on her father."

George did something truly astonishing to me then. He sent me a sad smile. "That's my girl," he muttered, staring down at the paperwork on his desk.

"Uh, Dad?" Lucas said as if about to point out something very obvious. "Is that it? You have nothing else to say about someone harassing Lauren in the park about Daniella? Telling her lies and preying on her feelings?"

George looked at him crossly. "You even have to ask that question?"

Lucas looked slightly chastised but mostly just peeved.

George sighed. He suddenly looked much older. He motioned to Lucas and said, "Shut the door please."

When Lucas did so, George looked at his son, then at me, and said, "Daniella didn't have a lover. I have no proof, of course, that this man is lying except for the fact that I knew my wife very well. She didn't have a deceitful bone in her body."

I held up my hand, and he looked at me in surprise. He didn't say anything, so I said, "Look, I'm not questioning you or her. I believed Lauren when she said she thought Claude was lying. I thought he was lying too. So don't feel like you have to defend her."

"I don't," George said, frowning. "And you shouldn't either. If Lauren has questions about her mother or about our relationship, send her to me. You don't have to do her asking for her."

*Oh, he's good.*

"I'll have someone look into Claude Keller, his story, and what he's doing in the city. Until then, if it makes you and Lauren more comfortable, I can hire some security to go out with you," George said, scribbling something on a post-it.

"Or I could," Lucas said suddenly, looking as if he just realized something very interesting. "I have a lot of free time coming up, I don't mind going with Lauren and Heidi when they need me."

I prayed the panic wasn't showing on my face. "No, no," I said hurriedly, putting my hands up. "That's okay. We'll be fine. We totally held our own today, and, besides, we had Greg there. So if it had gotten bad, we could have just called Greg. Please, Lucas, we don't need an escort."

"If someone is harassing my little sister—"

"Just let me do my job," I hissed, glaring at him.

He had the audacity to smile. "I don't think you were actually hired to be a body guard. However, I know from experience just what you can do to a guy when provoked," he teased, guiding his hand along his jaw line to emphasize the fading bruise there.

I felt my cheeks redden. "You didn't provoke me. That was an accident," I said, then I lowered my voice so only he could hear me say, "Keep this up, and I'll show you what I'm like when provoked."

Despite my glare and the fact that I thoroughly meant my words, he smiled down at me as if he were addressing someone very silly and said, "Promise?" in the quietest, deepest voice I'd ever heard. I had to look away suddenly because of the power of that stupid, crooked grin. No product in his hair and a devilish smile. He must have made some sort of Faustian deal. Only explanation.

I looked back to George and said, "Unless you need anything else, I'm going to go check on Lauren."

He nodded as if dismissing me, and I started out the door. Lucas began to follow me, but I slammed the door to the study between us, effectively stopping him. I heard his laughter from the other side of the door, and that only made me angrier. Was he trying to get me fired? And since when had I decided I wanted to keep this job so badly?

Near the point at which I knew I would begin growling, I stomped up the stairs and into what I laughingly referred to as my bedroom. It didn't feel like my room, and I wasn't sure when it would start to, but until then I felt like I was staying in a hotel room—a hotel room with an incredibly annoying neighbor who stole my fresh towels every day (which I bet is the equivalent of an overbearing, over-attentive brother of the teenager I was being paid to entertain hanging around constantly and making me look like an idiot in front of my employer).

Lauren was waiting for me. She was stretched out on my comforter, her shoes kicked off, and was flipping through this month's *Vogue*.

"So?" she said, sitting up and closing the magazine. "What did he say?"

"Uh..." I had to work to get my mind out of the bitter barn and remember what we had discussed. "He said that your mom never cheated on him, but that he would look into Claude's story and why he's in New York. He also said that if you had any questions about your mother or your parents' relationship or anything else under the sun, to ask him, and he would answer you honestly."

Lauren smiled a little. "That's my dad," she said, playing with her hair. She sighed. "Did he act upset when you told him what Claude said?"

"Not so you'd notice." I kicked my shoes off and sat beside her. "He was more impressed with your kick-butt response to Claude than anything else."

She rolled her eyes, but I could tell she was pleased. Who wouldn't be? Her father put her above everything else in his life. My father put work and golf above everything else in his life. Third would probably be the steak at Chez Pierre's. I wasn't sure I would break the top fifteen, and I didn't say that to sound sorry for myself—there were just more important things to my father than his kids, and he'd made no bones about letting us know that. Unfortunately, that's a trait that had been passed on to my siblings. Max spent zero time with Maxie—in fact, he insisted

Susan quit her job to be an at-home mom—and I couldn't see either of my sisters being hands-on parents.

"Ooh," I said, closing my eyes and scrunching up my face. "I haven't called Leslie yet."

"Your sister that just had a baby?"

"Yeah, I told my mom that I'd call Leslie by now. Not that my mother will remember that, but I will. Hand me my purse, will you?" I said, holding my hand out. Lauren obliged, and I dug around until I found my cell phone. I scrolled down until I found my sister's cell number and hit send.

"Hello?" My sister sounded more than a little distracted and a little irritated too.

"Hey, Leslie, it's Heidi."

"Who?"

"Heidi. Your sister," I pointed out dryly, and Lauren looked up from her magazine.

"Nuh-uh. She didn't know who you were?"

I rolled my eyes as my sister responded. "Oh, hi," she said casually, obviously less interested now that she realized she was just talking to her sister.

"So I heard you had a pretty big week," I said, trying to sound excited.

"What, the baby? Yeah, I guess. He's cute. Cries a lot, though. It's driving Brady crazy. He keeps saying he thought Isaac would stop crying when we got him home from that horrible hospital," Leslie said, and I could practically hear her rolling her eyes.

"The baby's name is cute," I lied. The baby's name was too long. Big name for a little baby. "Isaac Maxwell Brady Walden. Dad and Brady must be proud."

Leslie laughed. "Are you kidding me? Dad would put me out of the will if I had a son without the Maxwell or at least a Hart being in the name, and Brady doesn't care. I did that for his mom. When she found out we were naming him Isaac Maxwell

Walden, she threw a hissy fit. Why, I don't know, since we gave the kid Brady's last name. I think that should be enough, but we threw the Brady in there to make her happy."

I didn't know what to say to that. For one thing, it seemed weird that a new mom was calling her baby "the kid." For another, I couldn't believe Leslie cared what her mother-in-law thought. I didn't think Leslie cared what anyone thought.

"Well," I said awkwardly, "I just wanted to call to say congratulations. I know you and Brady wanted a boy."

"Thanks. What are you doing these days?" she asked pretty much as an afterthought.

"Uh, this and that," I said, hoping Lauren couldn't hear Leslie's side of the story. I knew if Leslie found out that I was currently employed as a nanny, she'd call my dad, who would only be too happy to call me and re-offer the position in his firm to me out of some sort of family obligation or pity. Besides, my dad was already under the impression that I had interviewed for a job with George Dayton, and he didn't need to know which job. "I'm staying busy."

"Well, good. Call me sometime when you're heading upstate, okay?"

"Sure."

I started to say bye, but she had already hung up the phone.

"Why does no one say good-bye anymore?" I complained, closing my phone. "They just hang up when they've completed their mission and that's that."

Lauren raised an eyebrow in amusement. "She should be shot."

I gave her a look and moved to look over her shoulder at the fall Gucci line.

# CHAPTER 4

I wish I could say that the rest of the weekend I spent every moment trying to convince Lauren not to look into her mother's death. I wish I could say that I worked tirelessly to persuade her that the past was the past, and the future was more important.

I am an idiot.

Because of course I didn't do those things. Those were things sane people would think of, things that a good nanny/companion—no, even just a run-of-the-mill, mediocre, C-average nanny/companion—would do. I, on the other hand, spent the weekend helping her practice asking Connor Whitson to be her escort, thereby letting the questions about her mother fester, simmer, stew, and come to a nice boil. I forgot all about them by Tuesday; on Thursday, when Lauren came home from school and asked me if I wanted to "get started," I was honestly confused.

"Get started on what?" I asked, looking up from my book. Lauren and I had gotten into the habit that while she did her homework, I read. She had been working on biology for half an hour, and I was absorbed in the lives of Jane Eyre and Mr. Rochester.

Lauren cleared her throat, obviously unsure about something. "You know. You said you'd help me find out about my mom. And how she died," she said in a hurry.

My mouth dropped open a little. Before I could come up with anything with which to dissuade her, I saw a flicker of something go through her eyes, and instantly I changed my mind. I couldn't let her down.

So I smiled and said, "You sure? Because your dad said if you wanted to know something, you could just ask him."

Lauren fidgeted in her chair and lowered her gaze to her lap. "Oh, right, because that's a conversation every girl wants to have."

I bit back a sigh. I guess I could see her point. When I was fifteen, the only thing I ever went to my dad for was money, and in our family that meant picking up our weekly allowance check from Dad's secretary, Gillian.

"Okay," I said, trying not to sound resigned to my fate. "Where do you want to start?"

Lauren looked at me blankly. "Uh, I don't know. Where do you think we should start?"

Great. I was being held at gunpoint on a forced march, yet I was in the driver's seat. I scratched my ear and squinted at her.

"Well," I said, "my investigating knowledge comes primarily from old episodes of *Charlie's Angels* and Nancy Drew books. I guess what we should do first is look at your mom's stuff. Did your dad keep any of it?"

Lauren's eyes lit up. "Yeah, he kept most of it. Everything that was important to us anyway. We have a storage unit upstate a ways, and he put it all in there."

I shrugged. "I guess we know where Greg is taking us this weekend."

Lauren shot me a highly satisfied smile before returning to her biology. I had just resumed reading when she said softly, "Thanks, Heidi."

"Any time," I said, not looking up.

A knock came at the door and Alexis poked her head in. "Hi, girls," she said, sounding rather perky. A week and a half ago, when I took this job, I had been in awe of Alexis's rather optimistic, chipper outlook on life. Now I was starting to wonder if she took Prozac.

"Hey," Lauren said, not looking up from her homework. She erased something feverishly and frowned deeply.

Alexis stood primly in the doorframe, her navy blue jersey dress tailored to first lady perfection, but there was a slight difference to her face than usual. Her eyes weren't smiling.

"Lauren, I hate to bother you during your homework time, but do you have a moment?"

Lauren shoved a lock of her blonde hair behind one ear, revealing a dangly silver earring. "Sure. What's up?"

Alexis hesitated, picking at her cuticles. I saw her swallow and then shift her weight from foot to foot. "I received a note today that concerned your father and I, and your safety has always been our first priority. So we want you to reconsider taking a bodyguard with you whenever you leave the house."

Lauren frowned. "You think I'm in danger?"

I cleared my throat and asked, "What did the note say?"

Alexis blinked rapidly, clearly flustered. "Oh, I'm not sure George would want me to say anything."

Lauren saved the day. "Dad just told Heidi that if I wanted to know anything, anything at all, I should just ask, and he would be honest with me. If you think Heidi and I need a bodyguard, I'd like to know why."

She delivered her speech with such aplomb, such grace, that I had to bite my tongue not to say, "You go, girlfriend."

Alexis gave her a small smile and said cautiously, "An envelope addressed to me came to the lobby today, and when Peter"—the apartment building manager—"handed it to me, I thought it must have been a tenants' meeting reminder."

(Apparently, when you live in a building as fancy and high-end as the Daytons did, you not only sign a lease or a rent agreement, you sign away a piece of your life, as well, in the form of bi-monthly tenant meetings.)

"It was a plain envelope, with my name typed on it very neatly, and when I opened it I found a picture of my brother and sister and I that was taken over ten years ago and a letter that said, 'I know everything you do, and I can destroy you.' I assumed it was some sort of blackmail, but George was worried. Apparently, Daniella had received some messages like this before her death," Alexis said, looking carefully at Lauren.

Lauren smiled. "I won't break. Promise."

Alexis shook her head. "I probably shouldn't have said anything. It's nothing. Your father just wanted me to offer you a little protection. He didn't want to scare you."

*Um, hi? Remember me? The nanny/companion (Possible title: Nanion) that has already been sufficiently weirded out by the current events since beginning this job? The person who takes threats against the well-being of others very seriously?*

*Yeah, my vote doesn't count.*

Lauren insisted that we would be fine, that we would be extra careful and report anything suspicious. She confided in me after Alexis left that if we had a bodyguard, her father would find out that we were going to research her mother's death, and he probably wouldn't be thrilled with it.

I was so getting fired.

While Lauren was at school, I was basically off the hook. I mean, from three fifteen in the afternoon to eight in the morning, I was at her disposal. On Saturdays, she told me what we were doing. Sundays were mine, but the last Sunday, I just hung out with Lauren. During the weekday, I was pretty bored. The first day was awesome. It felt like what summer vacation used to feel like when I was a kid. Back then, Leslie, Diana, Max, and I would load up in the limo with whatever nanny Dad could pay enough to take this trip, drive to the airport, and fly to the summer home in the Hamptons. Leslie and Diana spent the entire summer tanning and making their blonde hair blonder. Max made meeting after meeting with our powerful businessman neighbors—playing tennis, golf, racquetball, and shuffleboard with anybody with a 401K or a portfolio. I spent my summers swimming, eating sno-cones, and reading whatever pop culture magazines I could get my hands on.

Which was about what I did on Monday. I took a nap. I read a few gossip magazines. I made a sandwich. And I understood something about myself: I needed to stay busy. Sitting around all day was boring. I then fully understood why my mother was a member of every ladies' club on the Upper East Side. If I had to stay home all day, every day, with nothing of any significance to keep me occupied…well. It's a wonder my mother wasn't on Prozac.

So for the rest of the week, I tried to be more efficient with my time. I worked out in the building's weight room. I had all of my mail, bills, and identification cards updated to my new address. And I waited for people to get home so I would have someone to talk to.

On Friday, when Lauren got home, I was standing on the balcony that the hallway between out rooms led out to, staring down the side of the building.

"What are you doing?" she asked, peering over with me.

I grinned and pointed to a balcony two floors below us. "One of your neighbors spent the afternoon standing out there, yelling at her sister on her cell phone about the fact that they were dating the same man."

Lauren smiled and raised an eyebrow. "Interesting, but I don't think it's quite worth the avid ear you were giving it."

I raised my eyebrows at that and said, "Your neighbor was at least sixty-five."

Lauren wrinkled her nose. "Ew, old people love."

I laughed at that and went back to peering off the balcony.

"Can we go inside? Heights give me a weird tingly feeling in my back that is not pleasant. This is freaking me out," Lauren said, stepping away from the railing and looking dizzy.

"Have heights always done that to you?" I asked, frowning.

Lauren shrugged uncomfortably. "Everybody's got something. Lance doesn't do spiders. Alexis is afraid of bees, flying, cigarette smoke, snakes, caffeinated beverages, mice, and frogs, plus she's claustrophobic and hates blood. Dad doesn't like horror movies. I don't do heights."

I nodded. "Sure."

"What are you afraid of?"

It was an innocent enough question, but I didn't know how to answer it. So finally I sighed and said, "Myself. I am my own worst enemy. I can psych myself up, push myself down, or weird myself out. It's all up to my mind."

Lauren smiled and shook her head. "Oh, Heidi. You crack me up."

I followed her back inside the apartment and tried not to feel patronized.

"When are we going to the unit?" she asked, dumping her backpack on the floor of her room. I sat in her armchair and tried not to look lost.

"Unit?" I asked, checking out my fingernails.

"The storage unit. Remember, we were going to start there?" Lauren said, her voice tinged with something I couldn't quite put a name to. It sounded like fear, but she wasn't scared of what we might find, she was scared of me trying to talk her out of going.

I held back a sigh and said, "We can leave first thing in the morning, if you like."

She smiled and nodded, and I resigned myself to a Saturday in a musty old storage shed digging through boxes of a dead woman's belongings.

I should have realized that if the Daytons were involved, it wasn't musty or old. The storage shed was actually a super ritzy facility that celebrities, politicians, and really rich people used to hold their expensive but slightly out of date stuff. We had to show ID to get in, and Lauren had to use three keys to open up the rooms (yes, plural) that George rented every month.

The first room we walked through had mostly furniture. Cribs, old dining room sets, toddler beds, a chandelier, some rocking chairs, a trunk. Everything was beautiful and expensive. I just wanted to touch everything, but I restrained. It wasn't what we were here for.

We walked through another room that had literally dozens of boxes marked either "clothes" or "dishes" or "Lance's assignments, K-12" (which I found hysterical). Lauren looked around the room quickly, almost in an agitated sense, and exhaled.

"Nothing," she muttered, opening another door. She stopped in the middle of the doorframe. I would have bumped into her, but I stopped right in time. I glanced over her shoulder and saw a look of absolute, unadulterated pain brushed across her face. Her bright blue eyes were even brighter than usual, and her cheeks had no color. I put my hand on her shoulder and said, "Lauren?"

# CHAPTER 5

She sniffed and said, in a broken voice, "Look at this. Thirty years of life boiled down into one room."

I smiled and rested my chin on her shoulder in a sort of weird hug.

"Honey, I think you're living proof that Daniella's life extends past just this room."

She smiled at that and wiped her eyes with her wrists. She moved inside the room and went to the first box she could reach. She unfolded the flaps slowly, carefully, and smiled when she saw what was inside. She lifted out a cashmere sweater and raised it to her face.

"She wore this every time we went to Central Park. She loved the park in the fall, with all the leaves."

I didn't know what to say. I moved over to another box and opened it. There were dozens of CDs, mostly country and pop, stacked alphabetically. I left the box open so we would know that we already checked that one.

Lauren pulled a gray linen jacket out of the box next, then a few other pieces of clothing. She put everything but the sweater back in. The next box she opened was filled with old stationary and desk supplies. After several boxes of clothes, I opened one and went, "Hello."

Lauren was by my side in a heartbeat. I pulled out several thick photo albums and handed her one.

"These should help," I said, sitting down on the floor and opening one up. Lauren followed suit. I was treated to Lauren's third birthday party, whereas Lauren had George and Daniella's wedding. I was tempted to trade with her since that couldn't have been easy to look at, but I didn't want to put her on the spot.

It was surprisingly fun looking at these pictures. Lucas and Lance were fourteen and eighteen, and it was obvious that they both adored their little sister. Daniella was so pretty that it actually hurt. To know that someone that beautiful met such a sad end was like lighting a Monet on fire. I flipped through the pages and watched as Lauren opened presents, blew out her candles, and posed with every member of her family, including someone I had never seen before. She was tall with red hair and green eyes, and it wasn't until I really looked at her eyes that I knew who she was. Those were Lucas's eyes. It must have been Maureen, the first wife. She was pretty, but she looked bitter.

I turned the page and saw a family picture with George, Daniella, the boys, Lauren, and Maureen all crowded around a huge birthday cake in the shape of a three. I started to smile until I saw something odd. George had his arm around Daniella's waist, and he was smiling down on her. She was smiling down at Lauren, who was at the center of the picture. The weird part was that Maureen had one arm around Lance, and the other arm looped through George's. He didn't even look like he noticed. I wondered what Maureen was thinking, lacing her arm through her ex-husband's at his daughter from another wife's birthday. Awkward!

I closed that book and picked up another one. Summertime with the Dayton family looked like an episode of a cheesy TV show. Everyone was smiling; everyone was together.

I was amusing myself by watching what appeared to be Lance teaching Lauren how to swim when Lauren said, "Oh. Oh, Heidi, I think I found something."

I looked over her shoulder and saw that she was staring at a picture of a boat.

"Is that…"

"Yeah. It was called *The Renegade*. See? In the picture you can kind of see the name across the side of the boat," she said, pointing.

I looked closely. The boat was a pretty standard party boat; several of my friends' parents owned them. I moved to the next picture, a picture of the deck. Several women in party dresses were standing arm in arm, laughing and smiling at the camera. Daniella was in the middle, wearing a blue dress and the most gorgeous earrings I'd ever seen. They were perfectly round, beautifully cut sapphire earrings, and they made her blue eyes look even bluer. In fact, at the center of both perfect circles, the blue was so dark it was almost black; they sort of looked like irises.

"Those are gorgeous earrings," I said, pointing them out.

Lauren smiled and said, "I forgot about those. She wore them all the time. Dad got them for her on their first anniversary."

"What happened to them? Did he give them to you?" I asked.

Lauren frowned. "I don't know. He probably put them in the safe or something. I've never asked."

I looked back at the picture and something caught my eye. The women were leaning up against the railing of the deck, and the bar came up to most of their shoulders. It hit Daniella, who was a bit taller, a little above the elbows.

"Lauren," I asked, frowning, "Lucas told me that your mother fell overboard and drowned. Is that true?"

She nodded, trying to see what I was seeing.

"How could a person fall off a boat with a railing that came up so high?" I asked, pointing to the slim, white railing. "In order to go overboard, you'd have to have help, or you'd have to jump."

"Are you saying my mother killed herself?" Lauren asked sharply, looking at me with anger in her eyes.

"No," I said quickly. The anger on her face decreased a little. "I'm just saying that there would have been a big hole in the railing or something to have allowed her to fall. And even then, most people would have tried to fix it in some way. For safety and all."

Lauren's nostrils flared slightly and her jaw clenched. "So you think someone killed my mother."

I closed my eyes briefly. This wasn't going well. "Look, Lauren, I'm just thinking out loud, okay? I'm not Nancy Drew. I don't get hunches that turn out to be uncannily correct. I'm just working through some stuff, okay?"

Lauren nodded, but I could tell my questions had left burning markers in her head.

I took the pictures out of the book and slipped them in my purse. Lauren stared down at another photo album, filled with pictures taken from the year before Daniella died. I rubbed her shoulder and then stood, moving to another box.

The pictures were the only important thing we found at the storage unit. I was a little upset that we had found something suspicious at all because now I knew with absolute certainty that Lauren was going to want to keep looking for answers. I also knew that I couldn't tell her "no" because now I was too invested in this. Between Claude and the pictures, I knew something horrible had happened on that boat, and that someone—somewhere—was covering it up.

I totally understood why Nancy Drew risked getting knocked unconscious all the time. The determination to get to the bottom of things, to fix everyone's problems, was intoxicating.

Which is why I suggested that Lauren and I ask some of the women that were on the boat that night some questions.

I don't know why I do these things to myself.

The only woman that Lauren knew for sure had been on the boat that night was Susie Engle. Susie lived in upstate, about thirty minutes from where we were, and she had been in several ladies clubs with Daniella. Susie had a daughter around Lauren's age, Brianna, and a son a few years younger, Hugh, that went to Lauren's school. Lauren said that Susie used to bring Brianna to the house a lot and that she and Daniella were pretty close.

We rang the bell at the Engles' very impressive mansion and waited, one of us patiently, one of us not so much. Lauren was tapping her foot, checking her watch, and glancing around like she was about to commit a crime. I smiled at her and shook my head.

A pretty blonde woman about my height answered the door dressed in Armani and looking confused. She had dull brown eyes and a string of pearls on, and I could smell a vague hint of scotch on her.

"May I help you?" she asked, and she even sounded confused. Looks like my mother wasn't the only member of the Rotary Club that dipped into the hops before quitting time. "Are you collecting for something?"

Lauren stepped forward and said, "Mrs. Engle, my name is Lauren Dayton."

I could practically see the light click on in her eyes. "Lauren! Of course! Oh, I feel so silly. I just didn't recognize you at first."

*Probably because of said scotch.*

"But you look just like your mother," Mrs. Engle continued, clasping her hands and bringing them to her chest.

"That's what we're here about, Mrs. Engle," I said, smiling at her sweetly. It doesn't hurt to suck up a little bit.

She looked at me, and I could see the confusion swim back into her eyes. "Who are you?"

"I'm Heidi Hart, Lauren's…friend," I simplified, throwing a wink at Lauren, who grinned. The whole nanny/companion thing was too confusing to explain, least of all to a drunk woman.

"Oh, all right. Come on in, girls."

We followed Mrs. Engle into her home, through a spacious and eccentrically decorated entryway (it had a sort of jungle theme to it, very odd. I thought at any moment I might see a monkey) and went to the den, a room done entirely in different shades of pink.

Lauren and I sat down on a couch the color of Pepto-Bismol and tried to get comfortable. Mrs. Engle stared down at us for a moment as if silently debating something in her head, and finally she said, "Would you girls care for a drink or a snack?"

We shook our heads. I was vastly amused. It had been a while since I had been lumped into the "girls" category. When Mrs. Engle sat down across from us in a pale pink armchair that had been stuffed like a Build-A-Bear by an over-eager four-year-old. Lauren looked at me, clearly not knowing where to begin. I smiled at her encouragingly, prompting her to speak up.

"Now what were you girls wanting to talk about?" Mrs. Engle asked, picking her cuticles. The woman couldn't sit still.

"We wanted to ask you some questions about my mom," Lauren said, shifting where she sat. She was impatient to get started, but I put my hand on her arm and motioned for her to calm down. I wanted her to ask most of the questions, but I didn't want her to jump in headfirst.

Mrs. Engle smiled and said, twisting some of her hair around her finger like a little girl, "Dani and I were such good friends. We'd known each other since high school. We both attended St.

Agnes School for Girls, and Dani was the most popular girl in school. She was beautiful, bright, and so funny. She loved practical jokes. She never played a mean one though, and she never played one on someone who wouldn't think it was funny."

I smiled. "Sounds like she was a good friend."

"I was in her wedding. We were close. She held my hand through most of my doctor's appointments when I was pregnant with Brianna because my husband, John, had to work a lot back then. He hadn't made partner yet," Mrs. Engle said, and her eyes slid over to stare out the window. She was obviously reminiscing about something.

"Did you go with her for her doctor's appointments?" I asked.

"No, not really. George went with her to every appointment, and three's a crowd," Mrs. Engle said in a singsong voice, as if she were reciting something. "All the girls were so jealous of Dani where George was concerned. No man was ever more adoring of his wife than George of Dani."

"The girls?" I asked to clarify.

"Oh, the old gang. We haven't done much together since Dani died. Dani was the glue, turns out," Mrs. Engle said, her voice becoming strained. She raised a trembling hand to dab her wrist against her cheek, wiping up a stray tear.

I reached down and got a pen and pad out of my purse. "Mrs. Engle, can you tell me who was a member of the, um, old gang?"

Mrs. Engle nodded, putting on a fake smile. "Let's see, there was me, Dani, Amanda Honey, Tonia Barton, Ashley Snyder, and Joyce Miller. We'd all been friends for ages. After we all got married and some of us started having children, we started weekly lunches—every Thursday at Martinelli's—and once a month we went out for a girl's night. Sometimes it was clubbing, sometimes we would go to a concert, and other times we would go out on Ashley's boat…"

Mrs. Engle trailed off, biting on her thumbnail. She gave us another smile, this time a watery one. "Haven't been on a boat since, to be honest."

Lauren cleared her throat, and I looked over at her. "Is Joyce Miller the mother of Amy and Oscar Miller?"

"Yes. Oh, I forgot, they go to school with you and Brianna, don't they?"

Lauren nodded. I turned back to Mrs. Engle and asked, "Did Daniella seem different the night you all went boating?"

Mrs. Engle seemed lost in thought for a few moments. She finally shook her head. "No. Sorry, girls. I can't remember much of what happened that night. It was all kind of a blur."

I smiled at her and stood. "We won't take up any more of your time, Mrs. Engle. Thank you so much for answering our questions. We really appreciate it."

Lauren stood up and said, "Thanks, Mrs. Engle. Tell Bri I said 'hi.'"

"Of course I will, dear. Have a nice weekend."

Mrs. Engle walked us out and watched us get back into the limo. Greg pressed the intercom button and asked where we wanted to go.

"What time is it?" Lauren asked, looking a little pale.

"Quarter to three," I responded, trying to tell from her expression if this was too much for one day.

"Fifth and Marriott," Lauren told Greg, sounding tired. "Fourteen twelve Marriott."

I raised my eyebrows and asked, "Where are we going?"

"The Millers. I didn't realize Mom and Joyce were friends. Joyce Miller remembers *everything*. She's never flaked on even one of Amy's recitals or Oscar's games, and she remembers everyone's birthdays and anniversaries. She's practically a walking PDA," Lauren said, and her excitement spread across her face prettily.

I shifted in my seat. "Are you sure you're up for this? I mean, this is a lot of information in one day. We can wait and go to the Millers tomorrow, if you want."

"No," she insisted, as I knew she would. "I want to do this. I need to do this. Even if we don't find out anything else ever and I never know what happened to her, I owe this to my mom. I want to try and find out what happened to her. Especially now that, well, now that those pictures have brought up some questions."

I nodded, still skeptical. "But you'll tell me if it's too much? For real now. You have to promise me."

She smiled and nodded. "I promise."

Greg let us out at the Millers' townhouse, and we ran up the front stoop and rang the bell. After a few seconds, a redheaded teenage boy answered the door dressed in a soccer uniform. He immediately blushed when he saw who was standing on the front step.

"Hey, Oscar. Is your mom home?" Lauren asked, shifting her purse from one shoulder to another.

Oscar swallowed visibly and blushed harder. "Uh, yeah. Come on in. What are you doing here?"

He moved aside, and we walked in the door. The entryway was done entirely in black and white modern furniture and artwork. Oscar's red hair was the only thing in the room with real color. Even his uniform was bleak—gray and forest green.

"We're here to ask your mom a few questions," Lauren explained. She seemed cool and comfortable and completely oblivious to the fact that Oscar Miller obviously had some sort of a yin for her.

Oscar showed us into the living room—also done completely in black and white—and told us to sit down. He walked out of the room and returned a few minutes later with two cans of Coke, a veggie tray, and his mother.

Joyce Miller was a statuesque redheaded woman dressed in a black pantsuit and a white ruffled shirt. She had a forty-thousand-dollar gold watch on her wrist (I knew because Max had bought one for Susan when Maxie was born) and wire-rimmed glasses on her nose. She gave us a tight smile and said, “Hello, girls. Are you interested in a snack?”

Oscar offered us the veggie tray, off which I quickly grabbed some carrots and celery. We hadn’t eaten lunch, and I was starving. I was about to dive for one of the Cokes when Oscar went to the drink cart and scooped ice into two tumblers. He brought the cups and two coasters over to us and sank into the background of the room, an amazing feat for someone whose hair is that bright.

“Hi, Mrs. Miller,” Lauren began, smiling winningly. “This is my friend, Heidi Hart, and I just wanted to ask you a few questions about my mother.”

Joyce nodded, never dropping the businesswoman demeanor. “Ask away.”

“How long did you know my mother?” Lauren asked, starting with an easy one. Oscar was listening intently in the corner.

Joyce smiled more authentically and crossed her legs. She tapped her foot quickly, the pointed toe of her Marc Jacobs pumps peeking out from her extra long slacks.

“I met your mom through our sorority in college when we were twenty. Daniella was so much fun. She’d stay up three days straight to get a paper done, crash for two days, and then talk us all in to making some kind of road trip on the weekend. Then she’d start all over.”

“Was she big into the partying?” I asked, taking a sip from my Coke.

Joyce shrugged. “You know how it is to be twenty and in college, I assume,” she amended, smiling. “Dani liked to have fun.

She liked to flirt and dance and have a good time, but she never over-indulged. She knew the limits on everything."

"Did Daniella ever say anything to you about her marriage?" I asked carefully, not looking at Lauren.

Joyce looked surprised. "I beg your pardon?"

"I don't ask to be nosy, it's just that…that…" I couldn't come up with something to say that wouldn't raise a major red flag.

"I'm just trying to get a better idea of Mom's life," Lauren supplied. "The good and the bad."

Joyce relaxed a little and said, "Well, as far as we knew, Dani's life was all pretty good. Her marriage was filled with love and support, and you were a great blessing to her. She always wanted more children, actually. She loved her stepsons very much and wanted to adopt them."

Lauren raised her eyebrows. I didn't know what of that was new to her, but something obviously was.

"Do you remember much about the night she died?" I asked, hoping against hope that Joyce Miller, the human PDA, would remember something of use to us.

Joyce looked like she was thinking hard. "Dani was wearing a new dress. Blue, to match her favorite earrings. She said she needed to leave early because she was spending some time with George. She was so excited; they were going out for a late dinner, and she kept checking her watch."

Wow. Joyce *was* good.

"We all went down to the hull to toast Ashley and Bob—they had just announced their engagement a few days before—and…" Joyce trailed off, squinting, as if she were remembering something, or trying hard to remember something. "Dani's cell phone rang. That was back when no matter where you were, you had bad reception, so she excused herself and went to the deck to hear better. When she never came back down, Amanda went to check on her and found her, found her in the water. Mandy screamed, and we all came running. Ashley called the coast guard, and Tonia—who was a champion swimmer—jumped in to try and save her, but it was too late."

Lauren was staring at Joyce in a mixture of horror and intrigue, and I was staring at Lauren with caution. This was a lot for me to hear, let alone Lauren. I mean, it was her mother, for crying out loud. I wasn't overly fond of my mother at all times, but she's my mom and I loved her, and if I ever had to hear—in detail—the time line of the night she died, I'd probably be sick to my stomach.

Joyce cleared her throat and shook her head a little as if coming out of a reverie. It must have been a horrible memory, reliving one of your best friend's deaths. I didn't even like reliving Rachel's wedding.

I figured that we had mentally bombarded Joyce enough for one day, so I stood up and said, "Thank you so much for answering our questions, Mrs. Miller. I know this isn't the easiest thing to talk about, so we appreciate you helping us out."

"Yes, we really do," Lauren chimed in, standing and smiling almost convincingly.

Oscar watched her intently, waiting for one last chance to say something to her. So adorable.

Joyce smiled and said, "I hadn't thought about it in a long time. If you need anything else, Lauren, or you want someone to talk to, please give me a call."

Joyce handed Lauren a business card, and I peered at it over her shoulder. *Of course.* Joyce was a shrink. She probably thought Lauren was about to go off the deep end, morbid-wise, and wanted to be there with the happy pills just in case.

Oscar walked us to the door, staring at Lauren, even comically bumping into a table in his eagerness to walk beside her. I kept my mouth shut and just smiled. He was a sweet kid, and he liked Lauren. We would have to talk about this later.

When we got back into the limo, Lauren slumped against the seat and covered her face. "That was intense," she said, rubbing her temples.

"Yeah," I agreed, sliding my arm around her shoulders. "Probably too much. Definitely enough for one day. Hey, Greg," I called, rapping on the screen. "We need ice cream!"

The screen went rolling down and Greg said, "There's a Baskin Robbins on the end of this street. Does that work?"

"Yes, please!" I said, rubbing Lauren's arm. "Everything is a little better after a big scoop of fudge mint. Promise."

She smiled and rested her head against me. "It's tiring, all this putting on a brave face. I feel like my cheeks are sore from fake smiling all day."

I laughed and said, "Well, we got a lot of information today. More than I thought we would find out. Did you know that your mom was going to adopt Lance and Lucas? Is that even legal when the birth mother is living and has custody?"

"No idea. I hadn't heard of it, either. I knew Mom always thought of Lance and Lucas like her own kids, but I don't know. I didn't know that Mom and Dad wanted more kids. I had never heard that before today. Very weird," Lauren said, rolling her eyes.

I excused myself and hopped out of the limo long enough to get two fudge mint cones from Baskin Robbins. I slid back inside and handed Lauren one.

"So what now, Chicken Little?" I asked, licking a drippy spot.

Lauren gave me a sheepish grin and said, "You wouldn't want to go shoe shopping at Chanel, would you?"

I rolled my eyes. "Somehow I don't think dropping a couple grand on shoes is really going to make you feel that much better in the long run. Besides, I shop as a celebratory exercise, not a pick-me-up. It's healthier that way."

Lauren frowned and pretended to think very hard. "Julia Roberts marathon? *Pretty Woman*, *Notting Hill*, and *Runaway Bride*?"

"Now that, I can support," I laughed, and we told Greg to head home.

# CHAPTER 6

October in New York is my favorite time of year. I mean, sure, December is pretty awesome, what with Rockefeller center; and summer time is cool because of all the street fairs and the festivals, plus they're always filming something on Fifth. I've been a "person in the crowd" on three different TV shows. But October is perfect weather, and the trees in Central Park start to turn colors. Best of all, the new lines come out in all the department stores.

I had been at the Daytons' for exactly a month. Two and a half weeks had gone by since Lauren and I had taken our turn as the girl detectives, and she hadn't brought it up again, causing me to wonder just how draining hearing all about her mother's last days was to her.

Things had been pretty good for me. My sister-in-law, Susan, had her second son, a boy named William Rigby Maxwell Hart. I tried to call her to congratulate her on the baby, but I kept getting her voicemail. My mom showed no sign of excitement over her third grandson, saying only that she hoped Diana and Barry had a girl, because she was tired of buying blue. Ah, priorities.

Lucas was around almost all the time. He always seemed to be available if we were going to the movies or out to eat. And he started doing the weirdest thing: He started making comments that veered a little too close to the edge of flirting.

Like, once, when Lauren, Lucas, and I went out to eat, he sat across from us in a booth and kicked my foot the entire meal. I shifted in my seat, thinking he didn't realize what he was doing. The next thing I knew, he must have kicked Lauren, because she yelped, "Ow!" and glared at him.

"What was that for?"

"Sorry," Lucas said, completely cool with having been caught. "I was aiming for Heidi."

Lauren had narrowed her eyes and asked, "Why were you trying to kick Heidi?"

Lucas had then developed the audacity to shrug and say, "We were playing footsie."

My jaw had dropped, and I cried, "Um, hello, it can't be playing footsie if I wasn't kicking back!"

He had made some snide remark about how he was giving me a learning curve since I was younger than him, to which I believe my exact words were, "Okay, now I *want* to kick you."

Lauren had laughed hysterically through most of this.

Another time, when Lauren was arguing with George about her curfew—her argument: if I was with her, what trouble could she possibly get in?—she appealed to Lucas by asking, "You wouldn't care if your kids stayed out until one with their nanny/companion/person, would you? I mean, it's just a late movie. It's not like we'd be clubbing or something."

Lucas had totally *not* helped the situation by saying nonchalantly, "Ask Heidi, she's going to be the disciplinarian, not me. I want our kids to like me more."

I nearly swallowed my tongue at that one. I wanted to throttle him for saying that in front of his father, my employer. That had been the worst of the bunch. I could handle all the innuendos and the flirtatious eyebrow wagging (seriously, who does that if they aren't John Cryer in the eighties?) because they were all innocent and discreet. He never crossed any lines of indecency, and he never made me feel threatened or belittled. Actually it was all pretty good for my ego, considering how many times he complimented my outfit, hair, brain, wit, and overall appearance.

But, seriously, he needed to stop. He was giving Lauren entirely too much ammunition against me. She was starting to get ideas, and none of them were good.

Which was why, when she came home shrieking and carrying on like a wild woman the second Friday of October, I was psyched. She obviously had something new to distract her. I had a lot of respect for the girl, but she was a little flaky—wag something shiny in front of her, and she totally loses her concentration.

"I asked him, I asked him, I asked him," she chanted, jumping up and down and grabbing my arms. "I asked Connor Whitson to the cotillion, and he said 'yes.' He actually said that he was hoping I would ask him!"

I smiled and hugged her. "This calls for celebration. We are so doing something special this weekend."

Lauren bit her lip and said, "Actually I think I want to interview Amanda Honey. I gave myself some time to recover from the last time we went fact finding, and I want to keep trying. I want to make sense of some things we've found out about."

I gave her a half-hearted smile and nodded. "I'll get out my sleuthing kit."

The next morning, bright and early (okay, nine-thirty, but it was early enough for me), Lauren and I ran down the stairs. Lauren was dressed in jeans and a blue T-shirt with a purple hoodie and Converse, me in jeans and a white turtleneck and black boots. We stopped in at the kitchen, where we sweet-talked Eliza out of two blueberry muffins and two large orange juices in Styrofoam cups.

We were on our way out the door when I heard someone say, "And where are you ladies headed this early Saturday morning?"

Lucas, dressed in jeans and a red sweater, was nursing a cup of tea and looking at us suspiciously. "Sale at Barney's?" he asked, raising an eyebrow.

I rolled my eyes. Lauren grinned and said, "No, we're going to ask some people questions about my mom."

I think Lucas was about an inch away from having his eyebrows disappear completely into his hairline. He looked at me in complete and total shock.

"Heidi? A word?"

I gave Lauren a frustrated glance and followed Lucas to the empty dining room. He set his coffee mug down, turned around to face me, and crossed his arms. "Now what are you doing with my little sister?"

I swallowed and said defensively, "It was her idea. After that whole Claude thing, she wanted to find out what she could about what happened to her mother. It's not that big of a deal. We're just interviewing the women that were on the boat the night Daniella died."

Lucas shook his head. "I'm going with you."

"No, Lucas, we're fine. We never do anything dangerous, and Lauren knows her limits. We're just going a few blocks over to interview Amanda Honey. That's it. No muss, no fuss," I said, trying to smile innocently.

Lucas put his hands on his hips and said, "You aren't talking me out of this."

I smiled winningly at him and said, "Oh, come on, Lucas. You don't want to crash a girls' day, do you?"

His lips quirked up into a smile, and he said, "If it involves hanging out with you, then, sure. I can put up with some girl talk. I'll grab a jacket."

I exhaled and said, "You just don't give up, do you?"

Lucas shrugged. "You haven't given me a reason to, yet."

"What are the odds I'll be able to come up with that reason in the next ten minutes?" I asked, tilting my head.

"Slim to none."

"Slim like no-fat yogurt slim or slim like anorexic celebrity slim?" I asked, smiling a little.

Lucas shook his head again and blew air out of his mouth, a sign of amusement for him. "Your brain makes me worry."

I sighed and rolled my eyes. "Fine. Come on. But you stay out of our business, understand? You are to be perfectly silent. Lauren and I ask the questions, and you sit there quietly and look pretty, okay?"

Lucas cocked his head to one side and grinned smugly. "You think I'm pretty?"

I let out a bark of laughter. "Can you say digging?"

I turned and walked out of the dining room, still amused. Lauren raised her eyebrows at us, but I shook my head and motioned her onward. Lucas grabbed a leather jacket and followed us, doing a bang-up job at the not talking rule. Greg opened the door—this time to a new black Range Rover—and the three of us filed into the back seat, me in the middle.

Lauren leaned forward and recited the address to Greg, then sat back and buckled her seatbelt. She turned to me and whispered, "I don't really know Amanda Honey. She may not be so willing to talk to us as Mrs. Engle and Mrs. Miller. I just picked her next because she...she found the body."

Lucas coughed. As if I hadn't known he was listening. We were in a Range Rover, for crying out loud. I could practically read Lauren's mind, we were sitting so close.

"Would you like to add something?" I asked, turning to look at him.

"How does she know who found the body?" Lucas hissed, glaring at me.

"Um, *she* is sitting right here and can hear you," Lauren reminded him sweetly.

"Joyce Miller told us," I replied, feeling tired. He looked pretty mad, which was surprisingly more upsetting than when he was flirting with me.

Lucas rolled his eyes and pursed his lips. Finally, after a long pause, he said, "Amanda Honey is a well-known interior designer who enjoys sailing and Merlot. She uses her appearance to make friends and win clients, but she's no dummy."

Lauren and I stared at Lucas with raised eyebrows and small smiles.

"And how do you know all this?" I asked, trying not to laugh.

Lucas looked like he was thinking about blushing but held it in.

"She was married to a buddy of mine for about five minutes. Nice lady, but she really just wants to have fun and decorate stuff."

"Uh huh," Lauren said, smirking. "Sounds like maybe she wanted to decorate you too."

Lucas rolled his eyes and looked out the window. "Oh, look, we're here," he said brightly as Greg slowed the car and pulled to a stop. Lucas unbuckled, opened the door, and said, "Party time."

Lauren and I exchanged a smile, and we climbed out after him. The three of us jogged up the steps and rang the bell, waiting anxiously on the stoop. A few minutes later, a truly gorgeous woman answered the door.

"Hello?" she said sweetly, taking us all in, lingering on Lucas. Her eyes lit up, and she said, "Lucas Dayton. How are you, darling?"

Lauren giggled but recovered nicely. Lucas looked pained, and I felt sorry for him until he grabbed my arm, yanked it upward to bring my hand out of my pocket, and laced his fingers through mine.

"I'm doing well, Amanda, how are you?"

Before I could kick him in the kneecap, Amanda moved to one side and said demurely, "Please come in."

Lauren walked in first, and Lucas pulled me through the door next. Amanda shut the door and led us to an absolutely beautiful living room. Amanda stood in the middle of the room, her white blonde hair cascading down her back, her dark brown eyes accented by the brown leather furniture in the room, her beautifully cut turquoise dress bringing out the Indian print pattern in the floor-length curtains. Huh. She matched her living room. Interesting kind of designer.

"Please, sit down," Amanda purred. She sat down on a dark purple settee and crossed her long, very tan legs at the ankle. She looked like a modern day Cleopatra. "What can I help you all with?"

"Ms. Honey, I'm Lauren Dayton. I believe you knew my mother?" Lauren asked, sounding perfectly pleasant and sweet.

Amanda took her gaze off Lucas and fixed it on Lauren. "Dani was a doll. I miss her dearly. You look like her, you know, and you should take that as a compliment. Dani Dayton was a beautiful woman."

Lauren nodded and said, "Ms. Honey, can we ask you a few questions about my mother?"

Amanda propped her chin up a little with her knuckles, a pose that perfectly highlighted her lovely profile. "Lauren, please call me Amanda. Everyone does. And you can ask me anything you want. I am an open book."

I refrained from making the four snide remarks that came to mind at that point.

"Did my mother say anything to you about her marriage before she died?" Lauren asked, leaning forward a bit in her eagerness.

Amanda blinked, her long lashes fluttering rapidly. "Oh. Those questions. Well, Dani was nuts about George. He was... older, but he kept up. That was an accomplishment, believe me. Dani was so full of life. She used to drag you around the city like it wouldn't be there the next day."

Lauren smiled at that, and Lucas shifted uncomfortably in his seat next to me. He hadn't dropped my hand yet, despite the fact that I had pinched him three times, twice with nails. He either wasn't getting the hint or he was a champion at ignoring pain.

"Amanda," I asked, and her eyes flicked to me, even though her smile lessened considerably. "We spoke to Joyce Miller a few weeks ago, and she told us that you found Daniella's body. Can you tell us everything you remember about that night?"

Amanda's perfect face blanched. "That was ten years ago. I barely remember what happened last week."

Lucas cleared his throat. "Try," he suggested, sending me an "I give up" grin. I wasn't buying it. He still had a death grip on my hand.

Amanda sighed and appeared deep in thought. "Well, we were celebrating Ashley and Bob's engagement. Ashley wanted to take a sail. Bob had gotten her a boat for her birthday. She had always known how to sail, so we figured it would be a blast. Dani told us all a hundred times that we could sail around for an hour or two, but that we couldn't be far from the coast because she was leaving early to meet George for a late dinner. She said they were celebrating something."

I felt Lucas stiffen next to me, but when I glanced at him, he just had a frown on his face. I couldn't tell if he was upset or if he thought she was lying.

"So we had a toast for Ashley and Bob, and, halfway through the clinking, Dani's cell phone rang. Only she couldn't hear anything or something, so she went up to the deck. I, um, I went to check on her after about twenty minutes or so because I thought maybe she got some bad news since she hadn't come back down, and I couldn't see her. I called her name..." Amanda trailed off, staring into space. "I tripped on some...some rope or something, and I caught myself on the railing, and that's when I noticed her. In the water. I screamed, and the other girls came running."

I narrowed my eyes. "Are you sure it was rope that you tripped over?"

Amanda shook her head and bit her perfectly lined lip. "No," she said, with regret. "A lot of that evening was a blur. I loved Dani, she was a wonderful friend, but I think I repressed a lot of that night."

Lauren nodded. "I understand. Was...do you remember if Mom was drunk?"

Amanda looked offended for some reason. "No," she said, giving us a disgusted glance. "Who have you been listening to? Did Joyce say that? None of us were drunk. Well, maybe Ashley a little bit, but she was the guest of honor. Dani didn't drink a thing that night. Maybe one sip of champagne for the toast, but that's it. Tonia wasn't drinking either. Never did. Susie had made this big deal that she didn't want to ever come home drunk because she didn't want her kids seeing her that way. I wish I'd known that earlier. I spent over eight hundred dollars on wine and champagne that night, and we didn't even go through one bottle."

"The police told us that you were all drinking," Lucas said, his voice very non-threatening.

Amanda shook her head. "Look, I know it was ten years ago and that we were a bunch of stupid kids, but I remember very clearly that we weren't drunk. I don't know how it got into the police report that we were, but believe me when I say that we were not drunk."

She said this with so much certainty, so much authority, that I instantly believed her. That's why I said, "I believe you. I really do. And we really appreciate you answering all our questions. I know they can't be easy for you to think about."

Amanda softened a little. "I hadn't thought about that night in a long time. I think about Dani a lot, and I even wondered from time to time what you were doing, Lauren. You were too little to remember, but your mom and I used to take you for walks. I was Aunt Mandy for a little while."

Lauren smiled. "I didn't remember that actually. I don't remember very much at all from before Mom died."

Amanda tilted her head and said, "You know, I think I have a bunch of pictures from about that time. Would you like them? I can dig them up and send them to you."

Lauren looked delighted, and it warmed my heart. It almost made me forget that my hand was asleep from the pressure there.

"I would love that," she said, jumping up. "Thank you so much."

Amanda stood up and hugged Lauren. I stood up too, nearly dislocating my arm when Lucas was a little slow on the uptake.

Amanda showed us out the door, promising to messenger over the pictures as soon as she found them. When she shut the door and Lauren opened the Range Rover door and slid in, I yanked my hand out of Lucas' iron clasp. "What were you thinking?" I demanded, flexing my fingers. "You didn't have to hold my hand the whole time, you know."

"I know," he said, grinning a little. "But it made the experience marginally more enjoyable."

I smiled and shook my head. I slid in next to Lauren and rubbed her arm. "How you feeling, babe?"

"Not bad," she said, shrugging her shoulders. "I liked her. Once you get past her exterior, she's pretty nice. I can see why Mom liked her. She seems so young and fun."

"She's only forty," Lucas said, slamming the door shut. "She isn't that old."

I gave Lauren a mock-serious glare. "Gosh, Lauren, I think Lucas feels like you've said something against his lady love."

"Don't you start something you can't finish," he warned, buckling his seatbelt.

"What is that supposed to mean?" I asked, buckling my own seatbelt.

"If you can't take it, don't dish it out."

I rolled my eyes. "Oh, please."

I turned to Lauren, fully intending on ignoring Lucas for the rest of the ride—possibly for the rest of all time—and said, "Where do you think I could get a copy of the police report from the night your mom died?"

"What would you need that for?" Lucas asked, sounding suspicious, but I simply held up my hand and shushed him.

"Did you just shush me?" he asked, sounding entirely too amused. "If you aren't careful, I'm going to hold your hand the rest of the way home."

I immediately brought my hand down to my lap and clenched it into a fist.

"Why do you want the police report?" Lauren asked, apparently choosing to ignore her brother, as well. Solidarity and all.

I shrugged. "I want to know why the police thought everyone was drunk. I want to know if the police even thought that the women were drunk. That story was circulated somehow, and I want to know how."

"Since when did you become Nancy Drew?" Lucas asked, and I shook my head and ignored him.

Lauren was nodding. "I see. Because if the women weren't drunk, then Mom's death wasn't the result of...what's the word? Negligee?"

I coughed. "Uh, negligence. I think that's the word you're looking for. I hope that's the word you're looking for."

Lauren sank back into her seat, lost in thought, and I began to feel guilty. I mean, I knew it was her choice that we were doing this. I knew that it was her idea that we do this, but it was still hard on her. I glanced at Lucas, who shrugged his shoulders, and I sighed. "Let's go do something fun. I want to go to Central Park. Greg," I said, leaning forward, "can we go to Central Park?"

"Right away," he said, turning down a side street.

We rode in silence until Greg let us out at the park. We wandered around for a few minutes, not saying anything, until we came to the big carousel. Lucas glanced at us and then said, "Come on, let's ride."

Lauren grinned and I laughed. "Seriously?" I asked. Somehow, I couldn't picture Lucas—or any six foot, two inches, one-hundred-and-ninety-pound man—riding the carousel. But he paid for our tickets, and we selected our horses. Lauren was in front of me, and Lucas was on the horse next to me.

I glanced at him, started to say something, and changed my mind.

He laughed. "No, go ahead and say it. I know you want to say something to me."

I looked at Lauren to see if she was listening, but she was staring into the crowd that always forms to watch the carousel riders. She was smiling like a little kid.

I leaned closer to Lucas's horse and said, "Look, I don't mean to pry, and I know this is a crappy thing to ask you after you were so nice and helpful today, but how are you available to spend so much time with us? And don't give me some flippant answer about how you make time or whatever. Be straight with me."

Lucas sighed. He spared a glance at Lauren before saying, "Listen, can you keep a secret?"

I raised my eyebrows. "Hello? My job is basically boiled down to being a confidant to a fifteen-year-old girl. I'm like the CIA."

He smiled at that and said, "Okay. I'm sorry I doubted you. I haven't told anybody yet because I don't want to deal with all the grief that my parents are going to give me. I quit my job last month."

My mouth dropped open a little—completely involuntary—and I snapped it shut.

"You were…you worked in PR, right?"

"Yeah. My dad got me into it when I was in college. I was good at it. I figured, why not? But I never loved it. I was sitting in my office one day, signing off on a budget plan for a charity dinner, and I realized I felt old. I'm twenty-six years old, and yet I felt like I had bags under my eyes and rust in my joints. My dad and Lance, they love their jobs. I didn't want to spend another moment doing something that was aging me," Lucas said, looking at the mirrors on the carousel.

"That's a good thing, though, right?" I asked, not sure what to say. "I mean, you want to be happy with your job."

Lucas nodded. "I haven't regretted it yet. I guess because it was the right thing to do."

We rode in silence for a few moments. "So what are you going to do now?" I asked, turning my head to look at him.

Lucas shrugged. The carousel lights glittered red and blue, sending a purple glow all over him that reflected off his leather jacket. "I have some ideas. None my parents will like."

"I can't speak for George because, well, I don't think anyone can and live to tell the tale, but I'm sure Alexis will support you in whatever you choose to do," I said, trying to be helpful.

Lucas' lips held the ghost of a smile. "Probably, but that's not who I was talking about. Alexis isn't my mom, remember? No, my mother was thrilled that I had a good job that put me in contact with high-profile people. The only way she ever saw for me was up. Lance always knew he would be in the same business as Dad. Mom made sure of that. I got plan B, but it wasn't what I wanted."

It sounded like Maureen Dayton was good at railroading her kids into doing what she wanted them to do. It also sounded like Lucas was afraid of going up against her.

It sounded miserable.

For the first time, I realized what it must have been like for Lucas and Lance before Daniella and Lauren came on the scene. Maureen sounded like she was the boss. With George at work and Maureen alone with the boys…

*Stop it*, I told myself. *You are being ridiculous. You have no reason to believe that Maureen is some controlling mama. You are just feeling sorry for Lucas. Why, that's not certain. Just get over it.*

Lucas was laughing when I came out of my little reverie.

"You look like you're having a little conversation with yourself. Anything interesting?"

I turned up my nose at him. "Oh, look, the ride's slowing down. Time to get off."

I swung my leg off the horse and planted both feet on the ground, placing my hands on the saddle of the horse. I spread my fingers out and something clicked in my head. I looked up at the pole that held the horse. I wrapped my hand around it and held on as tight as I could. "Lucas," I said over my shoulder, "push me."

"Excuse me?"

"I want to try something. Just…just pick me up and try to carry me off the ride, okay?" I said, knowing that I was going to regret this, but I had to know something.

Lauren laughed. "Are you sure you want to do this?"

I sighed. "Just do it," I said, losing my patience—or more importantly, my nerve. I tightened my grip, and Lucas let out a sigh of resignation. He put his hands on my hips and hesitated.

"They are waiting for us to clear the ride," I said through clenched teeth. "Just do it."

Lucas picked me up and tried to step off the ride, but I held on for dear life. He slid his hand until his forearm rested against my abdomen and pulled harder. Finally, after another valiant tug, I lost my grip, and he took a big step back to steady himself. He sat me down and let go just as an elderly woman and three little boys rushed up to us.

The woman swung her handbag as hard as she could into Lucas's stomach.

"You pervert!" she shouted, her tiny little glasses glinting in the autumn sunlight. Her hair was curled tightly against her head, and she was wearing a loose flowered dress and a baggy mauve sweater. She looked like a typical grandma, only she was beating the crap out of Lucas.

I gasped and Lauren covered her mouth.

"Ma'am," I said, trying to get her attention, but she slammed her purse into Lucas's back as he had doubled over when the bag made contact with his abs.

"I'll teach you not to grab some poor girl," the woman cried, and the three little boys all watched in awe.

The oldest of the bunch, who I guessed was about nine, although I could be way off because I haven't been around little kids since I was one, said, "Gram, you're gonna kill him."

The second tallest boy said, "Hit him again, Grammie!"

"Look, ma'am, he's my friend. I asked him to try to get me off the ride as an experiment. He wasn't trying to grab me," I explained, trying to get her to back off.

The woman looked at me like she didn't believe me. In fact, she squinted up her wrinkled little eyes and said, "Don't you defend him, dear. If he hurt you…"

Lauren couldn't help it at this point. She burst out laughing.

"Ma'am, this is my brother, and I promise, he's not a creep. He really was trying to help."

The woman relaxed her arm, dropping her defensive stance and swinging her purse by her side. She fixed me with a hard look. "Be more careful, young lady. The next time, it could be a pervert. I watch the news. I see all those reports about those men who grab innocent girls and take them Lord knows where to do Lord knows what with them. I'd hate for a pretty girl like yourself to be the next poor girl they show on the news."

I smiled and said, "Thank you. I appreciate your…concern."

The woman gathered the three little boys up and huffed away amid their whining that they wanted to stay and play. I shook my head.

"And that's why my grandmother doesn't have a television. She'd drive us all crazy if she knew what was going on in this city."

Lucas glared at me. He brushed his hand across his stomach and said, "You."

I smiled sheepishly and said, "I didn't think Jackie Chan's grandma would come attack you. But it was really funny."

Lauren and I burst into giggles.

"She kicked your butt," Lauren said, barely able to stand up straight from laughter.

"I couldn't exactly fight back," Lucas said, scowling. "I mean, what was I going to do? Put my palm to her forehead and hold her at swinging distance? Freakin' homicidal grandma."

That made us both laugh even harder. I had never seen Lucas lose his composure before, but it was pretty funny.

"Would you like to explain why I had to haul you off the carousel so I can determine if these are even good pains I'm having?" Lucas grumbled, straightening a little more.

I blinked. "Oh, that. I forgot for a second, what with all the... interruptions. The pole to the carousel was about the same size as the railing in the pictures of the boat Lauren and I found. I wanted to see how hard it would be to pull someone away from that railing if they were holding on for dear...I mean, holding on really tightly."

Lucas closed his eyes, presumably in frustration. Lauren raised her eyebrows and said, "So you think Mom was pushed off the boat, don't you?"

I shrugged. "I don't know what to think. I mean, I agree with what you said before. I don't think Daniella killed herself. And I can't figure out how she could have drowned. I really wish I could get my hands on the police report..." I trailed off, having trouble hiding the epiphany I had just gotten. I smiled. "But you know, we've done a lot today. We should go home. I'm starving, and there should be leftovers from that roast Eliza made last night, right?"

Lucas and Lauren laughed. "Alexis always takes leftovers to the homeless shelter on her way to the charity's office. All the women who work there do. That's why we make so much. Eliza usually doubles the recipe," Lauren explained.

Rats. So I took that as a "no" on another slice of the chocolate cake. If I smuggled that from the table before Eliza took the dish away and hid it in my room, would I get fired? Probably. Or sent to a home.

I grinned at Lucas. "You okay to go home, or should we get you an ice pack?"

Lucas shook his head, trying to hide a smile. "I think she had a brick in her purse. Something gave that thing a punch."

"Sure it did," I said soothingly, blatantly patronizing him.

"Sure, laugh at me," he said bitterly, pulling the hem of his jacket in emphasis of his irritation. "It's not like it was your fault or anything."

I smiled angelically. "Next time I ask you to do something, don't hesitate. We could have been done and off the ride long before that lady came by if you'd just done what I asked when I asked."

Lucas looked at me incredulously. "And the sad part is, I don't think you're kidding."

# CHAPTER 7

Since I had Sundays off, I decided to get my trip to see my newest nephew out of the way. William Rigby Maxwell Hart was now three weeks old, thus past that whole red body, scabby thing in the belly button stage that babies have that kind of freaks me out. I mean, yes, I realize all babies are beautiful and that they are a gift from God and all, but newborns kind of send me into a blind panic. I never know what they're thinking. Are they uncomfortable? Am I holding them too tightly? Too loosely? And they're so wiggly. Babies are nice and all, but I like them in pictures and stuff. When a new mom wants me to hold her baby, it literally sends shivers down my spine. Toddlers, I can do. As soon as they start talking and can say, "No, thank you, I would not like another cracker, and can you please let me down before I vomit on you?" I am all about little kids.

Portia, Max and Susan's housekeeper, let me into their house, and I looked around as I handed her my sweater. Max had married someone a lot like our mom; Susan had expensive taste, and she always got what she wanted. Despite those two things, I actually liked my sister-in-law. She's short—way shorter than me—and tiny, like a little fairy or something. She had strawberry blonde hair that she doesn't have to color every six weeks like my sisters do. Maxie inherited her hair, but everything else was his father (and his grandfather). Maxie, like his father, would never be tall or slender, but his broad shoulders evened out his thick chest. His soft hair fell over his forehead, making it almost impossible for me to walk by the kid without touching his hair, as it makes him so adorable (his dad doesn't have this problem, as his hairline started receding at age nineteen).

Susan, always fashionable, was dressed in various shades of peach that day. She was sitting at her desk, writing thank you cards for baby gifts, when I walked in.

"Hi, Suz," I said, using the nickname that I'm pretty sure only I called her.

She looked up and smiled pleasantly. Everything about Susan was pleasant, all the time. I'd never seen her visibly upset. She stood up, brushed her skirt (as if sitting perfectly still with pristine posture could have wrinkled her skirt), and reached out to give me a society hug (gently clasping one's hands to the other person's shoulders and air kissing both cheeks).

"What are you doing here?" Susan asked, but not rudely. She looked glad to have a visitor.

"I thought I'd come see the baby. I brought this," I handed her a blue box, which held a toy zebra. Lauren had picked it out because she said that the train set (which was so cool—it had a bridge and a post office station and little people that rode said train and picked up their mail at said post office station) that I wanted to buy was too old for a baby. Whatever, I almost bought it for myself. It was awesome. I was just relieved that I had money to buy the kid a gift—George certainly hadn't been kidding when he showed me my initial salary figures. If I'd known nanny companions (cannies?) made this kind of money, I wouldn't have majored in business. Although, I suppose working for a multi-millionaire (he had to be close to being called a billionaire by now) may have more to do with it than the services I actually provided.

Susan led me to an armchair, motioned for me to sit, and then sat down in her desk chair. She carefully opened the present, gave me the appropriate amount of thanks for the gift, and then asked me if I would like to see the boys.

I nodded. I hadn't seen Maxie since the summer, and he was getting close to being four.

As Susan and I walked through her powder blue hallway, I asked, "How is William? Is he a good baby?"

Susan turned to look at me and said, "We call him Rigby, actually. Maxie liked it. It was from a picture book the nanny reads to him, and Max and I thought it was nice. Dignified."

I thought it sounded like a sport where men hit each other and got muddy.

"Does Maxie like being a big brother?" I asked, trying to get my information before seeing the kid. Forewarned is forearmed.

"I suppose. He likes to dangle things in front of him, anyway, which I'm not sure I should let him do," Susan said, putting her hand to her cheek in reflection, and I shrugged because I had no idea.

Susan opened the door to the children's suite, a powder blue room filled with beautiful and expensive toys and furniture. This was where the nanny—a young woman named Addy—kept the boys occupied all day. Addy had been with the family since Maxie was one, and I liked Addy. She was nice. Quiet, but nice.

Addy was sitting in a rocking chair, rocking what appeared to be a massive mound of blankets, while Maxie sat on the floor playing with a puzzle. Addy hadn't changed any since the last time I saw her. Her black hair was pulled into a tight French braid, and her pale skin had no make-up. Maxie was wearing a button-up shirt, khakis, and a sweater vest. Nope, not kidding. He looked like he went to Harvard Law preschool.

Rigby peeked out from behind the mountain of blankets. His pink skin and dark curly hair made him a pretty cute baby, but I declined the offer to hold him, saying I thought I had a cold. It was for the kid's own good, believe me.

"Oh, he's adorable, Suz," I said, smiling at her. "Maxie, do you like having a little brother?"

Maxie blinked at me, looked at his mother, and then said, "Yes. Rigby is too small to play with though. I have to wait until he's bigger."

I nodded. "Of course," I said, feeling awkward. I had no idea what else to say, so I turned to Addy and asked, "How are you?"

Addy smiled politely and said, "I'm doing fine. Maxie and I took Rigby to the park yesterday. Maxie likes to scare the geese at the pond."

"Huh," was all I could come up with to say. I liked the geese at the pond. I used to feed them when I was little. Poor geese, you didn't ask for a future sociopath three-and-a-half-year-old to come chase you around, did you?

I looked back at Susan and said, "Well, the boys look great. You look wonderful. I can't believe how fast you got your figure back."

Susan blushed. "Well, I've always eaten my vegetables, and I'm religious with my Pilates. I can recommend a few excellent instructors, if you like."

I wasn't sure if she was simply endorsing Pilates or if she was calling me fat, so I simply said, "Maybe. I've been pretty busy."

Complete and total lie. For eight hours a day I longed for something to do.

I extricated myself from my brother's house. Since the day was already going so well—I mean, I got in and out of Max's house without having to actually see Max—I decided to give Jennifer a call and see what she was doing.

When she answered the phone, she sounded really weird. When she wouldn't tell me what was wrong, I told her I was coming over and hung up the phone. I hailed a taxi and tapped my foot impatiently as he drove me to Jennifer's apartment.

When she answered the door, her face was red, and her eyes were watery. She had on a cute little black V-neck sweater that showed off her little pregnancy belly—I did some mental math and figured she was about four months along or so—and her hair was in a ponytail. Somehow, with her face so red and splotchy, her hair looked even blonder, and for a moment I was sure it had finally just lost the will to hold color and faded to white.

"What's wrong?" I asked, grabbing her arm as we walked to the living room.

Jennifer wiped her eyes with her shaking fingers, and I realized that for the first time since we had been friends she wasn't wearing makeup after 9:00 a.m. She was religiously diligent about never being caught without makeup on, yet here she was looking like she didn't even care. That was not a good sign.

"Heidi," she whimpered, leaning dejectedly against the back of the soft, gray couch, "I think Kevin is having an affair."

I raised both eyebrows. Kevin Pierce? I'd known Kevin for about five years now, and he'd never struck me as the type that would even think about being unfaithful.

"Oh, Jen, are you sure? I mean, Kevin loves you," I said, brushing her bangs out of her eyes.

Jennifer shook her head, letting her bangs fall back into place.

"They're supposed to be in my eyes, Heidi. That's the way people are wearing their hair now."

I held back a sigh. Maybe I wouldn't blame Kevin for—No. That was horrible. I couldn't believe I even thought that.

"Jen, why do you think Kevin is having an affair?" I asked, trying to remember that she was hurting right now, and besides, you're not supposed to yell at pregnant women.

"He's been working really late, and he's always in a bad mood when he comes home, like he'd rather be somewhere else," Jennifer said, sounding miserable.

I felt awful. Jennifer may have been the kind of person that could drive you up the wall any given time of day, but she was a good person with a good heart who had been my friend for years. I didn't want to see her hurting.

"Maybe he has a really big project at work right now. Or maybe he's worried about a promotion or something," I said, trying to find a bright side or at least an excuse.

"Maybe," Jennifer said, playing with the hem of her sweater. "Heidi, he's been weird for a while, though. He hasn't made it to any of my doctor's appointments in the last three weeks, and he's been distant. He hasn't eaten dinner here two days in a row since September. I just don't know what to do."

Neither did I. I still couldn't believe that Kevin would cheat on Jen, but I didn't want to minimize her anxiety. It was very real to her, and I had to respect that. I cleared my throat and said, "Jennifer Kaye, stop this. Kevin loves you. He's loved you for a really long time. Everyone goes through tough times, and you just have to stick to what you know."

"What do you mean?" Jen asked, her voice breaking. I handed her a tissue out of my purse, and she blew her nose.

"Tell me what you know for one hundred percent sure in this world," I suggested, feeling rather deep. *Maybe I should write a self-help book.*

Jennifer looked thoughtful. "Nothing fits or feels better than a little black dress from Bergdorf's?"

I blinked. Maybe not so much on the self-help book.

"What I meant was about your life. About Kevin."

"Oh," Jennifer said, sounding less confused. She smiled a little through her still pretty weepy expression. "I know that Kevin is excited to have a baby."

I smiled. "Uh huh. Go on."

"I know that he wants to name it Spencer if it's a boy," Jen said, staring at her feet with a slightly bigger smile on her face. "I know that he wants us to get a place in Connecticut, and he wants a dog so we can take it on walks. I know he's always talked about going to Paris for our fifth anniversary."

I nodded. "It sounds like you know Kevin pretty well. Think, Jen. Would the Kevin Pierce that you know—the Kevin Pierce that you love—cheat on you?"

Jennifer shook her head, fresh tears appearing on her eyelids. "No," she whispered, rolling her eyes and exhaling. She smiled a little. "I guess I'm pretty stupid, huh?"

"No," I said, laughing. "You're not stupid. You're a little paranoid, but I hear that's a symptom of pregnancy or something."

Jen looked at me for a few minutes, as if evaluating something. "Heidi? Are you seeing anyone right now?"

I shook my head. "No."

"Are you working?"

"Yeah. I have…I have sort of a weird job," I said, hoping she wouldn't ask what it was.

Jen raised an eyebrow. "Really? What is it?"

*Shoot.*

"Um, I'm working as a nanny for George Dayton until I can find something else," I said in one breath, trying to get the worst over with.

Jen looked surprised. "I didn't think you liked children."

That surprised me a little bit. I didn't have the burning need to produce as many adorable offspring as some women I knew, but I certainly didn't dislike children. I might have one. Someday.

"No, I like kids. I mean, George's daughter is actually fifteen and pretty cool. He just wants someone for her to be able to go to if she needs something."

Jennifer squinted a little, as if she were trying to figure something out.

"Didn't George Dayton's wife die? Like, she drowned or something?"

"Yeah," I said, intrigued. I hadn't ever heard of this before working for the family, so I was curious to see what Jen had heard. "Ten years ago."

Jennifer nodded slowly. "Yeah, I guess it would have been. I was in eighth grade, and Sarah came home saying that Lucas and Lance's stepmom had died. Sarah dated Lance for a little while. He was a cutie."

*Wow. Small world. Jen's sister dated Lance Dayton at the time of the accident?*

"Um, Jen, do you have a new number for Sarah? I want to send her a Christmas card this year, and I don't have an address or a number for her," I lied. I was getting pretty darn good at the lying thing. Maybe I should stop that.

"Sure," Jennifer said, getting up and leaving the room for a few minutes. She came back with a slip of stationary with Sarah's new number and address written on it in Jen's loopy cursive handwriting. I tucked it into my wallet and turned back to Jen. She had a weird smile on her face.

"Hey, Lucas was a little older than us, right?"

"Yeah," I said, more focused on the new person I had to interview than what she was asking.

"He was always so hot," Jen said, looking at me closely. "Did he grow up well? He's not fat or balding, is he?"

I shook my head, narrowing my eyes a little. "No, he's pretty good-looking. Why?"

"You should so date him," Jen said, sounding pretty excited.

I burst out laughing. "Oh, jeez," I said, hitting my forehead with my hand. "Am I on one of those hidden camera shows? Between you and Lauren Dayton and Lucas himself, I am sick of hearing all about our inevitable love connection."

Jennifer grinned knowingly, putting her hand on her stomach. "Oh. I see. I'm sorry, I won't bring it up again."

"Good," I said, standing up. "Listen, I have to go. It's getting late, and I don't want to keep you. If you need to talk, please don't hole up here in the apartment and cry. Call me. We can talk it out."

"Okay," Jennifer said, hugging me. "I'll call you."

On my way back to the Daytons' (I still couldn't consider it my home yet), I thought about what I was going to do the next day. I would have to be sneaky about it. Manipulative, even. And I would have to lie some more.

It was surprisingly easy to make my peace with that.

# CHAPTER 8

After Lauren went to school Monday morning, I started putting my plan into action. I called Lucas and asked him to come over, something he was only too happy to comply with. I put on black jeans, a white T-shirt, and a charcoal men's vest. I added gray Converse and pulled my hair into a ponytail. I found the biggest bag I had (a Prada over-the-shoulder bag) and waited for Lucas to get there.

When he arrived, I was fully prepared to use the advantage I knew I had: Lucas liked me. I figured I could use that to get him to do what I wanted. Sneaky, yes, and below the belt, but sacrifices had to be made.

I was sitting on the bottom step of the stairwell, facing the front doors of the Dayton apartment, my elbow on one knee, my hand under my chin, getting more and more anxious by the second, when Lucas finally opened the door. He had on jeans and a black sweater and looked like a male model. Perfect for my plan.

"Hi," I said, sending him the biggest smile I could produce and not show him my wisdom teeth.

"Hey," he said, sounding a little confused. We didn't hang out without Lauren, so this was probably a little new for him. I was such a horrible person, but using his crush on me to get him to do what I wanted was all for the greater good, I reminded myself.

"I need your help with something," I said, crossing my arms and smiling up at him. Might as well just cut to the chase.

"Sure, what?" Lucas asked, looking pleased. I felt a little guilty about that, I'm not going to lie. He was eager to spend time with me, yet I was about to use him shamelessly.

"I want to go to the police department and try to see the police and coroner's report for Daniella's death," I said quickly, trying to make it sound like this was everyday stuff and not enough for him to get pretty mad at me.

Lucas narrowed his eyes and looked at me in dismay. "Heidi, come on. You've got to be kidding me."

"Hey, it may not even work. They may not let us see anything. That's why I need you to come with me. If they won't let us look at it, I need you to distract them while I try to, you know, sneak a peek," I said, talking as if it were the simplest thing in the world.

"Oh, so I'm needed for another little clue search," Lucas said dryly, his jaw tightening. I didn't know why he was suddenly upset.

Okay, maybe I did know. He wasn't an idiot. He probably totally got that I was using him.

"It's just an experiment. It may not even work," I said, putting my hands on my hips.

"An experiment," Lucas repeated, raising an eyebrow.

"No harm ever came out of a little experiment," I said, fully aware I was going to have to sweet talk my way out of this if logic wouldn't work.

Lucas glared at me. "Oh, yeah? Look," he said, lifting his shirt.

"What are you—" I cried, completely shocked, but then I realized what he was doing. He was showing me the large bruise that had come from that little old lady's purse.

"Ouch," I said, grimacing. The bruise was at least six inches wide and light purple. I raised an eyebrow. The bruise spread across his abdomen, which was flat and tan and rather sculpted. Who'd have guessed that Lucas Dayton had the core of a hottie?

*I did not just think that.*

Lucas grinned. "Something wrong, Heidi?"

I frowned and looked up at him. "You wish."

Lucas laughed and then sighed. "Yes, I do."

I almost changed my mind at that point. About the plan, I mean. Would he actually go along with this? If I managed to drag him down there and he had to play decoy, would he freak out? I opened my mouth to say never mind, I'd do it myself, when he shook his head and said, "All right. But if you go to jail, I won't bail you out until I get a picture of you in an orange jumpsuit."

I grinned. "Okay. Deal."

Lucas and I took a cab down to the police station because Greg had driven George upstate to a meeting, and Lucas didn't want to mess with parking. The ride over was pretty quiet since I was rehearsing my speech in my head and Lucas was text messaging furiously. I didn't ask who he was talking to, though. I was already asking a lot of him.

When we got to the precinct, Lucas paid the cab driver and turned to me. "Okay, I assume you have some kind of plan?"

I grinned. "Yeah. We go in, ask to see the police report for Daniella's crime scene, and if they refuse, you distract them while I try to find it."

Lucas shook his head, looking at me in utter disbelief. "Oh, sure, because nothing could go wrong with that plan. You watch too much television if you think it's going to be that easy."

I smiled at him and raised my eyebrows. "Chicken?"

"Reverse psychology. Cute, but not that cute. If I'm going to risk a felony charge, you better go in there and sell it."

"Don't worry. I'm a surprisingly good liar," I said, pulling open the front door.

"Comforting," Lucas muttered. "That will completely convince a judge."

I didn't know what he was talking about. I mean, I was the one that was going to be digging around in the police files. It's not like he was going to have to do anything but ask for very detailed directions to somewhere very far away (that was the plan I had come up with, anyway). I put my hands on my hips and said, feeling a little irritated, "Are you in or out?"

Lucas sighed, looked around the block, and then nodded his head.

"I'm in. Let's go."

He held the door open to the precinct and let me walk in first. The secretary that sat out front was in her thirties, with pale blonde hair pulled back with a headband and held off her neck in a dizzying knot of butterfly hair clips. She had wire-rimmed glasses on, and she was very pale. She looked like an egg that hadn't been cooked all the way. Very unfortunate, but true. On her desk, behind the guard fence that reached all the way to the ceiling, was a line of porcelain bobble-head cats in various hues, all with shiny metallic collars and rhinestone eyes that stared unblinkingly in all directions.

*This may be easier than I thought.*

I leaned up against the desk ledge, putting my face near the four-inch-by-four-inch square through which all forms of communication went in and out. "Hi," I said cheerfully. "I'm Heidi. This is Lucas. We were wondering if we could have a photocopy of a police report from about ten years back. Can you help us?"

The woman—her nametag said her name was Jeanine—blinked at me, as if she were unused to human contact.

"Oh," she said faintly, looking back and forth between Lucas and I but dwelling on Lucas. "Well, when the clerical aide gets back from vacation, sure, she'll make you a photocopy, but you'll have to wait until then. She should be back in a…week or so?"

I grimaced. I didn't want to come back to the police station if I didn't have to. I mean, what if someone brought a criminal in? *Law and Order* was about as close as I wanted my bad guys, thank you very much.

"Are you sure we can't get it now? We're in a bit of a hurry."

Jeanine blinked again, glancing at Lucas, then at me, a blush forming on her face. "If you and your…husband…would like to leave a number…"

I snorted—so ladylike—and said, "He's not my husband. He's my nothing. We're just friends."

Lucas coughed, shifted his weight to one side, and said, "Thank you. That needed to be cleared up."

I rolled my eyes and decided to plead one more time. "Please? We can photocopy it ourselves, if we need to."

Jeanine hesitated and I almost started celebrating, but then she shook her head regretfully. "I'm sorry. You'll have to come back."

I frowned, grabbed Lucas's arm, and pulled him outside.

"So what do you want to do now?" he asked, looking around, presumably for a cab.

"We aren't leaving," I said, looking at him as if he were crazy. "You're going to go in there and flirt with her."

"I'm going to what?" Lucas asked incredulously, raising his eyebrows.

"I need you to be the decoy while I sneak back into the records room and try to find a copy of that police report," I explained through clenched teeth.

"Why do I have to be the decoy?" Lucas hissed, glancing back into the office at the secretary. She was adjusting her cat figurines sadly. "You're so good at getting people to do things they don't want to; you should talk to her."

I rolled my eyes. Apparently Clark Kent here had never done anything slightly devious in his entire life. "I would, but she obviously thinks you're cute. You should do it."

"I don't know…" Lucas said, trailing off, staring at the secretary through the window with obvious guilt on his face.

I sighed. Time for some sweet talk. "Oh, come on, Lucas! You're smart and quick on your feet! You're attractive and charming! Go use your God-given talents to manipulate that woman!"

Lucas looked at me blankly for a moment before saying, quite mildly, "You really missed your calling as a motivational speaker, didn't you?"

I didn't say anything. I just gave him the biggest puppy dog eyes I could manage and bit my lower lip. I was a little afraid the lip thing was a little much, but it totally worked. Lucas ran a hand through his hair and stared at the sky for a moment before exhaling loudly and saying, "Fine. Let's go."

I squealed, grabbed his arm, and gave him a little hug. "You're the best," I said, dragging him back toward the door. I pushed the door open and walked straight to Jeanine. I smiled apologetically and asked, "Can I use your bathroom? I hate to impose, but I can't wait until we get to our next stop."

Jeanine blinked and said, "Of course. Straight through that door and to your left."

I changed my smile to one of gratitude and slipped out. I lingered on the other side of the door, peeking out the little window at the top, watching to see if Lucas would catch on. He was staring at the floor, tapping his foot, and finally he stepped up to the window between him and Jeanine and said, "Uh…I like your cats."

I shook my head. What a waste of a hottie. I walked down the hallway on my tiptoes, hoping I wouldn't run into a cop. I grinned as I saw the door marked "Records Room," and I crossed my fingers as I opened the door. It was unlocked! I refrained from doing my happy dance and slipped in. I was immediately greeted to the sight of dozens of filing cabinets. I groaned and looked closer. It took me a few minutes to find the year Daniella died, and a few more minutes to locate the month. I rifled through hundreds of files, so many that it depressed me. There were this many crimes committed in one month? Just in this precinct? It made me want to move to some place like Iowa or Ohio to a town that had more cows than people.

Finally I found it. I stood, looked around, and spotted the copy machine. I made a copy of every page as quickly as I could, breathing hard. Was this a felony? I mean, Jeanine had told Lucas and I that we could have a copy, just not this way. I stuffed the copies in my purse and the file back into the cabinet.

I slipped back out of the records room and oh-so-casually strolled back into the front room. Lucas was talking quite passionately about something, and I squinted and tried not to smile as I listened to him.

"How can you say that? He's a brilliant actor! Have you ever seen his Shakespeare, or are you just judging him from his eighties stuff?" Lucas demanded, and I watched Jeanine blink rapidly as she tried to come up with a response.

"Um, hey. We can go now," I said, waving, since neither of them had acknowledged my presence yet.

"Heidi! Tell her how great Denzel Washington is!" Lucas said, frowning at me and resisting as I tried to drag him toward the door.

"He is, he really is," I said over my shoulder, tugging on Lucas's arm until I got him outside. "Jeez, Lucas, that woman looked as if you'd been verbally whaling on her."

"She thought *Training Day* was an awful movie," he explained, still looking shocked.

I hailed a cab and pulled the papers out of my purse, brandishing them proudly. "Look what I got," I said proudly, waving them in the air. "Check it out. The police reports."

Lucas got a weird grin on his face. "You…found them? No one tried to stop you?"

I paused. "No," I said, a little surprised. "It was shockingly easy. I mean, they took a while to find, but its not like they were locked away somewhere. That's kind of weird."

Lucas nodded, not saying anything. He still had this odd grin on his face. "Yeah. Guess so."

I sighed as a cab pulled up next to us. "What?"

"Excuse me?" Lucas said, opening the cab door for me.

"Is there a reason you look so amused right now?" I asked, sliding in and across the seat.

Lucas shrugged. "I may have…helped you out a little."

"May have? How?" I asked, narrowing my eyes at him.

Lucas buckled his seatbelt and looked at me sheepishly. "I'm friends with a couple of cops, and I asked them if they would leave the records room unlocked. That was who I was texting this morning. I knew you were excited about this, and I figured I would let you think you were doing it on your own."

I glared at him for a minute, but I couldn't keep it up. I cracked a smile and took his chin in my hands. He looked surprised, to say the least, and wary. But I simply said, "You're a good man, Lucas Dayton. Thank you," and let him go, looking out the window.

# CHAPTER 9

I couldn't sleep that night. Probably because I was sure I would have nightmares. I hauled myself out of bed and pulled out the police report again. I hadn't shown them to Lauren yet—I didn't know if she should read them or not—but Lucas and I had looked over them during the cab ride home.

I spread them out on my comforter and began reading them over again. The body was found by one Amanda Leigh Honey, age thirty, at 8:17 p.m. The responding officers were Fred Garcia and Bill Forrester, and Daniella Marie Hallbright Dayton was pronounced dead at the scene. This was all stuff that Lucas knew already.

Something that Lucas hadn't known, and hadn't been mentioned by any of the women we'd talked with, was that Daniella had long, thin scratches across her abdomen. The police officer had written that it was most likely the result of broken railing. The officer who had typed up the report had written that there were four shallow scrapes running diagonally down Daniella's stomach, starting out deeper than they ended up.

Ew. I was majorly creeping myself out.

I kept reading. Amanda had been right. Daniella didn't have any alcohol in her system, per the coroner, who had a few notes scribbled at the bottom of the police report.

*That must have been a rumor or maybe even a police officer running his mouth,* I thought. *Happens all the time on* CSI: Crime Scene Investigators.

Daniella had drowned, that was the official cause of death, but something still didn't feel right to me. If Daniella could swim, how could she drown if she wasn't drunk or disabled or something?

The "something" was what was bugging me. Nothing added up, and I got very good grades in my math classes.

I took one last look at the copies, shuddered, and stuffed the pages into a drawer on my desk. I sat down on my bed, biting my thumbnail. I grabbed a lilac-colored post-it note and a lime green gel pen—oh, shopping with a teenager—and scribbled a few things down. I had people to see, places to go, and a lie to come up with for a fifteen-year-old girl.

The next morning, I got up to see Lauren off to school. She was excited because at lunch she and Connor Whitson were supposed to meet to talk about the cotillion, which was now six weeks away, the second week of December. When she was gone, I called Lucas.

"No," he said by way of answering the phone.

"What?" I asked, laughing. "You don't even know what I'm going to say."

"I know I'm probably not going to like it, and I know I'm not going to get what I want, so no."

I rubbed my forehead. "Please, Lucas? I'm bored. I want you to come hang out with me."

"Liar."

"What if I'm not lying? What if I want you to come over here and sweep me off my feet?" I teased, knowing I was flirting shamelessly but not really feeling bad about it.

"Don't mock me." He sounded stressed, and considering it was only eight forty in the morning, that wasn't a good thing.

"Just come over, okay? We can go have breakfast if you want," I offered. Coffee and Danish were my own personal olive branch.

I threw on a sweater and some jeans and braided my hair before he arrived. He looked dead tired and a little ticked.

"Something wrong?" I asked as I rifled through my purse for my Chapstick.

Lucas shrugged and didn't say anything.

I smiled and said, "I read the police reports again and thought of some new people to talk to. You game? After breakfast, I mean? I think we could make a lot of progress with the people listed as witnesses and maybe even the primary detectives."

Lucas groaned, shoving his hand through his hair. "I can't believe this. I cannot believe this. You know, before I met you, my life was so simple. I didn't go trying to chase down mysteries or get beaten up by little old ladies in the park or used as the decoy. The only mail I got was bills and the mounting wedding invitations because apparently all of my friends are getting married this year in some sort of conspiracy that I'm pretty sure was orchestrated by my mother in an attempt to get me to hop on the train. I never got hate mail or threatening letters. But now, here I stand, talking about the police report of my dead stepmother, and all I can think about is that you look good in that sweater. How is that a normal thought process?"

I glanced down. It was an old sweater that I really liked, pale pink and crew neck, and I only wore it when I wanted that warm, comfy feeling you get when you drink hot chocolate. I glanced up at him and said, "Really? You like this sweater?"

Lucas laughed, but it was an amused laugh more than a "that was funny" laugh.

"That whole speech, and the only part you picked up on was the sweater part. Man, to have your filter system."

I smiled at that. "I'm sorry. I wasn't ignoring the bulk of the speech. I'm just really good at compartmentalizing. Talk to me. Why don't you think you're normal? Because your life is different than it was four months ago?"

Lucas closed his eyes and smiled softly. "I'm not complaining. I'm just…I don't get it. I really don't. There was a time in my life that if someone told me I'd be standing here, trying to figure out what to do next in an amateur mysterious death investigation…I just feel weird. I feel like I should be on a TV show."

I leaned against the stair railing and asked, "Which one?"

Lucas shrugged and grinned. "*Lifestyles of the Rich and Crazy*?"

I laughed and his smile widened.

"I guess it isn't that bad," he admitted, looking at something over my shoulder.

I rolled my eyes. "Yeah, you're so put upon." Then the other shoe fell. "Wait, hate mail?"

Lucas nodded, pulling something out of his back pocket. "This was in my mailbox this morning when I went down to get the paper."

I opened an envelope and read, "Stop snooping where you don't belong."

I looked up at him and said, "This is your idea of hate mail? You've obviously never been in a sorority."

He blinked. "Um, it's not addressed. Whoever left this went into my building and left this for me. That's pretty creepy. I don't want some stranger leaving me notes."

I hated to point out the obvious, but it needed to be done. "Lucas, if someone left these for you at your home, they probably aren't strangers."

He closed his eyes briefly and said, "I was afraid you were going to say that."

"Did you ask your doorman if anyone came in wanting to see you?" I asked, studying the note—typed, unfortunately, and I doubted there was anyone I could sweet talk into doing a finger print test on it.

"Yes. But he said it must have come in between seven thirty and eight fifteen, because that's when everybody leaves for work and school, and the lobby is crazy. He didn't remember seeing anyone out of the ordinary," Lucas replied, and he earned a few brownie points. At least he had tried to get some information.

"Okay. Come on. I want to go see the police officer that responded to the scene," I said, slinging my purse over my shoulder and heading toward the door.

Lucas sighed deeply and started to follow me.

"Heidi? Are you going out?" I heard a voice behind me say.

I turned around to see Alexis standing in the doorframe between the entryway and the dining room. She was wearing a crimson sheath dress with dark tights and Marc Jacobs pumps, her hair pulled back in a sleek French twist, her expression nervous. She'd looked nervous for several days now.

"Um, yeah. Lucas is going to come with me to run some errands," I added by way of explanation for the nanny leaving with the older brother of her charge first thing in the morning.

Alexis handed me an envelope and said, "This was with the paper this morning. It's addressed to you."

I took the envelope, not too surprised. In fact, I was pretty excited. I assumed this would be some hate mail of my very own, and with every piece of written evidence, I knew the sender would get sloppy and give himself—or herself, excuse me—away. I anxiously opened the envelope and read, "Leave the dead alone. It would be a shame to see you join them."

I blinked. Okay. That wasn't like Lucas' letter or even the blackmail-like letter Alexis had gotten a few weeks back. That was down right threatening, and a little morbid. I handed my note mutely over to Lucas, who frowned at me when he read it. Oh, I knew we were going to have words about that one.

Alexis hesitated, but then asked, "Everything okay?"

"Uh, sure. I just got my very own blackmail letter, like yours," I said, rolling my eyes to try to present an "I so don't care that someone is threatening to kill me" attitude to Alexis.

She closed her eyes and shuddered. "I've gotten more, you know," she admitted, looking completely freaked. I felt kind of bad. No wonder she had been nervous so much lately. If her notes were like mine, I wouldn't blame her.

I raised my eyebrows. "Can we see them?"

Alexis didn't answer right away. She looked like she was having a great debate in her head. Finally, Lucas said, "Alexis, we're just curious to see if the notes you've been getting look like the note Heidi got. You know, to see if they're from the same person."

She nodded, obviously relieved about something. Maybe the help was getting too nosy for her taste. Oh, now that was a horrible thought. Alexis had been nothing but lovely to me for the six or seven weeks I'd been living here, and doubting her was unfair. Lucas and I followed her into her office where she pulled out a folder with about five envelopes in it. The first note was the one she had told Lauren and me about, the one that threatened that someone knew everything about her and could destroy her. The other notes were creepier.

One said "Watch your step," which was a little junior highish for me, but whatever. Another threatened to ruin her reputation with some deep dark secret, and another asked if Alexis was pleased with her new pedicure, which was creepy because it sounded like she'd been followed or watched or something.

The worst—and thus most interesting—was the one threatening her life…if she didn't leave George. Alexis was convinced someone hated George and didn't want to see him happy. Seeing the note, Lucas and I were inclined to agree.

"Have you thought more about a bodyguard?" Lucas asked softly, obviously seeing that his stepmother (which was so weird because I asked once, and they are like six years apart, which is pretty much the same as me and Max) was truly upset.

Alexis nodded. "I feel so stupid. I mean, I run a children's charity. I married a nice, loving man; who would have ever thought I would have to hire a bodyguard?"

I rubbed her arm. "It could very well save your life," I pointed out, giving her a small smile.

She still didn't look especially convinced, but she nodded and said, "I don't want to keep you two from your errands. I'll see you at dinner, Heidi. Are you staying, Lucas?"

"Probably," Lucas said, glancing at me—for what, I'm not sure.

We told Alexis good-bye and very quietly left the building. Neither of us said anything until we got down to the street.

"I think we should call the police," Lucas said, putting his hands on his hips.

"What? Why?" I asked. Surely he wasn't serious.

He looked at me incredulously. "Do I need to recap for you? Have you been following along?"

I grabbed his shoulders and tried to shake him, but he was stronger than he looked. So that didn't work. Instead, I simply said, "What are you going to tell the police, Lucas? That the nanny and the third wife of your dad are getting mean letters? I think the police have more important things to worry about than anonymous note writers."

Lucas shook his head and said, "I don't know why I even try to reason with you. You're obviously insane."

"Come on. I don't want to hit the lunch break at the police station like yesterday," I said, trying to catch him off guard.

Lucas grimaced and said, "You don't forget anything, do you? Come on."

He hailed a cab—saying he didn't want to try to explain to Greg why we were going to the police station at nine in the morning—and when one pulled up to the curb, he opened the door for me and watched me slide in. For a few blocks, we were silent. Finally, he cleared his throat and said, "Heidi, what are you doing?"

I didn't think I had been doing anything, so I looked at him in surprise and said, "Um…sitting here?"

"I'm not trying to make you feel bad, but I kind of thought you were doing this whole Scooby gang thing with my sister because she needed some sort of closure or something. It kind of feels like you're taking this a little too seriously, seeing as how the last two days when Lauren was at school you've continued to Daphne your way through this little investigation with me as your Fred," Lucas said, not unkindly.

I laughed. "Fred? Please. Try Shaggy."

"Thank you. I appreciate that. I'm sitting here trying to have a serious conversation with you, and you're making fun of me."

I gave him a little smile and patted his hand. "I'm sorry. I'll be serious. I know what you're talking about—I've wondered how involved to get too. But I started something, and I want to see it finished. I need to see it finished."

"Have you told Lauren what we've been doing?" Lucas asked seriously.

I winced. "Uh…no. Not really. It hasn't come up."

"You mean she didn't randomly look at you and say, 'Hey, Heidi, have you and Lucas been sleuthing your way around the city, stealing things from the police department?'" Lucas mocked.

I rolled my eyes. "We didn't steal from the police department. You set that up, remember? If you were so shocked by what I'm making you do, you wouldn't have called in that favor," I pointed out, starting to smile.

Lucas looked embarrassed. "Yeah, well," he said, trying not to smile, "you know I only do it to spend time with you."

"Lucas…" I said warningly, wishing that the backseat in the cab was bigger so I could sit farther away from him. "Stop it."

"I'm sorry. I can't help it. I like you. And to be honest, it's been a while since I've pursued someone that hasn't…you know… responded to me."

That I laughed at. "So I'm throwing off your average?"

Lucas shifted in his seat and said, "Oh, look. We're here. Darn. This conversation has to be over."

I unbuckled and said, "Have you ever met a woman? Conversations never end. Things may be postponed, but things are never dropped. Consider that your second lesson in women."

"What was my first lesson?" Lucas asked, looking suspicious.

I smiled at him. "You will never, from here on out, win. It's as simple as that. Even if you're right, I'll very seldom admit it, much less acknowledge it, so get used to losing."

Lucas looked at me blankly. "Are you serious?" he asked.

I shrugged. "You'll see. Come on."

# CHAPTER 10

He followed me into the police station, where Jeanine immediately straightened when she saw us. She had her hair pulled into a complicated French braid, and when she noticed us, I saw her discreetly add a layer of pink lipstick. Aw. Jeanine had a crush.

"Hi, Jeanine," I said warmly, giving her a little finger-wiggle wave. "Are Fred Garcia or Bill Forrester here?"

Jeanine brushed a small strand of hair over her ear and said, "Bill is here today. Fred is on administrative leave—his wife just had a baby."

"Can we talk to Bill?" Lucas asked, and I would like to point out that he didn't seem in the least bit begrudging. He was so into all of this. Little faker.

Jeanine smiled shyly, blinking her eyelashes so fast that it made me dizzy. "Of course. Let me page him."

She typed something complicated into the phone, and we waited in silence—somewhat uncomfortable silence, since Jeanine kept stealing glances from her computer screen to gawk at Lucas, and Lucas was shifting back and forth nervously.

A man in a navy police uniform came out a few minutes later. He was probably in his forties or fifties, a big guy with a gut, and he looked like he was fighting off balding tooth and nail.

"Detective Forrester, they have some questions for you," Jeanine said softly, eyeing the man timidly.

Detective Forrester looked at us, looked at Jeanine, and then said, "Come on back."

He led us down a hallway and into a—no, I'm not kidding—mirrored interrogation room. I felt like a criminal or something, and I really wanted to flip the table like I saw on *The Closer* once.

Lucas and I sat down in two of the hardest chairs ever made, and Forrester sat down across from us.

"What can I help you with?" he asked in a deep voice.

I smiled at him. "We heard that you were one of the responding officers to the Daniella Dayton case ten years ago."

Forrester looked at me blankly. "Hold on," he said, getting up and leaving.

I blinked. "Was it something I said?"

Lucas shook his head. "He works hundreds of cases a year, Heidi. He probably went to go get a report or something to make sure he doesn't give you information about a different case by accident."

Lucas was right. A minute later, Forrester was back, holding a familiar looking folder—to me, anyway—and another folder I didn't recognize.

"Why do you want to know about this case?" he asked warily, giving us a suspicious glare.

"I'm her stepson, and my sister—Daniella's only biological child—has been asking questions about her mother lately, and I want to be able to answer them as honestly as possible," Lucas said immediately, completely calmly. I guess when he wanted to be, he could be pretty good at this stuff.

Forrester nodded and sat down across from us. "This is the police report and the coroner's report. What do you want to know?"

Lucas looked at me expectantly, obviously turning the floor over to me from here on out. "Well," I said slowly, trying to think of a good question to start off with that wouldn't make it very clear that I had already seen that police report and I was dying to get my hands on that coroner's report, "was there anything, um, suspicious about Daniella's death? I mean, she drowned; yet she knew how to swim. Her friends said she wasn't drunk or anything."

Forrester flipped open the police report and skimmed it. "Well," he said, and he sounded pretty reluctant about something, "there were four long scratches starting at her rib cage and ended at her lower abdomen. The coroner didn't know what they were from, he assumed there was broken railing or something, but we didn't see any at the crime scene."

"Are there…pictures?" I asked, feeling morbid. Lucas elbowed me under the table. "I mean, I've seen pictures of the boat, and I just wanted to see if the scratches could have come from railing."

Forrester hesitated, then flipped open the coroner's report and rifled through some papers until he found what he was looking for. He slid a picture of Daniella's stomach across the table.

Lucas flinched so badly that I felt it, despite the fact we were sitting two feet away from each other. I reached out and patted his hand, thinking it was the least I could do since this had to be pretty painful for him. Then I took a good look at these scratches.

"Oh my gosh," I said, my mouth dropping open a little.

"What?" Forrester and Lucas asked at the same time.

"Uh…nothing." They wouldn't have liked what I was thinking, which was basically, as someone with two sisters that were only eighteen months apart and fought all the time growing up, those scratches looked to me like finger nail marks. Leslie always fought dirty with Diana growing up, and Diana often had three or four diagonal marks like that running across one of her cheeks or down an arm. That's exactly what it looked like to me.

But that didn't make any sense. All those women on the boat were each other's alibis, and none of them that we had met with so far seemed like they were capable of killing someone.

"How much did Daniella weigh when she died?" I asked absently, staring at the photo.

Forrester frowned deeply. "Are you a P.I.?"

"No," I said, looking up at him. "I'm just curious. Lauren is a good friend of mine, and if something is off about the way her mother died, I want to figure out what really happened."

Forrester didn't look any more satisfied than before, but he scanned the coroner's report and read, "Daniella Dayton was five foot, three inches, and weighed approximately one hundred and seven pounds."

I thought about that. I weighed around one forty, but I was five foot eight, so that weight is a little more distributed. Diana was about four inches shorter than me and about twenty pounds lighter (well, when she wasn't nine months pregnant). And I was pretty sure I could pick her up, especially if she wasn't squirming around.

I rested my chin on my hand and my elbow on the table, thinking hard. Daniella was a young mother who didn't work. She was a former socialite. Those things didn't add up to any motive I could think of.

"Did you ever look at her death like it was a murder and not an accident?" I asked, and Lucas looked at me sharply.

Forrester seemed to take mild umbrage to this question. "We investigate until the truth has been discovered," he said haughtily, sounding a little like a television cop on a soapbox. "We had no reason to suspect foul play, and neither should you."

I shrugged. "It just doesn't make sense for things to have happened the way it's written in that report. It's not logical."

"Nothing is logical in this world anymore, little girl. We have people leaving babies in dumpsters, beating up their girlfriends, offing some old man who may have been in the wrong place at the wrong time. Twenty-six years on the job, and after a while, nothing is logical anymore."

I felt inexplicably sad for Detective Forrester. To have to see such evil every day and then to try and find good in the world? I didn't know that I could do that. And I was an optimist.

"Do you have any more questions?" Forrester asked, giving us a tired look.

Lucas looked expectantly at me, obviously waiting for me to answer. I sighed and said, "I can't think of any that you could answer. Thank you for your time, Detective Forrester."

He nodded at us and opened the door, apparently more than ready to be done with us. Lucas walked out first, obviously just as ready to be out of there as Forrester was for us to be gone.

I paused and said, "Do you remember the crime scene?"

Forrester looked down at me. "Yeah."

"And you don't remember anything weird?"

He rubbed his head as if it were giving him great pain. I didn't feel too bad about giving him a headache.

"Lady, I don't remember much. I just remember thinking it was a real shame that a woman like that had died so young. Her friends were all pretty eaten up. Lots of crying, lots of hysterics. You say she had a little girl? She's, what, a teenager now?"

I nodded. "Fifteen."

He shook his head. "It's a shame. I feel for her."

I didn't know what to say to that. I suppose it was a stoic man's offering of comfort to a horrible tragedy, so I just smiled at him and walked out after Lucas.

"What was that?" he said evenly, glaring at me.

The door to the police station slammed shut behind us, and I blinked. "What was what?"

"Those questions! Those pictures! I didn't want to see her like that. I don't want to remember her like that. That was like walking into…" Lucas trailed off, visibly upset, and I felt like a jerk.

"I'm sorry. I didn't think—"

"You never think. You've got a one-track mind right now. I appreciate the interest that you've taken in my family, but these things hurt, Heidi. Did you notice how much Lauren looks like her mother? Do you think it's easy to see that and then have to look at my little sister every day?" Lucas ran a hand through his hair and shook his head.

"I am so, so sorry. Really. I didn't think about the pictures. I…I don't know what else to say, Lucas, other than I'm really sorry. Please don't be upset," I said, tugging on his shirtsleeve.

He looked down at me with irritation. "Sorry, but you don't get to flirt your way out of this. I'm not upset with you directly. I'm taking it out on you, and eventually I will feel bad about that. But right now it's making me feel better."

Okay, that was honest. Painfully honest. Very painful. I bit my lip and looked away from him, guilt flooding over me and making my face flush. So he knew about the flirting technique, huh? I had kind of thought he liked that enough that he didn't care when I used it to manipulate him. *I am such a horrible person.*

I grabbed his arm and rested my forehead against his shoulder. "I'm sorry," I said softly. I moved to look up at him. He was staring down at me suspiciously, as though he thought I wasn't completely sincere in my apology, so I gave him my most take-me-serious look and said, "You and Lauren are important to me. I'm so sorry that I hurt you in any way. I just want to give Lauren some peace of mind. And I won't lie; I want to find out what happened. There are a lot of things about this that don't make sense, and that doesn't sit well with me. However..." I trailed off, taking a deep breath, "I will stop if you ask me to."

Lucas raised an eyebrow, still not smiling. "Really?"

I nodded, hoping he wouldn't take me up on it. "Really. If you asked, I would stop."

Lucas narrowed his eyes and tilted his chin up. "But you wouldn't be happy."

I shrugged. "Don't worry about that. If you want me to stop, say it."

He smiled his sly, slow smile, and I had to work not to smile back. "I would never do that to you. You obviously enjoy this. Promise me something, though, okay?"

"Sure, what?"

"Be careful. Someone knows you're doing this, and someone isn't happy about it. Be more discreet. Have Greg drive you and Lauren everywhere if I'm not with you. Don't go out late at night. Just be aware, okay?" Lucas said, and I could tell he was completely serious.

I nodded and said, "Okay. I promise."

I let go of his arm, and he sighed. "It's bad enough that you're getting away with it, did you have to stop doing that, too?"

I held up my index finger and pushed it against his surprisingly hard chest. "Don't start with that. We just had a very nice moment, and you're about to ruin it."

Lucas rolled his eyes and then paused. "Oh, man," he said, making a face. "You're rubbing off on me. I used to never roll my eyes."

I smiled. "You can thank me anytime."

# CHAPTER 11

I was waiting in Lauren's room when she got home from school. She slung her backpack onto the floor and flopped down face first on her bed. "School sucks," she said in a voice muffled by purple comforter.

I raised my eyebrows. Usually Lauren loved school. "What happened?"

She lifted her head and said, in the most disgusted voice I'd ever heard, "People were talking about my mom again."

I raised an eyebrow. "Why?"

She rolled onto her back and covered her eyes with her hand, her rings—silver from Tiffany's—glittering with the reflection from her overhead light. "Amy Miller. Apparently Joyce told her that we were asking questions, so Amy is telling everyone the story about my mom all over again. Do you think Dad will let me transfer?"

"Do you?" I asked, smiling.

"No. He'd tell me that life isn't easy and that it's only worth living if you are tested. Or something else off a businessman's quote of the day calendar," Lauren mused, kicking the side of her bed with her Marc Jacobs boots.

I flinched, feeling sorry for the leather. Those boots were works of art; they didn't deserve the fate they were receiving. Oh, the buffing bill.

"It will blow over in a few days. That's what I remember most about high school."

That and the boys.

"I have to figure out what to tell Connor. He asked what everybody was talking about, and I didn't know what to say. Will you help me?" Lauren asked, playing with the fringe on one of her throw pillows.

"Sure, what do you want me to do?" I asked.

Lauren bit her bottom lip. "Well, I kind of invited Connor to come to Isobel's fifth birthday this weekend."

My eyebrows shot up, partly because I couldn't believe she had been brave enough to invite a non-boyfriend boy to a family function, and partly because I had forgotten about Isobel's party. Alexis had told us a few days ago that Lance, Julie, and Isobel were coming to spend the weekend with us and that there would be a big party for Isobel. I was looking forward to it because I'd never met any of the older Dayton son's family, and they all sounded like fun people. Also, Maureen was going to be there for the party, and I was dying to get a look at the woman who brought Lucas into the world.

"You want to bring Connor to the house to meet the family?" I clarified, knowing I sounded as appalled as I felt and feeling guilty because of it. I needed to learn to not feel guilty, because all this guilt could not be good for my skin.

"I figure if he sees how normal we are, maybe I won't have to explain everything. It's probably a cop out, but I don't know another way," Lauren said, tilting her head back to look at me upside down.

I shrugged. "Huh. Okay. If you think that's a good idea, then I will help you. I'm just worried about your dad and two older brothers he will meet all at once. Your father doesn't own a shotgun, does he?"

Lauren giggled. "I hope not."

We sat in comfortable silence for a few minutes before I cleared my throat. "I have something to tell you," I said, popping my knuckles.

Lauren sat up, her hair falling across her face. She brushed it aside and propped herself up on her elbow. "What?"

I took a deep breath. "Um, Lauren, the last few days, Lucas and I…we, um…"

Lauren's expression changed to one of complete ecstasy. "Did he ask you out?"

I burst out laughing. "No, no, no! That's not where that was heading at all. What I was going to say was that we went down to the police station and interviewed the responding officers that were at your mother's crime scene."

Lauren stopped smiling and looked sober. "Really? What did you find out?"

"Well, the coroner's report didn't say anything about her being drunk, so that seems to have just been a rumor. Also," I hesitated, not knowing how much to tell her. She already looked at little freaked. "Your mom had some long, thin scratches on her stomach that I think look like…fingernail marks."

Lauren's eyebrows shot up. Her hand covered her mouth, and she muttered something that I couldn't understand. She cleared her throat and asked softly, "Did…was she in pain when she died?"

I got up and went to sit next to her. "I didn't ask."

Lauren closed her eyes. "This sucks. This whole thing, it just sucks."

"I agree," I said, rubbing her shoulder. "Whenever you say don't, we can stop looking into this. Really."

Just like I had earlier that afternoon with Lucas, I hoped she wouldn't say yes. I hoped she would want to find the truth out. But more than that, I hoped she would feel comfortable enough to be honest with me. That meant more to me than figuring out an old murder mystery.

Lauren shook her head. "If anything," she said, looking at me very seriously, "it makes me want to search harder. I think I owe it to my mom to find out what happened to her. Do you…would you go visit the last two women on the list with me tomorrow?"

I nodded, pleased at her decision and impressed by her courage. "Of course I will. And then maybe we do a little shopping."

Lauren smiled. "You read my mind."

To say I was up at dawn, raring to go, would be a bit of an exaggeration. But only a bit. I was awake a long time before Lauren was, and I didn't know how to kill the time (I needed to invest in a TV/DVD combo), so I made lists.

Whenever I get stressed or overbooked or bored, I make lists. My college notebooks were filled with lists rather than notes, unfortunately. I make lists about everything, from things I need to do to things I want to do, even things that I wish I could do. My mother thought it was weird and told me I was obsessive; I liked to think of it as quirk.

So at six in the morning, wide awake with no hope of going back to sleep for a much needed extra few hours, I wiggled the bright green gel pen between my fingers. I started writing down all the things I needed to accomplish that day:

- *Talk to Tonia and Ashley, the last two women that were on the boat
- *Find Isobel a birthday present (The party is tomorrow!)
- *Call Diana and see if she's had the baby yet
- *Drop off dry cleaning so something I own will be ironed and clean to wear to this party
- *Pay phone bill
- *Get Lucas to stop flirting with me, *especially* in front of Lauren

Okay, so the likelihood of accomplishing everything on that list in one day (especially that last one) was slim, but I liked to aim big. Dad used to always yell, "Go big or go home," at our sports events (it wasn't until high school that I realized he was actually talking on his cell phone when he was yelling stuff like that, doing business while pretending to watch our games, but I guess it was the being there that was supposed to count), and it was a motto I took to heart.

I rounded up my dry cleaning and stacked it up, including a red wrap dress that I was planning to wear to Isobel's party tomorrow. I didn't know what someone wore to a five-year-old girl's birthday party. But I liked that dress, so it would have to work.

I wrote a check for my phone bill (must remember to mail it!) and dropped my list and the check into my purse. I took a shower and blow-dried my hair, taking time to actually put on makeup and fix my hair. Most mornings I was too lazy to do either. I put on jeans and a light blue long-sleeved shirt, adding a black cardigan because the weather had suddenly decided to suck and turn cold. I tore off yesterday's page on my daily calendar (I got it for Christmas last year, and it has a famous movie quote a day—I was pretty much obsessed with it) and was shocked to see that it was almost November. I am very much a live-in-the-now kind of person, sometimes so much so that I forget the surrounding days. I'm horrible with Christmas and birthdays because by the time I realize I should get something for a special event, nine times out of ten, the event has passed. I'm better than I was, though.

I read my quote of the day ("I love you." –Princess Leia; "I know." –Han Solo from *Star Wars Episode Five: The Empire Strikes Back*) and threw a navy and red Burberry scarf around my neck. I opened my door to leave and found Lauren waiting sheepishly outside. She had her hair pulled into a ponytail and wore a bright purple sweater dress with black leggings and black boots.

"I couldn't sleep," she admitted, grinning.

I grabbed my purse and my black Coach frames—I only wear my fake glasses when I feel the need to look very smart and savvy—and followed her out of our wing of the apartment and down the stairs. We sat at the table and told Eliza we would both take scrambled eggs and toast with orange juice.

George was already at the table. He looked over his newspaper and said, "You two are up early for a Saturday. Shopping?"

Lauren smiled winningly at her dad, and I kicked her. No need to rouse suspicion by being suck-ups. "Probably, Daddy, but we're just doing errands and stuff. Do you need something while we're out?"

George looked thoughtful for a minute. "I don't think so. Alexis is in charge of this party tonight, and she's already bought a dozen things and signed my name to them. You might ask her if she needs something. She's been slightly nervous lately, always jittery. It's kind of unsettling."

I forced myself not to wince. Lauren looked concerned.

"Is she okay? Why is she nervous? Is she upset about her letter?"

George cleared his throat. "She told you about her letters?"

"Letters? Plural? She got more than one?" Lauren asked, sitting up straighter.

*Oh, smooth, George.*

George frowned at her and said, “Yes, and I have half a mind to make you and Heidi have a bodyguard. It makes me very unhappy to think that someone is threatening my wife, and I still can’t find anything about that Claude fellow you two ran into a few weeks ago. It makes me very uncomfortable to think of you two out in the city alone.”

“They aren’t going alone,” a voice behind us said. I nearly groaned, but I managed to catch it just in time.

I turned around and shot Lucas a withering stare. I had wanted some alone time with Lauren today, to see what she really thought of all this and if she was strong enough to keep doing this or not. I knew she would totally put on a stiff upper lip for Lucas, but she might be more open with just me.

He looked like an ad for Ralph Lauren. Great jeans, dark green undershirt, charcoal pullover, and black leather shoes. I accepted my plate from Eliza and began eating, shoveling the food into my mouth in an effort to get out as soon as possible.

Lucas stole a blueberry scone off his father’s plate and asked Eliza for a cup of tea, sitting down across from Lauren and me. Lauren bit into her toast and asked, “You’re coming with us?”

Lucas smiled at her. “Would that be okay?”

Lauren nodded. “Of course. We might shop, though.”

“A price I’m willing to pay, I suppose,” Lucas said, picking a blueberry out of his scone and popping it in his mouth.

Okay, I was glad they were close and all, but this whole investigation thing would be going a lot easier if she would just tell him to stay home every once in a while.

George stood, stretched, and moved to kiss the top of Lauren’s head. “Have a good day. I’ll see you tonight, right?”

“Yeah. Oh. And, Daddy, I’m bringing someone, okay?” Lauren said, busying herself with her eggs.

Lucas paused, deliberately put his scone down, and asked oh-so-nonchalantly, "Who?"

George was fiddling with his wallet, but he froze when Lauren responded crisply, "Connor Whitson."

"A boy?" George asked, looking flabbergasted.

I did a mental eye roll. I mean, she was fifteen for crying out loud. He had to know fifteen girls dated on occasion.

"Yes, Daddy, Connor is a boy," Lauren said patiently, sipping her juice demurely, as if this conversation was in no way scarring her for life.

"What's he like?" Lucas asked, crossing his arms in what I could only assume was an effort to look formidable. It came off more fraternity president punishing an under classman than anything else.

"He's really sweet. A great listener. Very thoughtful," Lauren said, unable to stop the smile from spreading across her face.

"Oh, good grief," Lucas muttered, shaking his head, and I kicked him under the table. I glared at him, silently sending him the universal "shut up" sign by jerking my finger across my throat. He sent me that sly smile of his, and I sat back in defeat. Lauren was going to have to fend for herself on this one.

George didn't look very happy, but he dropped a few bills on the table next to Lauren and said, "Have fun with Heidi. Remember to ask Alexis if there's anything you can do for her while you're out. We'll talk about the boy later."

Lauren just smiled. I found myself envying her calmness all the time. She so rarely freaked out; it was kind of unsettling.

George walked out, and Lauren and I stood up, quickly followed by Lucas. I slid my purse over my shoulder and put my fake glasses on.

"I didn't know you wore glasses," Lucas said, looking at me closely. "Are you near-sighted or far-sighted?"

I looked at him blankly. I had no idea what he was talking about.

"They are visually pleasing," I explained, gesturing to them in a move that would have made Vanna White proud.

Lucas looked at Lauren. "Translation?"

"They matched her outfit," Lauren said, grinning. "She has perfect vision; she just wears them when they look cute."

Lucas looked at me like that was the weirdest thing he'd ever heard. "Just when I think I've got you figured out," he said, shaking his head, "you do something like that, and I can't tell where you're coming from."

"Upper East, dear, and that's where we're going, too," I said absently, digging through my purse.

"Did you hear that?" Lucas said to Lauren as I led the way to find Alexis. "She called me dear."

I rolled my eyes and pushed the door to Alexis's office open. She was sitting at her desk, writing out a guest list for her next charity ball, small Marc Jacobs reading glasses perched on her nose to match her killer forest green pumps and khaki sheath dress. The woman knew how to dress; I'd give her that.

"Hey," I said, smiling at her. "We're going out for a little while. Do you want us to pick anything up or maybe even drop something off for you?"

Alexis blinked and said, "I have a big stack of mail that I need sent out. And if you could pick up the ice cream for the party, that would be wonderful. I completely forgot to have Eliza go get some, and it's Isobel's favorite part. Chocolate is her favorite flavor."

She handed me a pile of mail, addressed, stamped, and ready to go; and a twenty for ice cream, but I put the money back on her desk and said, "We've got it. Don't worry about it. Relax. Enjoy having the house to yourself."

She smiled wistfully. "It seems like I always have the house to myself."

A general feeling of guilt flooded over the room. I mean, I couldn't speak for Lucas and Lauren, but I felt like a crumb. Poor Alexis did spend almost all day, every day, there at the house, working on her charity, with no one to talk to but Eliza. And Eliza gets fidgety if you try to talk to her for too long. I made a mental note to try and do some bonding with Alexis sometime soon, and we told her good-bye.

We loaded into Greg's limo and stopped first at the post office (where I mailed my phone bill in addition to Alexis's stuff) and then the dry cleaner's. When I got back in the car, I turned to Lauren and asked, "What did you get Isobel for her birthday?"

She smiled. "A stroller for her doll, but you don't have to get her anything, Heidi. I mean, you've never even met her."

"I know, but I figure if the first time she meets me, she gets a present, she'll like me faster," I said cheerfully, buckling up.

Lucas laughed. "Have you ever thought about just being yourself? That works on most people. Although I will have to intervene if you decide to introduce yourself to my niece the way you introduced yourself to me. Her parents won't be thrilled if you bruise her too."

I threw him a dirty look. "Thanks. You hadn't brought that up this week. Way to find a way to include it in the conversation."

Lauren giggled. "Do you want to stop somewhere before we go interview Tonia and Ashley?"

I shrugged. "Let's use it to break up the day. We can interview Tonia, then go shop a bit, then talk to Ashley, and shop a bit more."

Lucas's upper lip curled involuntarily. "Joy," he muttered, obviously not thrilled with the prospect of all day shopping.

"We warned you. We told you there would be shopping. You have no one but yourself to blame," Lauren said, fixing him with a look that reminded me so much of George when he was scolding someone that it almost made me laugh out loud. Lauren may look like her mother, but she's all George personality wise.

Lucas drew a halo around his head and said, "I'll be good. No more complaining from the male side of the car."

I turned back to Lauren and said, "Okay. What do we know about Tonia?"

Lauren rustled a sheet of paper out of her Coach hipster. "I wrote it out with her address," she explained, smoothing the paper. "Okay. Tonia Barton is married with three kids living in the Upper East—not too far from Susie Engle, actually—and, according to Joyce Miller, Tonia is the one who jumped in the water to try and save Mom."

I felt Lucas give a sudden shiver. I smiled at him reassuringly, and he closed his eyes briefly, as if he still couldn't believe he was having a conversation like this.

When Greg pulled up to the Bartons' apartment building, we filed out, talked to the doorman, and walked into the building, taking the elevator to the tenth floor.

A pretty woman with jet-black hair, chocolate brown eyes, and beautiful, smooth mocha skin answered the door.

"May I help you?" she asked, her voice soft and lyrical.

Lauren moved a little to be out in front. "Are you Tonia Barton?"

The woman nodded. "Yes, I am."

"I'm Lauren Dayton, and this is my brother, Lucas, and my friend, Heidi. I came to ask you some questions about my mother," Lauren said simply, choosing a more direct approach than with the other women. She was taking charge, doing it on her own, and I felt a wave of pride sweep over me.

Tonia blinked and looked taken aback. "Oh, well, sure," she said, moving aside.

As we entered the apartment, I looked around, mentally comparing her taste in decoration to the other women we had met. Tonia's house seemed more comfortable, more forgiving, than any of the other houses. It was homier, with pictures everywhere, and the furniture looked lived on, not there for display.

Tonia sat in an olive-colored armchair across from a leather couch, so the three of us sat on the couch. She looked at us expectantly.

Lauren cleared her throat. "Mrs. Barton, I've been asking some of the women that were with my mother the night she died to tell me what they remember from that evening. I want to understand why my mother died, I guess. I just need some answers."

Tonia nodded, scratching her forehead. She sighed. "I'll be honest with you, Lauren, I probably won't be a lot of help to you. I don't have the best long-term memory. However, I will try my best to help you. I know if anything ever happened to me, I'd want my kids to have peace of mind."

"How old are your children?" I asked, trying to put her at ease and be nice at the same time.

Tonia smiled. "My oldest, Sadie, is eleven, and I have twin seven-year-olds, Isaiah and Levi. Here," she said, reaching behind her and picking up one of the many frames that covered the little table sitting next to the armchair, "this is from the beach this summer."

I took the picture from her and looked at the two little boys in bright orange swim trunks and a pretty little girl with knobby knees in a yellow two-piece.

"They're adorable," I said, handing the picture back to Tonia.

"Thank you," she said, looking sad all of a sudden. "Sadie was about one when Daniella died. I remember when I got back from the police station that night I just picked her up and held her for hours. I couldn't stop crying, thinking of what Daniella had left behind," Tonia said softly, looking up at Lauren sadly. "But I guess you turned out just fine, didn't you? You would make your mother proud."

Lauren's lower lip trembled, and I slipped my hand under her arm trying to remind her that we were here for her. She smiled and said, "Thank you. That's what I aim for. I just want to make her proud."

Tonia crossed her denim-clad legs and adjusted her blouse, very business-like in her casual attire. "Dani was a wonderful friend and a lovely human being. She introduced me to my husband, and for that I will always think of her as my angel. I would love to tell you anything you want to know about her."

Lauren nodded and glanced at me. I gave her the go-ahead supportive look, and she took a deep breath. "Mrs. Barton, what can you tell me about my mother's relationships?"

Okay, that was a new question. I looked over at her, confused, and Lucas held my gaze over Lauren's head. That had surprised him too.

Tonia ran a hand through her short, curly hair. "What do you mean?"

"I mean, my mom's relationships with those closest to her. My dad, her kids, her friends, her family. Anything you can tell me would be helpful," Lauren amended, and I noticed she was picking her cuticles, a clear sign of nervousness.

Tonia looked thoughtful for a moment. "Well, she loved being a mom. I don't remember her ever complaining about you or your brothers. She was crazy over George. I think we were all a little jealous about how he doted on her. She had him wrapped around her little finger, but in a good way. They really loved each other."

Lauren smiled. "Yeah, I'm getting that."

"We were a close group of friends. We didn't gossip; we weren't backstabbers. We had a rule that if someone was acting inappropriately, in any kind of way, the others would say something. It kept us close. It kept us friends for a decade."

Okay. I loved Rachel and Jennifer, but if we ever tried that, we wouldn't be able to last a week.

Lauren glanced at me in hesitation before looking at Tonia and asking, all in one breath, "Did she ever mention anyone named Claude Keller?"

I sat up straighter, slid my arm behind Lauren's back, and pinched Lucas before he could say something because he had that look on his face that promised objections. He was so easy to read.

Tonia frowned, thinking. "I don't think so. Joyce and I were sort of new to the group, though. Dani, Susie, Ashley, and Amanda all knew each other in college. Joyce and I met them through mutual friends. He might have been around before me."

Lauren looked at me again, this time because she didn't know what else to say. She sent me a pleading look, so I turned to Tonia and asked, "Can you tell us what you remember about the night Daniella died?"

Tonia bit her bottom lip and stared at the floor. She shrugged. "Probably stuff you already know. We went out on the boat to celebrate Ashley and Bob's engagement. During the toast, Dani's cell phone rang. She couldn't hear anything; she kept saying something like 'Where are you?' and 'What are you doing?' in a sort of irritated voice. But I could be wrong on that, it's been forever. So she went up to the deck to hear better, and when she didn't come back for a little while, someone—I think it was Amanda—went up to check on her, and she screamed. So we all went running up there, and when I saw her in the water I jumped in and pulled her over to the boat, but by then it was... well, I guess we didn't find her in time."

I nodded my head sympathetically as Tonia cleared her throat and wiped her eyes.

"Tonia, I know this is going to sound weird, but do you remember anything odd about Daniella when you found her? Was her dress ripped? Was she bleeding anywhere?"

Lauren shuddered and Lucas glared at me, but Tonia frowned and looked thoughtful. "Her dress was torn," she said, as if just realizing something. "Across her stomach, her dress was torn. And she was bleeding a little bit, right here"—she pointed to her abdomen—"and here"—and then to her eyebrow. "Just a little, though. I think the water stopped the bleeding. I tried to give her CPR, but it was obvious by that time that it wasn't working. She had some rope around her ankle too, and no one could figure out how that got there. I think the police decided it got stuck there while she was in the water."

Light bulbs went off like fireworks in my head, but I didn't say anything. I checked my watch and said, "Thank you so much for your time, Mrs. Barton. You've been very helpful."

Tonia smiled at us and said, "Well, thank you for coming to see me. Lauren, here's my card if you need anything else. You wouldn't happen to baby sit, would you? I'm always in the market for someone to watch the twins."

Lauren smiled widely and stood up. We all followed her cue, and she hugged Tonia. "Sure. Call me anytime. We're at the same number we've always had. And thank you for your help."

Lucas and I said good-bye to Tonia, and we filed out of her apartment. We rode the elevator in silence, but Lucas kept sending me glances full of a good gripe I knew I would get later.

# CHAPTER 12

When we got in the car, we told the driver to take us to FAO Schwartz, and Lauren said brightly, "Well, I think that went well. I mean, we didn't really get anything case breaking, but it will help to have her story."

Lucas's hand brushed my knee, and he leaned forward to whisper to me, "We need to talk."

I ignored him and said to Lauren, "Yeah, and she was really nice too. And, hey, you might have found a good summer job."

She smiled and looked out the window to watch as we pulled up to the curb.

As Greg pulled to a stop, Lauren began to scoot closer to the door. We got out of the car, and she bounded up to the entrance, apparently very excited to go to a toy store. She held the door open for us and then took off, saying something over her shoulder about knowing the perfect thing to buy Isobel.

Lucas reached out, grabbed my arm, and pulled me next to him so that we had to walk side by side—literally.

"What was that?" he asked through clenched teeth.

I blinked and tried to shoot a nice smile at a couple that was looking at us like I was being abducted. I so didn't want another scene; although, the memory of that grandma beating the crap out of Lucas still made me laugh.

"What was what?" I asked.

"You asked Tonia if there was anything on the body," he hissed, and I realized he was pretty mad. I closed my eyes and sighed.

"I couldn't think of any better way to put it. I mean, it got me what I wanted to know," I said, keeping an eye out for Lauren because we had officially lost her in the web of stuffed animals, Barbie dolls, and Tonka trucks.

"Which was..." Lucas prompted, looking at me closely.

"Tonia said there was rope around Daniella's ankle. Amanda said that she tripped over some rope when she went up to check on Daniella."

"So?"

"So maybe someone knocked her out, tied her ankles together, and tossed her overboard. It's pretty hard to swim without your legs, and if she were knocked out, that's just added opportunity," I explained, excitement mounting. I knew I was right about this; I just knew it.

Lucas nodded, thinking hard. "What if she stepped in the rope coil, got her foot stuck, tripped, hit her head on her way overboard, and drowned?"

*Rats.*

I shrugged. "Maybe. It's definitely a possibility. But now we have possibilities. And, hey," I said, pointing my finger at him and frowning, "if she just tripped, how did her dress rip and four long scrapes get on her stomach? How did her eyebrow get cut?"

Lucas held up both hands in defeat. "I'm not saying you're wrong. I'm just saying that you need to have foolproof answers if you're going to tell these theories to Lauren. I mean it, Heidi, I don't want her to think her mother was murdered and then come to find out it really was just an accident. Okay?"

I nodded. "Of course. I don't want that either. But I owe it to Lauren to figure this out. I owe it to Daniella."

"How do you figure that?" Lucas asked, looking skeptical.

I stopped and thought about it for a moment. I had never met this woman, and I knew very little about her except what was important to her. However, that was something we happened to have in common.

I looked at Lucas and smiled slowly, taking my time in choosing my words. "She had a life. She was vibrant. I'd bet she was fierce in just about everything she did—fierce mother, fierce friend—and that's the kind of woman that's worth being diligent for. Besides, no kid should ever go to bed at night not understanding why her mother isn't there to tuck her in. I knew why my mom never tucked me in. Lauren went all those years without anyone to baby her the way only a mom can, and it breaks my heart that someone might have taken that away from her. I just need closure…for Lauren."

Lucas looked away from me to where Lauren stood at the end of an aisle, holding up different ballerina outfits and watching the glitter and sequins send shimmering light over the white tiled floors.

"For Lauren," he said, and he released my arm and motioned for me to go down the aisle first.

I couldn't explain it, but I had tears welling up in my eyes. I blinked really hard to get them to go away and walked toward Lauren. She held a pink princess dress out to me and said, "This would be fun."

I nodded, not convinced. That little thing was 10 percent cotton, 10 percent spandex, and about 80 percent toile. It didn't look comfortable in the slightest way.

I reached above Lauren's head and pulled down a fun silver tiara with hot pink rhinestones and fake diamonds encrusted all over it. It had a matching star-shaped wand that actually lit up.

"This is cool," I said, making the wand light up blue and then purple.

Lauren nodded, clearly more impressed with the dress, but my mind was made up. The wand and tiara looked way more fun than a dress.

I checked out, making an impulse buy at the register in the form of three Ring Pop suckers and a pink plastic locket with heart-shaped candies inside. The locket was for Isobel, but once we got into the car, I passed out the ring pops. I had cherry, Lauren got watermelon, and Lucas—under protest—ate grape.

Ashley Snyder no longer lived in the city, and her name was no longer Ashley Snyder. Her newest name was Ashley Bartlett-Bacon, and she moved upstate, about a half an hour without traffic (but when does that ever happen?) with her latest husband, Renaldo. Apparently, according to Mr. Lucas I-totally-don't-read-the-society-pages-but-I-seem-to-have-all-this-information-on-my-mental-rolodex-by-complete-and-total-accident Dayton, Ashley and Bob divorced after two years. She married Raul, her tennis instructor, six months later. They were married a little over a year, and, when that went south, Ashley married Jeff Bartlett—a friend of Lance's—and had her son, Denver, who is now five. Ashley and Jeff divorced two years ago and she married Renaldo Bacon (pronounced Buh-cone) last year.

Ashley didn't quite sound like the society wives we had been dealing with. I had no idea how to tactfully ask about her engagement party to her first husband that one of her closest friends happened to die during. I mean, how do you drop that into conversation?

When we finally pulled up to the house about forty minutes later, we were all eager to get out of the car, especially Lucas, who had been complaining of a leg cramp for half an hour. Because of how annoying that was, Lauren and I accidentally forgot to tell him his grape ring pop had turned his mouth purple.

We walked up the front steps and rang the bell—a bell that played "Take Me Out to the Ballgame." I kid you not. That seemed a little odd, considering the house was worth about four million dollars, and it barely looked lived in, let alone that the owners had any sort of personality required for American pastime themed doorbells.

A very sober man answered the door, dressed immaculately, and asked us in a dry voice what we needed.

"Could we see Ashley, please?" Lucas asked politely, but the waiter lingered on Lucas's purple lips just long enough that I had to bite the inside of my cheek to keep from laughing.

"One moment. Please wait in the entryway," the man said, sounding bored or maybe as if we were a tremendous waste of his time.

We waited for about five minutes before he came back and told us to follow him.

The house, or at least the part of it we were being shown through, was decorated in apparently one theme—money. Everything I saw was the most expensive of any brand, the best quality of antique, the newest technology. Ashley was obviously very indulgent.

The den we were led to had silk curtains, fresh flowers on every table, pure oak furniture, and an Oriental rug older than my great grandma. A woman who didn't look a day older than thirty—but had the kind of face that you immediately knew she worked hard and spent a lot of money to stay permanently thirty—was watching us from a leather armchair. She was wearing a Gucci watch with diamonds in it bigger than most engagement rings, an Alice + Olivia dress that a lot of young starlets had (and I had been lusting over for weeks), and Roberto Cavalli pumps that looked like they had been handcrafted for her specific foot. I nearly checked my mouth for drool, I was so in love with her outfit.

She stood and walked smoothly over to us, an inch shorter than me even in the heels and thirty pounds lighter. She had blonde hair smoothed back into a preppy chignon and clear blue eyes that I was betting were contacts (and if not, oh, I'd kill for that woman's genes) because they were the bluest eyes I have ever in my life seen.

"Ashley Bartlett-Bacon, may I help you with something?" she purred, her eyes moving over Lucas. Husband number five?

I took a sidestep away from Lucas, remembering what happened at Amanda's when he felt romantically threatened.

Lauren put on her brave girl smile and said, "My name is Lauren Dayton, and I'm Daniella Dayton's daughter. I was wondering if I could ask you some questions about my mother."

Ashley's smile faded minutely. She exhaled loudly and said, "You look like your mom, you know that?"

Lauren nodded, clearly unsure about how Ashley was going to react to us.

Ashley nodded, still looking completely unaffected, but then she raised a hand to bite her thumbnail. I realized she was shaking. She sent us a weak smile and said, "Please sit down."

Nowhere in the living room did it look comfortable to sit down. All the chairs were oak and leather, and they looked like the wrapping had just come off. I gingerly sat in a recliner, and Lauren and Lucas went to a loveseat. Ashley sat in a rocking chair.

There was an uncomfortable silence for a moment before Lauren said, in a fairly light voice, "How...how did you meet my mom?"

It was a question she hadn't asked anyone else, and I knew why. If we started out with the hard questions, Ashley, in her obviously very unstable state, might crack on us.

Ashley swallowed. "Um, I was friends with Mandy Honey in high school, and when we went to college, she wanted to live with these other two girls, Susie Breck and Dani Hallbright. Susie was kind of a wet blanket, but Dani was a blast. Susie and Dani both got married pretty quickly right out of college and had kids right away, but I didn't want that. I wanted to have some fun, you know?"

I looked around the room. Did she realize she was talking to a currently unemployed bachelor, a teenager, and a failed business-woman turned nanny? We so didn't know what she meant.

"What did you think of my dad? The first time you met him, I mean," Lauren asked, scooting forward on the loveseat.

Ashley grinned. "George may have been twenty-something years older than Dani, but he was adorable. We all thought so. And he treated her like a queen. He used to shower her with jewelry and the best dates a girl could ask for, but all she could talk about was that he was a family man. Dani wanted kids so badly I think it hurt her. George already had two, boys, I think, and she was crazy about them." Ashley paused to look closer at Lucas. "Are you George's boy? Levi or something?"

Lucas nodded. "Lucas, actually. But, yeah, I'm Daniella's step-son."

Ashley leaned back, suddenly very sure of herself. "Dani always used to tell us you'd grow up to be quite the little heart-breaker. She was going to adopt you, you know."

Lucas frowned. "My mother is still alive and had custody of us. Is that even possible?"

Ashley shrugged. Her shoulders were tiny beneath the navy blue satin. "Don't know. Didn't ask. Mandy would know. Toward the end, Dani and Mandy were super close."

"The end?" I repeated, thankful she had given us an easy segue.

Ashley looked at Lauren hesitantly before clarifying, "Before she died, I mean. Before Dani died, she and Mandy spent tons of time together with her little girl. You," she said, nodding to Lauren. "That was who Dani was closest to in the end."

I cleared my throat. "Ashley, what do you remember about the night Daniella died?"

Ashley shrugged. "We were on my boat. I sold that thing years ago. Actually, Bob may have gotten it in the divorce. I can't remember. Dani was kind of being a party pooper that night. I wanted to sail out really far so we could see the skyline better, but Dani kept griping, saying we had to stay within a mile of the coast so she could leave early. George had dinner plans for them or something, I can't remember. I just remember being ticked that she had to leave early and that she wouldn't drink for the toast. She kept saying the champagne would ruin her appetite or whatever. It gets a little fuzzy from there because I wasn't worried about my appetite, so I was drinking whatever I wanted."

I nodded, wishing I could fast-forward her. Talk about a rambler.

"So Dani gets a call on her cell and gets all mad because she couldn't hear or something and stomps up to the deck, saying she'll be right back. Forever goes by, and we all wanted to do presents. But Amanda wouldn't let us start without Dani, so she went up to see what was taking her so long and started screaming her head off. We all went up the stairs, and Tonia freaked out and jumped in the water. Joyce and Susie were screaming for someone to call nine-one-one, and then I think Joyce sailed us closer to the shore. By that time we weren't that far away from it, and that's when the police came."

"Do you remember anything odd about the accident? Anything that didn't seem right to you?" I pressed.

Ashley scratched her forehead. "Not really. I mean, Dani could swim and everything, so it was weird that she drowned. But there weren't any, like, reasons to believe something else happened to her either, if that's what you're saying."

"Did Daniella ever talk about a man named Claude Keller to you?" I asked.

Ashley's face went blank. "Doesn't sound familiar. Dani didn't talk about men unless she was setting up one of her single friends. Not the kind with wandering eyes, you know."

Lauren smiled at that, and Lucas looked a little nauseated.

"Thank you for your time. It was very helpful," I lied, feeling bummed. We hadn't found out anything new from Ashley, which was a big let down after my epiphany from Tonia earlier in the day.

"It was my pleasure. Lauren, it was nice to see you again. You too, Lucas," she said, saying his name slowly and almost seductively. He tried to smile, but it came out more of a grimace.

We left quickly, and when we got back into the car, Lauren and I were both pretty blue. Lucas was groaning about getting back into the car.

"Come on, don't be like that. You had a full day. You can't expect to learn new things from every person you talk to," Lucas said, trying to cheer us up as we pulled out of the driveway.

Lauren sighed. "I know, but I was so sure that we would find some major clue if we talked to all Mom's friends. I guess I'm just sad because I don't know where to go from here."

I knew how she felt. I didn't really know where to go from here either. We had talked to the police, all the witnesses, and none of them had any ideas to whether or not Daniella's death had been more than just a tragic accident.

"By the way, don't say anything to Lance at the party," Lucas said, frowning at both of us. "He'll be ticked. He was very close to Daniella, and her death hit him hard."

Something suddenly occurred to me. I had completely forgotten about my other link to the case. Jennifer's sister had dated Lance at the time of the accident, and she might have some inside scoop.

I made a mental note to call her as soon as I wasn't squeezed between Lucas and Lauren.

Lucas shifted in his seat and looked down at me. "So are you stumped? Do you give up?"

I shook my head. "No. I know something is there staring us in the face, and, when it comes to me, it will be a huge break. I just know it."

Lauren smiled. "You have way more confidence in our abilities than we do. You make me believe we'll find something."

"That's because I believe we will find something," I said, brushing some hair out of my eyes. "If you believe it, you can achieve it. Corny but true. I have always thought that if you doubt yourself, you're giving everyone else free shots at doubting you too."

Lucas laughed. "You've got to stop ordering in from the Chinese place. You're starting to talk in fortune cookie."

"You can mock me if you want, but I bet you can't say I'm not self-confident," I said, feeling suddenly very sassy.

Lucas frowned. "I think I followed that sentence, and you're right. You are very assured of yourself. That's a great quality in a woman."

Lauren giggled, and I glared at him. I turned back to Lauren and said, "Don't let me forget to pick up the ice cream on the way home. Alexis has so much to do. I would really like to do more to be helping her out."

Lauren nodded. "I know. She gets dozens of letters a day for her organization. She's been so stressed lately, and she hasn't gotten to them all. That's making her even more stressed. It's just a vicious cycle."

My eyes widened, and I felt zinging in my head. I held a hand up and said, in a shocked voice because I could not *believe* I hadn't thought of it earlier, "Wait a minute. The letters."

"What letters?" Lucas asked, sounding lost. Lauren frowned at me and motioned for me to go on.

"The letters that Alexis has been getting. The blackmail notes. Alexis said that Daniella got them right before she died. Lauren, weren't there boxes of papers from Daniella's desk in the storage unit?" I asked excitedly, grabbing her arm.

"Yeah, I think so," Lauren said, still sounding confused.

"If Daniella kept her letters, we can compare them to Alexis's and see if they were sent by the same people," I said triumphantly, smiling smugly.

Lucas raised his eyebrows, the very picture of skepticism, but Lauren gave me a broad smile and said, "Let's go!"

Lucas sighed and said, "Sorry to be the voice of reason here, but why would anyone keep blackmail notes? Furthermore, why would Dad save them after Daniella died?"

Lauren gave her brother a dirty look, and I elbowed him in the gut.

"Don't be such a Debbie Downer," I ordered, glaring at him. "It's a good lead, and we're going to go look. Do you want to come with us or not?"

"Sure. I'll play Ned to your Nancy and Bess."

Lauren grinned, looking back and forth between us. "You just want to be Ned because he dates Nancy."

Lucas shrugged. "You've always got to look for the silver lining, kid."

I rolled my eyes and asked, "How do you even know who Ned is?"

"Hey, I have layers," Lucas said defensively.

"Whatever. Peel off your sarcasm layer, and tell Greg to take us to the storage shed."

"You better be glad I like my women bossy," Lucas teased, leaning forward to talk to Greg. I shook my head, irritated that he had said that in front of Lauren because I knew I would never hear the end of it.

# CHAPTER 13

When we got to the storage shed, the sun was going down, and it was suddenly freezing. When I commented on the matter, Lucas looked at me witheringly and said, “That would be November you’re experiencing.”

I gave him a dirty look and shivered. Lauren punched in the storage unit code and opened the door. We walked into the first room with all the furniture, and Lucas started laughing.

“I had no idea Dad kept some of this stuff. Look, that’s your crib, Lauren. Daniella had it hand painted with all those flowers. I think she liked it more than you ever would have.”

Lauren smiled and skimmed her hand over the delicate rounded headboard. “I wish I could remember more about her,” she said wistfully, her hand closing around one of the small, intricately carved rails. “What her laugh sounded like, the kind of perfume she wore, her favorite song, whether she liked being called Dani or not. She’s such a mystery to me.”

Lucas sighed. “If you want information about your mom, we’re probably in the right place. Look around. It’s not like Dad threw much more than Kleenex away.”

Lauren hesitated. "Doesn't it feel like snooping to you?"

Lucas shrugged. "Lance and I used to listen in on phone calls, read mail, and rifle through Dad's date book. That's snooping. Getting to know your mom is kind of like…interviewing her through her belongings."

Lauren seemed happy with that analogy, but I raised an eyebrow.

"Little spy, were you?"

Lucas grinned sheepishly. "We wanted to be CIA or FBI. We were practicing. We never found out anything too juicy."

I laughed. "Oh, we are talking later."

Lauren was rifling through a box, looking confused. "This doesn't look like Mom's stuff."

Lucas stood behind her and looked over her shoulder. He frowned.

"That's my mom's stuff. I thought she had her own storage unit downtown. These must be from decades ago."

I ran my hand around the box and shoved it until we could see the back panel. The box was dated eight years ago.

"Not quite a decade," I said, showing them the date scrawled on the cardboard.

"That's Mom's handwriting," Lucas said, sounding really confused. "I guess maybe she has a key to this place too. I thought she would have given it back by now."

Uh huh. Because from everything I'd heard of Maureen Dayton so far, it didn't sound like letting go was exactly her forte.

I went to the next box and flipped open the lid.

"Ooh, home videos," I said, my eyes lighting up. "I wonder if any are of itty baby Lucas doing something embarrassing."

He grinned. "Most likely. But that's not what we're looking for. Here's something," he said, selecting a tape and squinting to read the label. "It's from the year you were four, Lauren. You want it?"

"Yeah, and any more you find in there with Mom on it," she said, but she sounded distracted.

I turned my attention to her and realized she was looking in a long box full of shoes, all lined up and paired up neatly. I went to her side and tried to see what she was frowning at. Lauren picked up a pair of navy blue pumps and said, "What does this look like to you?"

I inspected the shoe. There was a thin, barely there line of clear, hardened gel along the edge where the heel met the shoe.

"It looks like these shoes were broken and then fixed," I said, mystified by why this was any big deal.

"If you were a millionaire's wife, would you repair the shoes yourself or get them professionally done?" Lauren asked, running her finger over the sloppily dried glue.

I shrugged. "I'd probably just buy a new pair."

She nodded and then replaced the shoe carefully. She shook her head. "I must be crazy," she said, smiling apologetically. "I'm making mountains out of mole hills. It must be time to call it a day."

I held up a finger and said, "Not until we looked for what we came here for. Don't get sidetracked, Dayton."

She rolled her eyes and followed me into the next room, leaving Lucas to make a stack of videos for Lauren to take home with us. I went to one box of papers, and Lauren went to another. We shuffled through them wordlessly, trying to make sense of bank statements and day planners. Finally, Lauren said, "Hey, Heidi, come look at this."

I went to stand beside her and looked at the pale pink day planner she held in her hands. "This was from the year she died," Lauren explained almost breathlessly. "The month she died she had several appointments with someone named Dr. Mueller, and the week she died she had three things written down: on Monday she had lunch with Maureen, an afternoon appointment with Dr. Mueller, and on that Thursday, Ashley's engagement party."

I raised my eyebrows. "Good job, Lauren," I said, taking the day planner from her. "Who is Dr. Mueller?"

Lauren shrugged. "Never heard of him. We ought to be able to Google him, though. Right?"

"Probably," I said, looking at something scrawled in the margin that Lauren either hadn't seen or hadn't commented on. It was in loopy cursive, written in blue ink, and all it said was, "Lillian?"

I frowned. Who was Lillian? We suddenly had a whole new set of players. This late in the game, everything was getting complicated.

"Did you find any letters?" Lauren asked.

"Uh," I said, trying to shake myself out of my reverie and focus on what she was saying. "Not yet. Let's give ourselves a few more minutes and then take our stuff to go."

I shoved the day planner into my bag and went back to my box. I found dozens of Christmas cards, a Rolodex, three pencil sharpeners, some pale pink napkins that baffled me, and a picture colored by Lauren. I handed that off to her and watched her smile weaken as she obviously had some kind of memory tied to that picture.

There was barely anything left in my box. I pulled out a bank statement and a thank you card for a baby gift. I put them in my stack and went for the last three things in the bottom of the box. Pretty generic: a receipt for a prescription; an unfinished grocery list; and a picture of Lance, Lucas, and Lauren from about twelve years back. I smiled and put the picture and the receipt in my back pocket. I tossed the list back in the box and started piling the papers back where I got them. I heard Lauren sigh, and I looked over my shoulder at her.

"Nothing?" I guessed.

"Zip. Maybe she threw them away after all. I mean, I wouldn't keep blackmail notes if I ever got them," Lauren said, and I grinned. Mine was in my desk drawer.

"Let's go. We need to stop at Baskin Robbins and pick up ice cream on the way home, and I'm getting hungry. Ring pops don't make good lunches."

We walked out of the room and found Lucas standing by the door, his arms full of stuff—movies, yearbooks, photo albums. We left the building, and as we approached the car Lucas said, "Oh, man, I left my jacket in there."

"It's okay, I know the code. I'll get it," I said, jogging back to the unit. I let myself in, grabbed the jacket, and headed back toward the car.

I heard a squeal of tires and an engine accelerate. I turned around and watched with horror as a black SUV came tearing across the parking lot right toward me.

I felt like an idiot. I had always watched the cartoons where the roadrunner evades the coyote and somehow manages to turn the horrible thing the coyote is planning for him back around, squashing the coyote with an anvil/sledgehammer/falling piano of some sort. And even as a little kid, I had thought to myself, just move when you see it coming toward you! If you have enough time to hold up your little sign that says "Yikes!" or whatever and look miserably at the audience, you totally have enough time to sidestep the wrecking ball or run away from the train barreling toward you. Yet there I was, staring like a deer in the headlights at this two-ton machine racing toward me. All I could think was, *Where is my little sign?*

Well, that's a lie. I also had time to think, *This is going to hurt*, and even a small consideration too, *I wish I wasn't going to get killed in front of Lauren.*

Before I closed my eyes to the coming impact, I even thought, *It* had *to be an SUV. No one ever gets hit by a VW bug or a Smart Car.*

Then something did hit me, but it was from the side, not the front. And I felt a great gush of wind, and, suddenly, I couldn't breathe.

When I opened my eyes, I saw why. Lucas had knocked me down instants before the car had zoomed by us, and he was now pressing down on me, looking over his shoulder and shouting something to Lauren about tags.

*Tags?* I thought dizzily. *Who cares about tags when I am about to suffocate from one hundred and ninety pounds of unadulterated male pressing into my lungs?*

I coughed and gasped, "Lucas," in an effort to get his attention.

He turned and his elbow connected with my kidney (well, it could have been my liver, I have no idea where all that stuff is), and I said, "Ow!" and tried to push him off me.

He surprised the heck out of me by rocking back on his heels, hauling me to a sitting position, and hugging me in a bone-crunching embrace that nearly knocked the breath out of me again.

"Oh, thank God you're okay!" he shouted into my ear, and I winced. I could feel every bone in my body clearing their throats and saying, "For that, we will make you pay tomorrow," in a most apologetic voice.

He pulled away briefly to look at my face, his hands running over my cheeks, my shoulders, my neck, brushing away my messed up hair, and then he hugged me again. I felt a second body hit me, and Lauren's sobbing crept into my ears.

"Oh, Heidi, he almost killed you!" she moaned, her arms wrapping around my waist while Lucas still held my shoulders.

At that moment, reality sunk back in, and I started freaking out.

"That car almost hit me!" I cried, my stomach knotting. "He didn't even try to miss me! He was trying to kill me!"

Both sets of arms around me tightened, but I pushed against them, suddenly desperate to stand, to take deep breaths, to prove to myself that I was alive, that the car hadn't hit me. I stood up, my legs shaking, and looked around the parking lot. There were skid marks about twenty feet away from where we stood, and I knew they weren't from trying to stop; they were from accelerating.

I closed my eyes and brought my hands to my face, and that was when I realized I was still holding Lucas's jacket.

Greg came jogging toward us.

"I called nine-one-one," he announced, breathless. "They said they would send a cop and an ambulance out immediately. They want to check and make sure you're okay before we take you home, Heidi."

I could feel my arms and legs becoming stiff with the promise of bruises. My head was pounding, but I was beyond that. I was ticked off. "Who would try to kill me?" I said, completely dumbfounded.

Lauren rubbed my shoulder, wiping her eyes with her other hand. "I don't know, Heidi," she said soothingly, and I realized I probably sounded hysterical if Lauren was talking to me like I was four.

I crossed my arms and tried not to rock back and forth. A few minutes later, amid Lucas and Lauren arguing about whether or not they should call my parents (I was staying out of it until one of them won so I could either congratulate or shoot down the winner), I heard the sirens. A police car came to a skidding stop right before an ambulance tore into the lot.

A policeman got out of his car and slowed his progress when he realized he wouldn't be making an arrest. He started talking to Greg, who began answering questions mechanically. The EMTs got out and hauled me over to the ambulance, saying things to each other in some sort of abbreviated code. Lucas and

Lauren got into the ambulance with me and sat on either side of me while an EMT flashed a light in my eyes to check for a concussion.

"I don't understand this," I said, not bothering to pay attention to what the EMT was doing anymore. "I'm nice to animals, I recycle, I always clip the plastic loopy things that come on coke cans so the ducks won't die," I said as the EMT put a blood pressure band around my arm.

"Did she hit her head when she fell?" he asked Lucas in a hushed voice.

"Yeah," Lucas said dryly, looking down at me as I winced against the alcohol they were rubbing on my skinned hands, "but she's fine. That's how she always talks."

"Even the loopy things?" the EMT clarified, looking doubtful.

"You haven't seen a crazy person until you've met this one," Lucas said, and I glared at him.

"I'm here on a stretcher, being taken to the hospital, and you're making fun of me?" I griped.

Lauren smiled at the EMT and said, "They verbally abuse each other. It's how they like to flirt."

I was in the middle of a long protest of that fact when the EMT suddenly thought it would be a good idea if I were put on oxygen to help me relax while we drove. I think I was giving him a headache. He slid a mask over my mouth and told me to try and relax because it would ease the pain building in my muscles from tensing so hard and being shoved into the ground.

Once at the hospital, they ran a few tests and gave me x-rays. Lauren hit the vending machines and brought me a Snickers, some Baked Lays, a Coke, and a shady looking turkey and cheese sandwich. I ate hungrily, suddenly so starving that I couldn't seem to eat fast enough. Lauren informed me guiltily that Lucas had called my family.

Before I could sufficiently freak out, she stopped me and said, "Your mom and one of your sisters are outside. Do you want to talk to them?"

I rolled my eyes and slumped over, resting my throbbing head against my knees. "Fine," I muttered, still in that position. I sat up in time to see my mother and Diana walk through the door.

My mom could never be called anything but lovely. She's not beautiful, but she's never been plain either. Her light brown hair is cut into a bob, her face is nearly wrinkle-free, and her outfits are always stunning. Today, she wore a pale gray skirt and a lilac blouse that brought the blue out in her eyes. She held onto her Kate Spade bag and tapped her Dior shoes in irritation. I can only imagine the guilt trip Lucas must have given her to get her to come out here. I wondered what social event she was missing in order to make sure her daughter was really okay after nearly being hit my a car.

Diana was wearing a snow-white sweat suit with sparkling silver rhinestones along the seams. She had on J. Crew flip-flops and held a Burberry tote bag. It took me a second to realize she no longer had a huge stomach.

"Did you have your baby?" I said in surprise.

Diana nodded, looking at me oddly. "Like two weeks ago. Where have you been?"

"No one called me," I said meekly, knowing I probably should have called Diana to check up on her at least once during her pregnancy. I guess this whole information thing goes both ways, and I'm not the best at it, either.

"What did you have?" I asked, and I saw my mother roll her eyes.

"A boy. His name is Joshua Hart Connelly."

I nodded. *Better than Rigby, I guess.*

"So," Diana said, her eyes wide with innocence, "who is the boy?"

I was completely lost. I looked at her and shrugged. "What boy?"

"The one who called us and told us that you had nearly been killed and that we needed to get out here and check on you. Was that Lucas Dayton?"

I nodded. "Yeah. He got a hold of my phone while I was in the ambulance."

*And called you both, even though I would have never in my life called any immediate member of my family if it had been my choice,* I added silently.

"Are you dating him?" my mother asked, suddenly sounding hopeful. I knew why; the Daytons would be great in-laws, reputation wise.

I laughed. "No, not even a little bit," I said honestly, wishing I weren't confined to this hospital room. I vowed to make Lucas pay for this conversation.

"Why were you with him, then?" Diana asked, looking confused.

*Shoot.* I had been at the Daytons for a while now, but I had managed to keep the nature of my job a secret from my family. I didn't want to have that conversation with my parents. I was about to respond—and most likely lie wildly—when none other than Maxwell Hart himself walked in.

My father was the kind of man that you respected no matter who you were. He was fairly tall, though shorter than Lucas, and was built like a wrestler (not the gross pro wrestlers that have biceps as big as bowling balls, though; wrestlers that are kind of broad shouldered and heavy-set). His hair was still black, and he stayed fairly tan year round because of his frequent tennis dates with clients. He had brown eyes, and, despite the fact that they were the color of chocolate, they were the only things that truly frightened me. My dad could show his entire spectrum of emotions with a single glance, and, as a kid, I dreaded getting in trouble because his anger would pierce my soul before his words even left his mouth.

Today, he looked like the ever-professional businessman in his navy blue suit and gray tie, but when I looked at his face I immediately put myself on alert. He looked like the cat that caught the canary. And I had the weirdest feeling like I was the dead bird.

"Heidi," he said, looking me over, and I straightened, fixing my posture almost instinctually.

"Hi, Dad," I said stiffly, trying not to act as disappointed that he was here as I was feeling.

"How are you feeling?" he asked, and Mom glanced at him, as if thrown by his sudden sign of giving a care.

"Uh, pretty good, I guess, considering," I said, unsure of how to proceed. He looked like he was about to lay down an Ace, and I was dealing in Old Maid.

"George Dayton is a nice man. I'm sure he'll let you have some vacation time if you need it," Dad said, and suddenly I knew that he knew. I could practically feel the color drain out of my face.

At that exact moment, Lauren and Lucas came into the room, presumably to check on us and possibly procure an introduction. I felt my heart start to hammer faster.

"George Dayton?" Mom said, looking bewildered. "You're working for George Dayton, Heidi?"

"Um, yes," I said, not technically lying.

"Dear, Heidi is George's nanny," Dad said, utterly delighted to be sharing this news, and my heart sunk. "She's in charge of this young lady right here," he said, pointing to Lauren, who smiled, completely missing the Tony Soprano, not-a-nice-guy vibe that my father radiated.

My mother and my sister looked at Lauren in utter disbelief, and Lauren stuck her hand out, smiling warmly, and said, "It's so nice to meet you."

Diana gamely shook her hand, but my mother was looking at me in something oddly akin to horror.

"You're a nanny…for a teenager. This is…new…for you," she said, diplomatically, although her tone was borderline disdainful.

Lauren's smile began to fade, and Lucas glanced at me in disbelief. I didn't look at him because I knew I would send him a death glare.

I nodded at my mother, pushing the sleeves to my cardigan up my arms.

"Yeah, it's new, I guess. I like it, though, and it's a good job."

My mother began twisting the pearls on her necklace, her smile becoming more and more mechanical. "Heidi, darling, why on earth would you turn your father's job offer down when your other option is childcare?"

I closed my eyes so I wouldn't see Lauren's expression. "Mom, I'm good. I like where I'm at. You don't need to make a scene."

Those were obviously the wrong words to choose at that point because my mother clenched her fists. "Make a scene? Oh, is that what I do now? Excuse me if hearing that my daughter is wasting her best years on a child that isn't even her own, making, I assume, nothing like what she could be making at her father's company, doesn't thrill me to my very core. Especially since this is all about some irrational need to prove something about independence. Heidi, you aren't even engaged," my mother said, her tone dripping in dramatic anguish. My mother, the actress.

I started to say something, but Diana chose that moment to add, "You always said she would be the weird one, Mom."

Nine times out of ten, I didn't care what my parents thought. I didn't care when my dad was mad that I chose track over tennis and my college over his alma mater. And I really didn't care when my mom freaked out over my decision to break up with my college boyfriend, Charlie. But I felt my throat close up and my eyes start to prick with tears when I heard Diana's words. I felt like I was six years old at the Children's Junior League meeting all over again, sitting in stone cold fear as Mrs. Vanderbilt yelled at me for twirling my hair and not having good enough posture. I looked at the floor, completely beaten.

"Excuse me," Lucas said, looking pretty peeved at this point, "I know it's really not my place to comment on a family problem, but Heidi is doing a great job. And my family loves her. She's intelligent and caring, and we would be lucky if Lauren looked at her like a role model. She is quirky, and she marches to the beat of her own drum, but she is not weird. For you to say so is incredibly insensitive."

Diana and Mom looked at him in open-mouthed wonder, and my father had this "We'll see" glint in his eyes that had me wigging out. I slid off the chair I was sitting in and slid my arm through Lauren's, pulling her out of the room with me. I heard Lucas behind us, but I didn't turn to check because I didn't want him to see me crying. I had a feeling he might do something drastic like try to verbally abuse my family some more.

I tried to get into the elevator, but these nurses swarmed us, chirping something about discharge papers. I signed my name a bunch of times, not knowing if I was clearing the hospital of any sort of lawsuit or if I were buying ocean front property in Arizona. I was working so hard at not crying that I could barely see. I couldn't blink or tears would run down my face.

Finally, I signed my name enough that they let us load the elevator. Lauren held my hand, but she didn't say anything. Lucas pushed the button for the parking garage violently, muttering something about Greg waiting for us. My arms, legs, and lower back were starting to get sore, and my shoulder was throbbing.

I just wanted to get into bed and never come out from under the covers.

# CHAPTER 14

We rode the elevator silently, but there was so much unspoken conversation going on that my head hurt. Lauren was obviously upset, and whether it was about my accident, my parents, or the fact that I had been ashamed to tell my parents what my job was, well, I was just waiting for that shoe to fall. Lucas was visibly irritated; so much so that, at one point, I swear he looked like he was going to punch the elevator wall.

We loaded into the car, Greg yammering on about follow-up questions the police had and what George had said when Greg called him. Apparently, George had wanted to come out to the hospital, but Greg told him we were almost done and that he would make sure we got home.

At the mention of home, I groaned. "We still have to stop and get ice cream," I said, moving stiffly to unbuckle so I could be ready to get out.

"You aren't getting out of the car," Lucas said, but he didn't sound mad; he sounded incredulous. "How could you possibly think I would let you out of this car?"

I shrugged, something that turned out to be extremely painful. "Because you aren't the boss of me?"

Lucas rolled his eyes and said, "Someone tried to run you over not even two hours ago, and you think I'm going to let you out of my sight?"

I sighed. "Is this how it's going to be now? You saved my life, so now you're going to be my shadow?"

"I'll go get the ice cream, okay? You two make everything so much harder than it has to be," Lauren said, unbuckling as Greg pulled up next to a Baskin Robbins.

I glared at Lucas after she shut her door and ran into the shop. "You upset her."

"I upset her?" Lucas said, raising both eyebrows and laughing. "Who was the one who was rushed to the hospital in an ambulance because a car nearly ran her over? I think that's what upset her."

"She knows I'm okay. I'm still here, still breathing; yet here you are, making it seem like someone is trying to kill me or something. It could have been a one-time thing for all we know, and you're acting like it's going to happen all the time now," I pointed out, giving him my stern look.

Lucas shook his head. "Unbelievable. You are completely unbelievable. How do you know that someone isn't trying to kill you? No one knew we were at that storage unit. Someone had to be following us, which means someone was probably following you, most likely to hurt you. I can't believe you, the girl detective, didn't put those two things together."

Me neither. I frowned. Someone must have followed us. Who? And from where? The house or one of the places we stopped? Probably the blackmailer, my sensible side reasoned. My normal person side was still thinking in exclamation points, mostly about how I almost died, someone tried to kill me, blah, blah, blah.

"I can tell by the look on your face that something I said registered in that tangled web you call your brain, so just think about one more thing: Next time, if you're by yourself, you could die. If you had been by yourself today, you would have died. The next time you get it into your head to go do something dangerous with my little sister—"

I started to protest at this, because we weren't doing anything dangerous, unless digging through someone's old stuff was dodgy, and all I had to say to that was, "Who's going to tell the antique buyers and garage salers of the world? Because it isn't going to be me," when Lucas covered my mouth with his hand.

I was shocked at this sudden act of aggression, so I didn't push him away. He finished his original statement slowly, emphasizing his words. "The next time, remember that it could happen to her too. They could use her to get to you."

I looked at him, the truth of his words sinking in, and he nodded once. "Get it?" he asked, sounding a little dizzy.

I don't know what it was, but whatever was making him look like he was about to fall over was effecting me too. I just kept looking at him, completely unable to think of anything to say, which was fine considering his hand was still firmly over my mouth. I tried to nod my head to show him that I got it, that it wasn't just my life that was suddenly in danger, and he surprised me by moving his hand to the back of my head and whispering, "If something were to happen to you…or to Lauren…"

As if by cue, Lauren opened the door to the car and slid in, stopping halfway, probably because of the tension in the air. Lucas dropped his hand and turned away from me, staring out the window with a blank expression on his face.

I was reeling. I blinked, shook my head, and turned to Lauren, trying to form words. She was smiling, way too smugly, but she took pity on me and didn't comment about the uncomfortable situation I had suddenly found myself in. She held up her plastic sack and said, "I got the ice cream."

Greg pulled away from the curb as soon as he heard Lauren's door shut. We rode in awkward silence until we got home. Lucas hopped out of the car, and, instead of coming in with us, told us he was heading home and that he would see us tomorrow at Isobel's party. Well, he actually told this to the ground, considering he wouldn't look at either of us.

After he was out of earshot, Lauren grabbed my arm and hauled me into the lobby. When we hit the elevator she let me go, but only so she could jump up and down, something that wasn't the most comforting thing to see in an elevator. I'm always afraid of being in an elevator that suddenly stops and plummets to the basement. That ride at Disneyworld totally freaked me out for life.

"What happened in that car? I only left you alone for like five minutes!" Lauren demanded, grabbing my arm and grinning widely.

"I have no idea," I said, but I needed to clear my throat to do so. "One minute he was yelling at me about putting you in danger, and the next minute—"

Lauren rolled her eyes. "You aren't putting me in danger. He's being ridiculous. Heidi, don't get mad at me for saying this, it's just my opinion, but I think he would have kissed you if I hadn't opened the door just then."

So did I. That's why I said, grimly, "Thank goodness for your timing."

Lauren laughed. "Whatever. You didn't exactly look like you were dreading it."

I hadn't been. Oh, it would have been a terrible idea, and I would have felt lousy about it later for making him think I cared about him like that, but even though there wasn't anything in me that liked him like that, I was a little disappointed it didn't happen. It would have been nice, being kissed, especially after nearly being hit by a car and being forced to see both my parents in one day.

There was really only so much one person could take. Said person could have really done with a little affection.

When we stepped into the lobby back at home; George, Alexis, and Eliza were all waiting anxiously for us. Eliza had a tray with a huge chunk of my favorite chocolate cake and a glass of milk on it.

On second thought, who needed affection when there was cake involved?

Despite my best efforts to make a beeline right for the cake, George and Alexis started talking, mostly about how worried they were, how glad they were I was okay, etc, etc.

"I'm going to hire a bodyguard to go out with the two of you until we can get an idea of who did this," George said in a tone that clearly meant no arguing. Lauren handed the ice cream to Eliza and took the tray. Eliza went scurrying into the kitchen to put the carton in the freezer.

"Are you sure you're okay, Heidi?" Alexis asked, her eyes huge. I nodded and tried to smile winningly, as if in the course of a single day, my world hadn't been severely altered; well, maybe *shifted* would be a more accurate term. I figured it would shift back as soon as the police caught the guy.

"I'm sore. Tired. And starving," I added as my stomach rumbled. "Lauren got me some food at the hospital, but I've still got the munchies. I think I'd like to go rest now. I can take the cake with me."

Lauren smiled at that.

George frowned. "Yes, certainly, go rest. I'm sure Lauren has some homework or something to do for her cotillion."

Lauren rolled her eyes but headed upstairs after me. With each step, I could feel the tightness of the muscles in my back and legs where bruises were forming, and I had to work to keep from wincing.

Lauren busied herself arranging my covers and adding pillows while I traded my nicer clothes for gray sweatpants and a red T-shirt. I slid in bed, my muscles protesting, and Lauren propped the tray up.

I helped myself to the cake, letting the chocolate heal me the way no Western medicine ever could.

Lauren sat silently for a few minutes, watching me, before blurting out, "It was Claude."

I choked on my cake. I started coughing, reaching for my milk glass. After a good sip had helped the rest of the mouthful of cake to make its way down my esophagus, I looked at Lauren in surprise. "Claude? What was Claude?"

"The man driving the SUV. I saw his face when Lucas pushed you away. He looked…disappointed."

I felt nauseated. I put my fork down and asked, "Lauren, are you sure? Did you tell the police?"

She nodded. "Lucas didn't hear me. He was arguing with the EMT. The officer promised to look into it. He said the car was probably stolen, so the tags I wrote down probably wouldn't help that much, but you never know. Claude could slip up."

I doubted it. This guy was rewriting my book on being a nuisance. Come to think of it, we wouldn't have even been at the storage unit if he hadn't lit the flame of curiosity in Lauren two months ago. I closed my eyes. He sounded like a good candidate for a black mailer, and it sounded like he was following us around too.

The thing that bugged me the most was that I couldn't figure out why he was doing it. I couldn't figure out what in the world he possibly had to gain from tormenting a fifteen-year-old girl about her mother's past and how he would ever prosper from offing a nanny-companion (companny?).

Okay, now this thing was beyond helping Lauren find peace. This was officially personal.

I faked a headache—okay, that's not true, I had a headache, I just lied about how debilitating it had become—and told Lauren I wanted to nap. She told me to feel better and cleared out, taking the now empty cake plate and milk glass with her. As soon as the door was shut and I could be sure that she had walked away, I grabbed my phone and my address book and found where Jennifer had written her sister's phone number down.

I dialed and let it ring. A little kid answered the phone.

"Hi, is Sarah there?" I asked, hoping this was her son or something and that I didn't have the wrong number.

"Yeah, hold on," he said, and I heard him yell "Mom" at the top of his voice a few times.

Finally, a very agitated adult voice, sounding out of breath, said, "Hello?"

"Hi, is this Sarah Warner?" I asked, hoping I remembered the right last name.

"Yes, it is," she said, sounding cautious. She probably thought I was a telemarketer.

"Hi, this is Heidi Hart, Jennifer's friend?" I clarified, hoping Sarah would remember me.

"Heidi! Of course! How are you?" she asked, suddenly full of life and sounding glad to hear from me. I breathed a sigh of relief.

"I'm well, Sarah. How are you?"

"Oh, I'm fine. That was my son you just talked to, Morgan. And sorry, we're working on his phone skills," she laughed.

"How old is Morgan now?" I asked. I vaguely remembered when he was born. Jennifer had been pretty excited.

"Seven. Mason is four, and my youngest, Mallory, is two. Are you married, Heidi?"

"No," I said rather quickly and felt bad at the audacity implied by that tone. "I mean, no, not yet."

"Dating anyone new?"

"No, not since Charlie," I said, knowing Sarah knew Charlie's family a little bit.

"Oh, well, I guess he bounced back okay," she said sarcastically, and I was confused.

"What do you mean?" I asked. When we had broken up in April, Charlie had gone around like a heartbroken fool, crying to anybody who would listen. Let's just say that didn't exactly make me want him back.

"You heard he got married last month," Sarah said slowly, as if unsure how I would take this news.

My mouth dropped open. "He did what? Who did he marry?" I demanded, a little outraged. I mean, the guy had spent a month trying to convince me to take him back, and he had bought a ring before that. And now, just six months later, he was married to someone else?

"Cynthia Mayfield," Sarah said, and I nearly dropped the phone.

There are a few people in this world that I loathe. Child molesters. Pickpockets. Murderers. Hot dog venders. Cynthia Mayfield was one of the few people I hated personally. She was this dippy little sophomore that talked too loud, too fast, and too often. She had a to-die-for figure, real blonde hair, and the biggest blue eyes framed with the darkest lashes I'd ever seen. She was the epitome of cute and giggly and had flirted with every guy on campus.

Including, it seemed, the dipstick formerly known as my boyfriend.

"When did that happen? How did that happen?" I asked, feeling as though I had to know. It was like watching an autopsy on television. You couldn't look away, even though you knew you so didn't want to see whatever made the person die because it couldn't be pretty. Even though I knew this information would irritate me to no end, I simply had to know.

"Uh, well, Tess Newberry told me that Charlie was just devastated when you told him you didn't want to get married and that Cynthia was there for him at a really tough time in his life," Sarah said.

Translation: When Charlie got to the drinking everything in sight stage of mourning, he found Cynthia an all too willing companion for club hopping.

"Jennifer said you were over Charlie. Did you...do you still have feelings for him? Should I not have told you?" Sarah said, sounding guilty.

"No, I'm glad I know. It makes me feel a lot better about us breaking up than I used to," I said, although she didn't know the half of it. I had felt so responsible whenever I saw Charlie moping around campus. At the time, it had made me feel like a real jerk, yet here he was, obviously totally over it.

"So now that I've given you some not-so great news, is there anything I can help you with? That you needed?" Sarah asked, sending me back down to earth to pay attention to our conversation.

"Yes, actually. I'm working for George Dayton now, and I was wondering what you could tell me about your relationship with Lance Dayton."

There was a long, awkward silence, and I realized what I had just said. "Oh! I meant, when you were younger. You obviously don't have one now."

I heard Sarah breathe a deep sigh of relief. "Let's see, well, Lance and I dated a long time ago. Like ten years ago, I think. But we keep in touch a little. He married a real sweetheart, Julie Newton, and they have a little girl just a little older than Mason. We take our kids to the same private school."

I scratched my forehead, trying to figure out how to bring up Daniella, but she did it for me.

"He was never the same after his stepmother died. He got really distant. I understood, but it ended up driving a pretty big wedge between us. When it came down to whether or not I could deal with it, I backed out," Sarah said, and she sounded a little wistful about it. Probably guilt.

"Can you tell me anything about that?" I asked, crossing my fingers.

Sarah hesitated. "Well, I mean, it was really sad. The little girl looked so lost at the funeral. Lance didn't want her out of his sight. That was the saddest funeral I have ever seen."

Okay, this wasn't helping. Maybe an upfront approach. "Did anyone seem…weird…about the funeral or her death?"

Another long pause from Sarah's end; then she said very cautiously, "Well, Lance was really upset with his mom. She didn't seem too sad that Daniella was dead. I got the feeling they didn't get along very well, but it was totally one sided. Daniella didn't dislike anyone. She was very sweet."

"So you think Maureen had a problem with Daniella?" I asked quickly, eager to get her talking.

"Oh, I don't know if I would call it a problem. She was more jealous than anything, I think. Lance said his mom was upset when George changed his will."

My heart started beating faster. A will. Why had that never occurred to me? I made a mental note to try and find a will. That could tell me a lot.

"What did he change?" I asked.

"Oh, I don't know. I just remember Lance was dreading his mother finding out. Those boys were terrified of their mother half the time."

That tracked. Lucas still seemed like he was under mom's thumb.

"Did you spend a lot of time with Maureen Dayton? I ask because I'm meeting her tomorrow," I explained.

Sarah's voice changed from reminiscent to amused. "Meeting the parents? Are you dating Lucas or something?"

I laughed. That got less funny every time someone asked me. "No. I'm actually Lauren's nanny. Companion. Person. We're having Isobel's birthday party tomorrow, and she's going to be there. She's kind of intimidating."

Now Sarah sounded sympathetic. "Oh, I hear you. I remember meeting her for the first time. I think Lance was even more nervous than I was. Apparently Maureen likes to speak her mind. At least that's what Lance told me. I think most people would call her blunt to the point of rudeness. She was okay for the most part, though. Lance said to never mention Daniella in front of her, and I didn't. We really didn't see her that much, though. We spent most of our time over at his dad's house."

As I was trying to think of my next question, Sarah spoke up, sounding thoughtful, "Look, just between us, you're obviously fishing for something specific. Why don't you just ask me? It was a long time ago, but I'll try to help you out."

I wondered if she had mom radar or if she was just really good at reading people. Either way, it was tremendously helpful to be able to say point blank, "I'm really curious about the events surrounding Daniella Dayton's death. I've been trying to get information about the people that were closest to her."

Sarah laughed a little. "You always were the most interesting of Jen's friends. If you want the dirt, I'd talk to Amanda Honey. She was Daniella's best friend, and they spent a lot of time together. If Daniella wasn't with George or Lauren, she was with Mandy. If something was wrong, Mandy would have known."

I sighed. It was a good suggestion. I had no idea how to convince Amanda Honey to talk to me about her best friend's life before she died, but it was a good suggestion.

"Thanks, Sarah. I really appreciate you answering all of my questions. It was really good to talk to you again," I said, resigning myself to the uncomfortable phone call I was going to make next.

"It's no problem. Call me anytime. It was great to hear from you. Now that Jennifer is married and pregnant, I don't get to talk to her much. For a while you were like my adopted little sister, so it's nice to check in with you."

I smiled at that. "Be careful, or you'll convince me to let you adopt me. It would be very Angelina of you."

Sarah laughed and said, "Like I said, call anytime. Talk to you later."

I said "bye" and hung up. I slid back into the covers and stared at my phone, trying to get up the courage to call information for Amanda Honey's number. What was the worst that could happen? Apart from her being so offended about my questions that she called George to complain and me getting fired.

Okay, that would be bad.

My phone rang, and I crossed my fingers that magically Amanda Honey had decided she had something pertinent to inform the nanny-companion (nanion?) of her deceased best friend's teenage daughter and had taken the liberty of finding my unlisted number to call me.

Because that could happen.

I looked at the screen and saw Leslie's name flashing across the screen. I groaned but answered anyway, "Hello?"

"Hi. Diana sent Max and me an e-mail saying you almost got hit by a car?" she said, clearly disbelieving.

I was a little shocked. We weren't, to say the least, a call and check up on each other kind of family.

"Um, yeah," I said, feeling a little flattered. Leslie is pretty self-involved, and for her to call me to see how I was…

"Did your boyfriend really yell at Mom and Dad?" she asked, sounding eager.

"He's not my boyfriend, and he didn't yell. He just voiced an opinion at the lack of respect they have for my chosen employment," I said stiffly.

Leslie laughed. "Yeah, I heard you were doing that. Load of good four years of college did you, huh?"

I closed my eyes and slumped down in my covers. "Did you need something, Les?"

"I think you need to call Mom and Dad and apologize for that guy's behavior. They were really hurt by whatever he said."

"I could, but I'm not because I don't think he did anything wrong. Besides, I don't really want to talk to them right now," I said honestly.

"That's a little selfish, Heidi," Leslie said in what I assumed was her new mom voice. It was borderline scolding and very bossy.

"They'll recognize the gesture, then," I said, knowing I was being dramatic and not really caring.

"I don't know why I even tried to call you. Diana said you were being a brat at the hospital," Leslie said, but she didn't sound snotty. She sounded resigned, as if I were such a burden.

"Yup, that's me, the family brat. Now if you don't mind, I've got a migraine from being shoved to the ground to avoid the SUV speeding toward me. I'm going to take a nap."

"Fine. Are you coming to Thanksgiving?"

I rolled my eyes. "I don't know, Leslie. Maybe. I might be busy being a brat."

"Call me when you know."

She hung up, and I was tempted to throw my phone across the room. There were times when small doses of my family was okay, sometimes it's even nice, but most of the time it's just the most annoying thing in the entire world. I would rather go to a packed Saturday night showing of a super popular movie and endure people kicking my seat and whispering to each other about the plot and how hot someone was than spend an hour with my family.

Dramatic? Maybe, but I thought it was deserved.

I decided to do something productive and actually take a nap. I leaned off the side of the bed and grabbed my jeans, digging in the pocket until I found the old prescription slip. I dialed the pharmacy I had all my prescriptions filled at and asked for the head pharmacist. A few minutes later, she came on the phone.

"Hi, this is Dinah," a very pleasant voice said.

"Hi, this is Heidi Hart, and I was wondering if you could tell me what this prescription is for," I said, and then I read off the long, multi-syllabic name of the medicine.

"That's a prenatal vitamin," she said immediately, and I nearly dropped the phone.

"What does it do?" I asked, nearly coming off the bed.

"Excuse me?"

"Is it something you take to try to get pregnant or something that you take when you are pregnant?" I demanded.

"It's something you take when you're pregnant. However, some women take them for the health benefits. Many prenatal vitamins are great for bad skin, for growing your hair out faster, things like that. Just because someone is prescribed a prenatal vitamin doesn't mean she would be pregnant," Dinah said cautiously, and I felt the excitement balloon that had been swelling start to deflate.

"One last thing and I'll let you go, okay?" I said, taking a deep breath. "Do you recognize the name Dr. Mueller?"

There was a long pause, and finally Dinah said, "Not off the top of my head, but I can look him up for you. We keep files on the all the doctors we get prescriptions from."

I waited impatiently for a minute or two before she came back on the phone and said, "Well, if he was the one who prescribed the medicine, it tracks. He's an obstetrician."

I put my head in my hands and said, "Thank you for your time and help. You've been really nice."

"Oh, no problem. Have a nice day."

"You too."

I hung up feeling nauseated. I had no way of knowing 100 percent for sure, but everything was lining up. I thought Daniella was pregnant when she died.

Suddenly things were clicking big time. Nearly all of Daniella's friends had remembered her being really excited about something the night she died. One of them had even mentioned that Daniella and George were celebrating something. What if Daniella had been planning on telling George she was pregnant the night she died? What if he never found out?

I let the phone fall out of my hand, and I rubbed my eyes. This just kept getting worse.

Maybe if I called Dr. Mueller directly, I could get him to confirm my suspicions. I mean, there might be some sort of doctor/patient privilege, but on *Law and Order* people were always saying that if the patient is dead, what's the harm? I wondered if I could make that work for me.

Probably not. But I did know someone who I could talk to, because if anyone would know if Daniella had been pregnant, it would have been her best friend. I called information, got Amanda Honey's number, and dialed with shaking hands.

When she picked up, I took a deep breath and said, "Hi, Miss Honey, my name is Heidi Hart. I met you a few weeks ago with Lauren and Lucas Dayton?"

"Yes," she said, and then she added, "Oh, shoot, I forgot to send that box of pictures to Lauren. I've got it sitting here in my office. Do you want to pick them up some time?"

I raised my eyebrows. I never get this lucky. "Uh, sure. Should I come by your house, or…"

"That's fine. I'm home between nine and one every day. Those are my office hours. After that, I'm usually with clients."

"I'll be there on Monday. Thank you so much for doing this, Miss Honey," I said, meaning the box of pictures.

"No problem. It's my pleasure, really."

We hung up, and I was amazed at how well that went.

I definitely earned an hour-long nap, one I took then with relish.

# CHAPTER 15

The next day, Sunday, I got my dress from the cleaners and checked with Lauren that it would be appropriate. She rolled her eyes and said, “Only you have to ask what’s appropriate to wear to a five-year-old’s birthday party.”

I shrugged. “I’m meeting half of your family for the first time. I don’t want to look like an idiot.”

“Well, you won’t. Just as long as you don’t explain your bruises to everybody, I’m sure they will love you,” Lauren reassured me.

Yeah, the bruises were certainly a sight. I had one solid purple bruise on my shoulder where it hit the pavement, and my upper arm was scratched up and a little swollen from rubbing against the asphalt. My hands weren’t as bad, but I had a honey of a scrape on my knee that the nurse had told me would probably scar.

I slipped the dress on and slid my hands over it, smoothing the cotton material down. It came down to my knees and had three quarter length sleeves. Even though the neckline was a little low, as long as I didn’t bend over, I’d be good to go. I added a pair of black calf boots and curled my hair a little bit. Lauren came into my room while I was applying some makeup and said, "Which earrings?"

I looked over at her and gauged the two sets she held up for me. One set were dangly, silver, and glittered in the light; the other were large pink roses. I checked out her outfit: black flats, gray linen mini skirt, and black camisole, worn with a diaphanous black peasant top over it. "The roses. Adds spice to the overall ensemble."

She nodded and went back to her bathroom. I added some lipstick and dropped the tube back into my travel bag. I sighed. Every time I saw Lauren, I wanted to say something about what I had found out yesterday. And every time I chickened out. I mean, how do you tell someone that her mom might have been pregnant when she died? How do you tell someone that if her mother had lived, she could very well have a nine-year-old little brother or sister right now?

I couldn't do that to Lauren. Not until I had unequivocal proof that Daniella had been pregnant. And if Amanda Honey couldn't tell me tomorrow and Dr. Mueller, my back up, couldn't release that kind of information to me, I didn't know how I was ever going to find out. I prayed that Amanda would know. If it had been me, I would have told my best friend. That I was pregnant, I mean. I would have been dying to tell someone, especially if I was waiting for a special time to tell my husband. Then again, maybe Daniella was more private than I had come to think of her.

I shoved my makeup bag into the cabinet and walked out, fixing the bow that held my dress tied. It wasn't until I heard a whistle that I was aware someone else was in the room.

I let out a yelp and jumped, nearly falling into the wall. Lucas was sitting in my armchair, completely at ease, waiting for me.

"Don't you know better to knock when you're coming into someone's room?" I chastised him, recovering from my scare. "I could have been changing!"

He grinned. "I apologize. Next time I will wait for your signal to come into your room. You look great, by the way."

I rolled my eyes. "Is there something you wanted?" I asked, suddenly uncomfortable. I had just remembered that the last time I saw or spoke to Lucas, I was 99 percent sure he was going to kiss me. The life or death feeling was gone, however; and if he tried it again, I'd have to hit him.

"Just…checking to see if you're okay," he said, sounding a little uncomfortable himself.

"Fine. A little sore, but I'm all better. Really. So you can go downstairs now."

Lucas laughed. "Will you relax? I'm not going to bite you."

I refrained from commenting. It was too easy. However, a little voice in my head said, *Make him promise not to try and kiss you. That's worse than a bite.*

Lucas stretched. "I like your room, by the way. Very you."

"Thanks," I said, wondering at his sudden change of subject. "What are you doing here, again?"

He sighed. He appeared to be choosing his words very carefully. I took this time to look him over. He wore jeans and a plaid shirt with various shades of blue. The shirt brought out the different colors in his eyes—sometimes I was convinced they were blue; other times, I was sure they were green—making them look almost teal. He looked completely at ease and way less uptight than usual.

"Heidi, I was just going to tell you that…" Lucas trailed off, looking at me closely. He closed his eyes briefly and said, "Actually, I was just going to remind you that when my mom's around, don't talk about Daniella, and don't be surprised if she'd rude to Alexis."

I blinked. It didn't take an idiot to realize that the thing about his mom was so not what he was originally going to say, but I didn't want to put too fine a point on it. So I just nodded and said, "Got it."

He nodded and shoved himself out of the armchair. He strode to the door and stopped, and he appeared to be having an argument with himself. I almost laughed, but instead I said, "Just say it."

He turned to me and said, "Did you think about what I said yesterday? About being more careful?"

Technically, no. I had thought about other things he said and did yesterday, but I had kind of tuned out the warnings.

I shrugged. "I didn't exactly dwell on it..."

He had a disappointed look on his face. "Heidi, please. Humor me. I just want to make sure you're not going to go do something stupid and then get shot or something."

I swallowed. Probably not the best time to tell him that I was meeting Amanda Honey the next day. "I won't get shot," I said, not looking directly at him.

"What are your plans for tomorrow? Are you going somewhere, or are you going to stay in?" he pressed, ducking his head to try and look me in the eyes.

I shrugged. "This and that."

"That doesn't answer my question."

I wet my lips, trying to come up with something to say that wasn't a complete and total lie. I opted for, "You know, if I'm scared or threatened in any way, I'll give you a call. Okay?"

Lucas pursed his lips. "Do you have a death wish?"

"No," I said, trying to be patient. "Listen, I'll be careful. I'll stay on crowded streets, travel by cab or by Greg, and be home before Lauren gets home. I'll be safe as houses. Whatever that means."

Lucas got that look on his face that, since coming to work here, I had seen on Lauren and George as well. It was the "I'm a Dayton, and you can't tell me 'no'" look. So far I had been powerless to stop it.

I was less than thrilled when he said, "I'll be here tomorrow morning before you leave."

"How do you know when I'm leaving?" I challenged, taking a step toward him in my irritation.

He looked down at me with the quirk of a smile on his face. "I'll hedge my bets and be here at eight. I've seen you at half past that, and you're completely useless. So I'm betting that earlier than that would just be unheard of."

*Rats*. He knew me well. There was no way I could be up and lucid before eight. I sighed. He was forcing me to be rebellious, and I knew that I would now be sneaking out of the house at seven thirty, around the time Lauren went to school. Mental note to get some sort of IV full of coffee to keep me vertical.

I smiled at him and said, "You aren't going to like what I'm doing."

"Don't care. If you're dead, I can't date you, and that puts a big hamper on my future plans."

I laughed. "You're delusional."

"Nope. Optimistic."

I shook my head, thoroughly amused by him. The thing was, I did like Lucas. He was smart and funny and he always got me to smile even when I didn't want to. Plus, he was what my friends would refer to as a "hottie with a body." Unfortunately, he didn't do anything for me romantically. He was a wonderful friend, and I loved him as a brotherly type figure, but not as a boyfriend. So when he said things like that I just laughed because I'd grown tired of telling him that it was not going to happen. Besides, he got that look on his face like I'd run over his puppy, and I couldn't stand that.

Lauren opened my door and nearly hit her brother, who she grinned at like he was doing something naughty. "Lance and Julie just got here. You should see Is. She looks awesome."

I followed her out the door, Lucas at my heels, and we went down the stairs. The three new people stood in the dining room, surrounded by the two dozen pink balloons Alexis had purchased and protesting the mound of presents in the corner. Alexis was holding Isobel up to the Princess Sleeping Beauty balloon tied to the birthday girl's chair, smiling widely. She wore a beautiful cream-colored cashmere sweater with a black sheath dress that fell to her knees, and I realized that Alexis had great legs. She had these adorable Marc Jacobs kitten heels on with big bows on the heels, and she had a huge smile on her face. It had been several weeks since I'd seen Alexis that happy, and it made my heart glad.

Isobel looked at us and got closer to Alexis, recognizing a stranger in the room. She had dark brown hair parted down the center of her head and pulled into curly pigtails, big blue eyes, and fair skin. Her eyelashes were to die for—super full and very dark—and she had on an absolutely fantastic pink polka dot party dress. Looking at Isobel I felt, for the first time in my life, like I might actually want a kid someday.

Julie stepped forward and hugged her brother and sister-in-law warmly, and when she turned to me, she said, "You must be Heidi. I'm Julie. I've heard so much about you."

I smiled. I wondered who she had heard it from, because certain people could say drastically different things than others.

"It's nice to meet you. You have a beautiful daughter."

Julie smiled widely and glanced at her daughter. Isobel looked like her mom; Julie had dark brown curls too and fair skin, but she had brown eyes. I liked Julie immediately, partly because she was friendly in an honest, natural way, and partly because she wasn't stick thin and intimidating. She was beautiful, but in a healthy size eight or ten kind of way. I knew several size twos and fours that would have loved to have Julie's body. She just seemed perfect in a natural, happy way. Her pink sweater and gray slacks fit her perfectly, and the rings on her left hand were so stunning that even someone that worked at Tiffany's would have teared up a bit at their beauty.

Lance moved in my direction, glancing over my shoulder at Lucas with a sly smile on his face. He looked a lot like his brother, only more mischievous. His blond hair definitely had a little gel in it. His eyes were bluer than Lucas's, but they had the same build and were about the same height. Lance wore jeans and a navy sweater, and when he stuck his hand out to me, I knew instantly that he would be testing me because he knew Lucas liked me.

"I'm Lance," he said, shaking my hand. "We've definitely heard a lot about you."

I grinned. "Heidi. It's nice to meet you."

He let go of my hand, but he crossed his arms and swayed on the balls of his feet a little. "You're from New York, right?"

I nodded.

"Just out of college?"

"I graduated last May."

"So that would put you at twenty…"

"Twenty-three."

"Uh huh. Do you like living here?"

"I do," I said, shooting Lauren a "save me" glance. "Lauren and I have become great friends."

"Lance," Lauren said, moving past me to take her brother's arm, "help me get the piñata hung, will you?"

Lance, completely aware of what was going on, smiled at me but didn't put up a fight. He followed his little sister out of the room, and I could see her whispering something fervently to him while he laughed. Lucas grinned at me and followed them out.

Julie sidled back up to me and said softly, "Sorry. He does that. He's fiercely protective of Lauren and of Lucas, even though neither guy would ever admit it. You should have heard the things Lucas grilled me about when Lance brought me home for the first time."

I leaned in and said, "I feel for you, really, I do, but you know that I'm just the nanny/companion, right? Lucas and I aren't together."

Julie sighed. "Yeah. I appreciate your honesty, but I knew that. Lucas doesn't make stuff up, and he never said the two of you were dating. He just talks about you incessantly whenever he comes over, so Lance and I kind of hoped..."

"Why did you hope? You've never even met me," I said, unable to stop myself from doing so.

Julie smiled again, a wide, happy smile, and said confidentially, "Lucas hasn't had the best couple of years. I'm not saying he's some sort of sad story, because no one born into this family can complain too much about wanting or needing anything, but he's had some ups and downs. He's seemed really happy since you came to live here, and that's something Lance and I have always prayed for, that Lucas would find someone that would help all the bad stuff go away."

I was a little frozen, my curiosity completely spiked. It was on the tip of my tongue to ask her what kind of bad things had been going on when Julie's facial expression changed from one of easy going happiness to apprehensive nervousness. I looked over her shoulder and saw that Alexis had handed Isobel off to George quite quickly and retreated to sit down at the end of the table, staring at the tablecloth.

It was like the temperature had dropped ten degrees in here. Either that or someone had sucked all the fun out of the room with some special kind of Hoover.

I turned and stared at the person who had just come in. She was tall, about my height, with a metallic gold shirt on that went perfectly with her bright red hair. Her brown slacks were tailored to fit super well, and she had gold Gucci flats on. Her green eyes snapped with electricity; and, despite her beautiful, flawless skin, she looked like the kind of person one didn't want to mess with. She looked, to quote Tyra Banks, fierce.

Maureen Dayton—Lucas and Lauren had never mentioned why she never changed her name back after her divorce—looked over the room calmly, her eyes piercing everyone she looked at. She seemed to ignore Alexis completely. Her eyes rested on Isobel.

"Come give Grandma a hug, darling," she purred, her voice oddly smooth for someone who looked like she had so much energy pent up.

George put Isobel down, and she looked a little reluctant to cross the room and hug her grandmother, but she did. Maureen looked around and said, "Where is your help, George? I have presents that need to be brought up."

Instantly, I had serious misgivings about this woman.

George gave a forced smile and said, "Oh, Lance and I can grab them. Are you parked in the garage?"

"Of course not," Maureen scoffed, looking disdainful. "My car is waiting outside."

George walked out of the room quickly, presumably to hunt down his sons.

Maureen released Isobel, who ran to Julie and buried her face in her mother's leg. Maureen was looking at me now, and I felt like I was being inspected.

"You must be Lauren's new…friend," she said smoothly, her eyes cool on mine.

I nodded. "Yes. I've been here since September. I'm Heidi Hart."

Maureen seemed to acknowledge that. "Lovely to meet you, Heidi. You are rather young, are you not? Surely you aren't that much older than Lauren?"

"I'm twenty-three," I said, and, suddenly, an age that had once seemed without a doubt adult somehow seemed quite childish.

Maureen sniffed and nodded. "Well. That's…nice," she said, sounding as if it were anything but. She looked around the room and said, "Goodness, who decorated this?"

Alexis cleared her throat. "I did," she said softly, standing up.

Maureen laughed a little, as though highly amused by something. "You did a…nice job," she said, as if she were being highly generous in this praise. "The balloons are…festive."

I watched in outraged shock as Alexis slowly deflated. I knew firsthand that she had worked for hours on those decorations, and for Maureen to just show up and make that less than the gift it was…I cleared my throat, totally ready to give her a piece of my mind, but Julie elbowed me. At first I thought it was an accident, but then I looked at her. She shook her head sadly, as if saying, "Yeah, it sucks, but we can't say anything."

Maureen walked around the table, picking apart everything Alexis had worked so hard on. "Linen napkins? For a five-year-old's birthday party? How…optimistic," she said, batting her eyelashes. "And princess balloons! I'm sure Julie is thrilled at having to take them home with her afterwards. They can be so impractical, can't they?"

Alexis cleared her throat and said, "Excuse me. I'm going to tell Eliza we can eat dinner now." She walked out quickly, her head ducked.

I was livid. This woman was horrible. I glanced at Julie, who looked miserable, and then said, "You know, I bet I can find some paper napkins if you like."

Maureen shrugged. "Good luck finding anything in that kitchen, honey. It seems in the last few years to have gone completely crazy. I believe you have to have ESP in order to find a fork now!"

I smiled as if amused and walked out of the room just as Lance, Lucas, Lauren, and George came in, each carrying a present. I ignored them because I knew I would explode if one if them talked to me—to let this woman behave the way she did toward Alexis went against everything I believed—so I ducked my head and walked as fast as I could.

I walked into the kitchen, desperately hoping to find some napkins that didn't have a thread count higher than most people's sheets. I stopped short when I saw Alexis, standing in the middle of the room with her hands on her hips, eyes closed, frown marring her beautiful face. I started to back out, but she opened her eyes and said, "You're okay. Don't worry about it."

"Are *you* okay?" I asked, concerned. She looked really sad.

Alexis shrugged, her creamy sweater shifting on slim shoulders. The fake smile she had resumed weakened, and she said, "I'll be fine. I'm just having a tough evening."

"Anything I can do?" I asked, feeling bad for her. Alexis may have had her oddities, but she was probably the nicest person in the universe. To see her sad was cosmically upsetting.

Alexis shook her head, but her lower lip trembled a little. She sighed, resigned, and opened a cupboard, pulling out a tumbler. She opened a bottom shelf and reached way to the back to pull out a bottle of Scotch.

"I'm not a big drinker," she said, pouring an inch or so into the tumbler, "but some things cannot be endured without a little liquid courage. Don't tell George."

She sipped the honey-colored liquid, shuddering as it hit her throat. I smiled in realization. Maureen was putting Alexis into a panic. It had to be Maureen. She was making me pretty darn uncomfortable, and I wasn't even the source of her bitterness and subsequent wrath.

"I didn't see anything," I said, shrugging my shoulders. She sent me a small smile and relaxed against the counter.

She shook her head. "I just can't seem to remember I'm a grown woman when I'm around her. She terrifies me. Isn't that ridiculous?"

I shook my head vehemently. "Absolutely not. That woman is scary. That's the kind of person the monsters check under the bed for."

Alexis chuckled at that, swishing the remnants of her drink wistfully. "I try to be so nice to her, you know? But she hated me from the beginning. I wouldn't mind so much—I mean, I understand that I married her ex-husband, I didn't expect us to be best friends—but she told everybody I married George for his money. Who does something like that?"

I waited until after she had finished the contents of her glass to answer. "A bitter woman," I said honestly. "He did marry someone almost half his age."

Alexis rolled her eyes, something I had never seen her do, and I wondered if she could hold her liquor. "Just because I'm younger than him doesn't mean I had a motive for marrying him. I love George, and whether he was twenty or sixty, I knew I wanted to be with him. I don't see why that's so hard to understand."

I shrugged. "It just seems odd that a woman…that you…"

Alexis lowered her head a bit. "I realize that I'm going to have to do things most women my age won't have to do for years yet. I realize that while most of my friends are enjoying their kids and their grandkids, I'll be enjoying stepchildren and a step granddaughter who isn't even allowed to view me as a grandma because her 'real' grandma would be mad. I get that I won't ever get to have my own child. I made my peace with that a long time ago. George is more important than that. Do you know what worries me the most?"

I shook my head, suddenly unable to speak. Alexis had obviously been keeping this in for a long time, and it was rushing out so fast I'm not even sure she knew she was saying it aloud.

Alexis's lower lip trembled violently and she said, "I'm afraid of being forty and having to bury my husband."

She brought her hand up to her mouth, and her shoulders shook. I think she was working really hard not to cry and not succeeding very well.

My heart broke for her. In all my cynicism about marriage and children and having a family, I could still totally see what she was saying. I had never thought about everything that Alexis gave up to be with George, not the least of which was a "normal" marriage for a woman her age. Her stepchildren were nearly her age, and she could barely claim her grandchild because of her husband's anal witch of an ex-wife. Alexis knew the chances of her getting to have her own child were slim to none, and she knew that, barring tragic circumstances, her husband would most likely die twenty to thirty years before she did.

I don't know what caused me to do so, but I went to her and hugged her. I held onto her tightly and let her pretend she wasn't crying. I rubbed her back and stroked her hair, trying to think of things moms did in movies when their kids were upset.

She sniffed and pulled away from me after a minute. She wiped her eyes carefully, avoiding messing up her makeup, and looked much more composed.

"Thank you for listening to me vent," she said, looking embarrassed that she had shared something so personal with someone that she didn't know that well.

I smiled at her and pushed a big chunk of her hair that had come out of her headband behind her ear.

"Anytime. I'm always here if you want to talk. I know that might be weird for you, but if you need someone to listen to you, I am volunteering."

Alexis smiled stiffly, fixing her hair, and said, "I'll remember that. We, um, we better get back to the party."

"Oh, yeah," I said, remembering where we were. "Hey, where would I find paper napkins?"

Alexis blinked. "You'll have to ask Eliza. I have no idea."

I nodded and, when she left, I dug around in some drawers until I found a set of pink paper napkins. I grabbed them and headed back to the dining room.

When I walked in, I noticed that George had put his arm around Alexis, and he kissed the top of her head when she leaned into him, closing her eyes briefly. My heart hurt for Alexis. She kept so much inside, and I couldn't help but wonder what else was weighing on her. I put the paper napkins on the table and then tried to fade away into the background.

Lauren came up to me and said, "What do you think of Is? She's pretty perfect, isn't she?"

I nodded. "She's beautiful."

She leaned closer and said, "Lance and Julie lost a baby before they had her, so they're really protective of her. Lucas told me earlier that they're expecting again, and that Julie's four months along. But they aren't making an announcement until she starts showing and it's obvious, just in case."

I was beginning to wonder if every woman over the age of twenty-two in my acquaintance would reproduce in the calendar year. Since the only variable they had alike was me, I started to worry I was causing some chemical imbalance in my married female friends that was causing them to get pregnant.

*Okay, that freaks me out.*

"Dad, Alexis, and Maureen don't know yet. Lance told Lucas last night when he was over there, and he told me just now. She's due in March, I think. Just don't say anything yet, okay?"

I made the gesture as if zipping my lips, causing her to giggle.

George and Alexis sat down at the table, an unspoken sign to follow their lead. Isobel sat at the end, between her parents, and Lucas and I sat next to Lance. Maureen sat down next to Julie, Lauren next to Maureen, with Alexis on her other side, and George was at the other end of the table. Eliza brought out salads for everyone first, and I was shocked to see Isobel go to town on hers. When I was five, there was no way anyone could get me to eat a salad.

Lance and Lucas kept a conversation running so no one felt awkward. Lauren offered some comments too, but the rest of the room ate in silence. I felt like doing something wild like singing the theme song to *Friends*, standing on my chair, pelting Maureen with my salad.

When Eliza brought out the spaghetti, Maureen raised her eyebrows and laughed gaily. "Spaghetti? Ambitious. I hope Isobel doesn't ruin her party dress."

Julie cut up Isobel's food, looking miserable. "I'm sure she'll be fine, Maureen. She eats it all the time at home. It's her favorite, that's why I suggested it to Alexis."

Maureen nodded, clearly unconvinced. "When Lance was little, I never had to worry about his table manners. He behaved so well. Lucas couldn't keep his food in his mouth if it killed him. I don't know how he survived childhood; he never ate a full meal."

George frowned. "I don't remember that. It seems like Lucas was pretty good too. Not any better or worse than Lance, anyway."

Lucas and Lance exchanged a glance, and I had a feeling they had heard this conversation before.

"How would you remember, dear? You were at the office half their childhood." Maureen laughed as if she were making a great joke, but it didn't look like anyone was laughing.

George cleared his throat. "Maureen, this really isn't the time to fight. Let's just celebrate our granddaughter's birthday in peace."

"You don't have to sound so condescending. You aren't talking to a child," Maureen snapped, glaring at Alexis.

I don't know why I did it, but I had to do something. And the first thing that came to my mind to say was, "When I was three, I threw my spaghetti across the table, and it landed on my brother's head. For a year, my older sister called him Meat Sauce."

There was a surprised silence in the air for a few seconds, and then Lucas smiled at me. "When Lauren was two, she made cookies with the maid, and when no one was looking, she threw in a bag of shredded cheese. They were, I'm sorry to say, the worst thing I have ever tasted."

I could tell Lauren was about to make a rebuttal to that comment when the doorman buzzed the apartment and she froze. "Uh, I'll be right back," she muttered, scooting her chair back and dashing for the front door.

I gave Lucas a warning glance. With my newfound dislike of Maureen, I had temporarily forgotten that Lauren had invited Connor to dinner (never mind that he was super late, but I guess he is a sixteen-year-old boy). I had a good feeling that this kid was walking into an attack, and I was hoping that by sitting next to Lucas I could kick at least one person if the interrogation got out of hand.

Lauren walked into the room a minute later, beaming, leading a tall, kind of skinny, very cute boy to his doom. Connor seemed a bit uncomfortable, and I felt for him. Being an outsider to this family was scary.

# CHAPTER 16

"Everybody, this is Connor Whitson," Lauren said, sounding ridiculously happy, as only a teenage girl can sound when she's around her first real crush. "Connor, this is my dad, George, and my stepmom, Alexis; my brothers, Lance and Lucas; my sister-in-law, Julie; my niece, Isobel, the birthday girl; and my brothers' mom, Maureen. And this," she said, as if saving me for the extra special person of honor, "is my best friend, Heidi."

Assuming I was the safest person to greet first, Connor shook my hand and murmured how nice it was to be here. The poor boy's palm was super sweaty.

"Do you need a chair?" I asked him, but my question was more directed to Lauren.

"Uh, sure, if you've got an extra one," he said, and I noticed the glint of his braces when he smiled. He ran a hand over scruffy dirty blond hair, and I grinned at him reassuringly.

"Connor, is it?" Lance said, sitting back in his chair and crossing his arms. His eyes were narrowed a bit, as if inspecting something. I caught Julie's eye, and she sent me a grin. *Here we go.*

I turned to Lucas, who had moved to match his brother's position, and said, "Why don't you go get Connor a chair?"

He glared at me, as if telling me to be quiet, and I yanked on his shirtsleeve and said, "Come on. I'll go with you. It will be fun."

I finally managed to get Lucas out of the dining room amid round one of Lance's questions. Lucas looked at me, very crossly, and said, "I have a right to be suspicious of my sister's first boyfriend."

I nodded, patronizing him shamelessly. "Of course you do. But he's not her boyfriend yet, and until he is you will stay out of it. She's going to be furious if you and Lance embarrass her, so I would send him some sort of signal to back off."

Lucas went to the hall closet and pulled a chair out. When he turned back around, he was sending me a sly smile. "Did your brother ever embarrass you in front of a boyfriend?"

I laughed. "No. My boyfriends rarely met my family. I think maybe two made that sacrifice. Besides, Max had better things to do than grill anybody I dated. He liked Charlie, but only because my parents adored him."

Lucas frowned. "They liked your ex?"

"They loved him. When we broke up I think they wanted to keep him and send me on," I said, completely serious.

Lucas shifted the chair to his other hand and closed the closet door. "Why did you guys break up?"

"Who, me and Charlie?"

"That's who we're talking about, isn't it?"

I shrugged. "He wanted to get married. I didn't. He gave me an ultimatum, and I said 'no.' That's pretty much it." I didn't add the part where six months later, Charlie apparently married a little minion of Satan.

"Are we talking he wanted to get married in the future or right then?" Lucas pushed, looking a little put out.

"Then, I guess. I mean, he had a ring."

Lucas stopped and set the chair down, leaning against it. "Wait, he proposed to you?" he asked, sounding incredulous.

I blinked. "Um, yeah. That was the ultimatum."

"He had a ring and asked you to marry him, and you turned him down?" Lucas clarified, moving past put out to ticked off, though I couldn't figure out why.

"Yeah," I said, wondering where he was going with this.

"So you loved him."

I blinked. "No. We were dating, but I never told him I loved him."

"He must have thought you did if he asked you to marry him. I mean, people don't generally ask stuff like that if they think the other person is going to say 'no,'" Lucas pointed out.

I turned my hands palm up and said, "Look, I don't know what you want me to say. I don't get why you're upset. I mean, obviously, I didn't marry him. I didn't say 'yes.' He was just an over-confident jock that thought after seven months I'd be thrilled to get a proposal, especially since my two best friends were already married. It's not the crisis situation you are making it out to be."

Lucas shook his head, looking at me like he was really mad about something. I couldn't understand it. I mean, I got that he liked me. Goodness knows I heard it enough. And I even got that another man asking me to marry him might bug him because of that. But I turned the other guy down, and it was several months before I even knew Lucas. So I didn't understand why he was looking at me like I had ruined something for him.

"Look, Connor needs that chair. Are we going to go back in there or fight about this some more?" I asked, trying to change the subject.

Lucas turned and carried the chair back into the dining room, completely ignoring me. I sighed, cursing the moodiness of men, and followed him in.

The rest of dinner wasn't awful. Everyone was so focused on Lauren and Connor that no one even noticed that Lucas was pouting into his spaghetti and avoiding my very presence. Maureen didn't make any more comments about Alexis, and when it came time to do presents I almost cheered right along with Isobel. A change of scenery, of topic, seemed a welcome gift.

She got a ton of stuff. Super cute clothes, toys, books, everything a little girl could need, and so much more. She liked the wand I gave her, so I was pretty psyched. I knew it was cool.

Though Isobel could have played with her new stuff all evening, the rest of us were ready for cake. Eliza brought out a beautiful, pink, castle-shaped cake with green vines running all over it and yellow flowers growing on the vines. My mouth was practically drooling just looking at it. I heard Maureen make some offhand comment about how the green dye would color Isobel's perfect teeth, but Julie served her daughter a piece with tons of vines and flowers anyway.

The cake tasted as good as it looked. I was more into that than the ice cream, despite the fact that it was chocolate, and that usually guarantees a good time in my book. I was savoring my piece, enjoying myself thoroughly, when Maureen came and sat down next to me.

I instantly tensed up, not sure what she wanted, but I smiled anyway. I didn't want to stoop to her level by being snotty to her, but I certainly wasn't going to be all chummy either.

"Are you enjoying the party?" Maureen asked, sounding like a happy, ordinary grandmother—a complete turn around from how she had been acting all night.

"Uh…" I said, trying to think of a pleasant response, "yeah. It's been fun."

"Does your family have big events like this?" she pressed.

"No. We can barely be in the same room," I said, shaking my head.

"That's such a shame," Maureen said, and I couldn't tell if she was being sarcastic or not. Something was blocking my normally foolproof sarcasm radar. "Family is the most important thing in the world, you know. You should hold them as the dearest things in your possession."

I blinked at her word choice. *Possession?* I didn't think I owned my family. Sometimes I felt my family owned me, but never the other way around. I couldn't imagine thinking I owned anyone. I even have issues with overly-whipped significant others.

I managed to smile and say, "I'm just not very close to my family. I'm excited to be included in this family, though."

"How included?" Maureen asked innocently, glancing at Lucas, who was listening intently to something Lauren was asking Connor.

I refrained from sighing. My lack of a relationship with Lucas would have made a great drinking game—every time someone asked our status, take a shot! That party would have been easier to handle, that's for sure.

"Not that included," I said carefully.

She shrugged and looked doubtful, so I changed the subject. "Isobel is beautiful. She looks just like her mom."

Maureen nodded. "Julie is very pretty, yes. I think Isobel gets her looks from her father, actually. She has his eyes, and he's really in wonderful shape for a man with a family and a high-stress job. He does a great job balancing his life."

"Lucas does too. You did a great job with them," I said, ashamed I was sucking up to her. Maybe if she liked me, she would be nicer to people I liked, namely Alexis.

"Oh, that boy. He has so little direction in his life. Lance was married and a father when he was Lucas's age. Lucas seems to think he can be lazy with matters like these when he needs to be out looking. There aren't many women that are good enough for him, you know. I mean, I'm not saying Lance settled when he married Julie, but..."

I tried not to look shocked. What a horrible thing to say about both your sons and your daughter-in-law! I suddenly didn't care if she was being nice to me. If she wasn't going to be nice to anyone else, I didn't need her to like me. I excused myself and ran up to my room. When I got there, I took a deep breath and tried to control the growing irritation I felt in my chest.

Lucas may not have been anyone but a friend to me, but to hear his mother say, basically, that he should hurry up and get married before all the good ones are gone was appalling. Did his mother not realize just how great her son was? He could do so much better than just "settling."

And Julie! How dare Maureen imply that Lance could have done better than Julie! She seemed like a completely lovely person, and I saw the way Lance looked at her and their daughter. He was clearly a man who loved his family and had no regrets about them.

I threw myself back onto my bed and rested my arm over my eyes, blocking out the brightness of the overhead light. There was a small knock on the door, and I sat up a bit, assuming it was Lucas.

"Come in," I said, preparing myself for round two of Heidi's past relationships.

Julie poked her head in and said, "I thought I might find you in here."

I catapulted up, feeling guilty. I was hiding out during her daughter's birthday party. I sucked as a person.

"Um, sorry, I was just getting, um—"

Julie held up her hand. "I hid up here during my first family event too. Only it was Christmas, and this was a guest room. It's quiet up here. No one telling you how much better off their son would be if he had married someone else."

I cringed. "Yeah, that kind of sucks."

Julie laughed a little and said, "Not kind of; it very much sucks. It's not bad enough that she's on us all the time about Lance's job, whether or not I should work, and whether or not we're raising our daughter right, but to put our marriage to question is just plain irritating."

I nodded. "If it's any consolation, and having just met you I can't offer my opinion about all those things, but I think you're doing an amazing job with Isobel. She's beautiful, and she seems like a great kid. And it actually means something that I'm saying that, because I don't really understand children that much. They very much bewilder me."

Julie rolled her eyes. "Oh, me too. Isobel is the scariest thing Lance and I have ever done, believe me. I get…nervous…thinking about having another one."

She looked at me sharply, as if she were afraid I'd start pestering her with questions about another baby, but I just said, "I'd think you were foolish if you didn't."

Julie sat next to me on the bed. "I like you. You're honest. That's a rare find these days."

I shrugged. "Yeah, well, coddling people—which is all lying is, most of the time—is really bad for the skin. It's all that denial and guilt. Goes straight to the pores."

Julie laughed. She started playing with a charm on her bracelet, a cloverleaf.

"That's pretty," I said, indicating the bracelet.

"Mother's Day present last year," she said, and she sounded pretty proud of it. "The heart is love, the clover is luck, the dove is peace, and the key is freedom."

I frowned. "How can a key be freedom? They go with locks. Locks aren't exactly freeing."

Julie smiled and shook her head. "Yes, but what can be locked can always be unlocked. And that's freedom to me—finding a way out of any situation by choosing where to be. It's not always about where you're escaping from; it should be where you're escaping to."

I smiled. "I like that. I guess it's the two sides of every coin thing, right?"

"Right."

We sat silently for a few seconds, but Julie obviously had something on her mind. "She likes you, I think," she said quietly.

"Who?" I asked, thinking maybe she meant Isobel.

"Maureen."

I snorted. "Yippee. I can die happy."

"Believe me, it will make your life here so much easier if she likes you. Lance and I have been married for seven years, and I have felt hated the entire time. She expects him to be president or something, I don't know. But I wasn't who she had picked out for him to pursue bigger goals, and she's pouted about it since we announced our engagement. She wore white to my wedding, just like Jane Fonda in *Monster-in-Law*," Julie said, as if that put the whole thing in perspective.

And, considering I was her audience, it totally did. I had seen that movie—which in my unbiased opinion was just okay, as far as movies go—and I now had a crystal clear image of what life must have been like for Julie at the beginning of her relationship with Lance.

I stood up and said, "Not that hiding out isn't the obvious choice in this situation, but I think there is a certain third wife of a millionaire downstairs that could use a little backup."

Julie nodded and shoved herself of the bed. "That's what makes me the most upset. Alexis is great, and she has really made George happy. When I first met him he was this broken man, still in mourning, with a child he didn't know how to raise.

And when he met her he was completely different. Lance said he hadn't been that happy in years."

I smiled. "I can see that, definitely."

"I can't help but think that's why Maureen doesn't like Alexis. Lance says that Alexis was like a breath of fresh air in George's life and that, after he met her, the change was instantaneous. He started smiling again. He started treating Lauren like a real girl instead of a doll he was afraid would break. And Alexis has been so good for Lauren," Julie said, opening the door.

I walked out of my room, and she shut the door behind us. I turned to her and asked, "How long were they together? Before they got married?"

Julie thought about it for a moment. "Their anniversary is in April, so it will be three years then. They started dating right around the time we found out about Isobel, I think, so they've been together for about six years or so."

"What did Maureen say when they announced their engagement?" I asked, justifying to myself that this was research not gossip.

Julie shrugged. "Nothing. She was nice to Alexis at first. Then she told half the wedding guests that Alexis only married George for his money. That was festive."

I giggled and shook my head. "She sounds like the Ice Queen."

"I'm pretty sure she's the entire Ice Court, actually," Julie said, and we had to control ourselves as we walked back into the dining room.

"Nice of you two to rejoin the party," Maureen said, in such a frosty voice that I almost started laughing again. This woman was unreal.

Lance slid his arm around Julie's waist and kissed her temple. She patted his back and smiled up at him. So cute.

Speaking of which, Lauren and Connor were eating cake and talking softly, and she had a big grin on her face. He looked like he had taken the iron rod out of his spine and learned to relax a little. Probably because George was nowhere to be seen. Neither was Alexis, and I silently hoped that she hadn't gone crazy from the constant pressure. Lucas was sitting at one end of the table, talking to Isobel, a very serious expression on both of their faces. I smiled at that. He was probably one of those uncles that kids loved. I couldn't imagine Lucas getting Isobel into trouble or being strict at all; in fact, I would bet a lot of money that he spoiled her rotten.

He glanced up and saw me looking at them. His smile faded a smidge, and he brought his attention back to Isobel.

*Um, ouch, what did I do?* I believe he was the one who went off in a tiff, not me. I was being completely reasonable.

I walked around the table (leaving Lance and Julie to pretend to listen to Maureen complain about the ridiculous decision to have a silk tablecloth at a birthday party for a five-year-old) and sat down in a seat next to Lauren.

"Your family parties are exhausting," I said, crossing my legs and resting my head on my hand, my elbow supported by the back of Lauren's chair.

"Sorry," she said, smiling a little. She knew, at least to some extent, I think, what I was talking about. I mean, she had to have noticed the Maureen thing. The Lucas thing, thankfully, seemed to be between us—more specifically, it was all him, and I was along for the ride by association—and she couldn't share an opinion about that. I was kind of curious to see why he was so put out with me, though. I couldn't imagine that Lucas, looking the way he did and being as nice as he was, had ever been at a loss for girls throwing themselves at him. Surely he'd caught at least one, at least for a little while.

The thought made me laugh. Maybe a fishing analogy wasn't the most appropriate way to describe it. I had a sudden visual of Lucas reeling in a girl, inspecting the catch, and throwing it back, saying it should be taller or something stupid like that.

To take my mind of all things unpleasant, I turned to Connor and said, "Are you having fun?"

Connor shrugged, his eyes cutting over to Lauren as his cheeks colored slightly. "I'm glad to be here."

I elbowed Lauren discreetly and hid my smile. What a cute thing to say! Connor, even if he didn't appear to have a lot of backbone, at least had a sweet side to him, and I hoped he would show a little more of it to Lauren. Every girl should have a good first boyfriend. Mine started out okay, but he turned into a real jerk the last few weeks we dated. So much so that I was relieved when he suggested we end our relationship. I didn't realize at the time that he had employed the oldest trick in the book on me—treat them so poorly the last few weeks, and they'll either end it for you or be glad when you finally end it. Luckily, I got to see him publicly humiliated by his next girlfriend at homecoming when she found him making out with a cheerleader and dumped chili cheese nachos down the back of his pants (those were the days it was cool to sag). Eight years later, it still brought a smile to my face to remember him walking out of the football stadium, holding the crotch of his jeans away from his body in order to try and keep the chili from seeping into his boxer shorts.

Lauren was looking at Connor like she was going to say something equally sweet and gooey back to him, so I excused myself. I adored Lauren, but our friendship was not to the point that I could listen to a "No, you're prettier" argument and not gag. I scanned the room. George and Alexis were still MIA, Maureen was showing Isobel how the new Barbie doll she had gotten could apparently change color under water and become some sort of mermaid (one of these days, I swear they are going to come out with a Barbie that reads or something), and Lance and Julie were talking with Lucas. I took a deep breath. I should make nice with Lucas while there were witnesses. And backup.

I sat down next to Julie and smiled, tuning into their conversation halfway through. Lance was apparently lecturing on something, and when I sat down he abruptly changed the subject. I mean, unless they had been talking about shrimp that heatedly, which I guess could be true, but I kind of figured Lance had changed the subject when he saw me coming.

"What's up?" I asked mildly. Julie put a hand over her mouth to hide her smile.

"Nothing. Nothing's up. I was just telling Lucas here about the great shrimp Jules and I had the other night," Lance said quickly. Lucas looked pained but, admittedly, entertained.

I nodded. "What kind of shrimp was it?" I asked, playing along.

Lance looked blank for a moment, and Julie took pity on him. "Coconut shrimp," she said, and I think she was biting the inside of her mouth to keep from laughing. "You know, the kind of shrimp that forms attachments and gets jealous when other shrimp get too close to the…tartar sauce."

Okay, I was a little lost, but Lance shot his wife an irritated glance, and Lucas stopped smiling abruptly. Julie wet her lips and said, "My husband has this…friend…who likes a woman he knows, and he got upset because apparently he had it in his head that he was the only man that ever got to like this woman, past, present, or future."

I was pretty sure she was talking about Lucas's problem with the fact that Charlie had proposed to me, and I really wanted to know why it was such a big deal, so I nodded and said, "And what did Lance tell his friend?"

Julie shrugged, and the Dayton brothers crossed their arms and glared at us, obviously aware we were patronizing them. "He told him that he has to be more aggressive in courting this woman. Lance seems to think that displays of affection like flowers, chocolates, empty promises, etc., are the best way to go. What do you think?"

I glanced at Lucas, who was staring at the floor, and at Lance, who was looking guilty at this point. I took pity on them and said, "Well, every situation is different, obviously, and since I don't know Lance's friend, I would think the best advice Lance could give is that this guy needs to look in the mirror. I mean, has he been in relationships before?"

Julie nodded. "A few. Only one fairly serious."

"Okay," Lucas started to object, sounding really mad, but I stopped him by putting my hand over his mouth, similarly to what he had done to me the day before. I looked at him solemnly, no hint of a joke on my face.

"Just keep that in mind, then," I said softly, speaking directly to him this time. "No one is perfect. Every body has baggage. If you can't accept that, then you've got a whole lot of hurt coming your way."

His eyes dimmed a little, as if he were accepting what I was saying but not particularly embracing it, and I removed my hand. Lance was looking at me with new respect, and Julie had a small, supportive smile on her face.

I suddenly felt very self-conscious. I didn't know what else to say. These people were going to drive me nuts. I couldn't get used to the whole sharing feelings thing. That was so not how I was raised. My siblings and their spouses expressed no interest in my personal life unless it directly affected theirs in some way. I could never imagine confiding in Diana or Leslie, and the thought of telling Max anything was comical. I rarely even talked when I was around Barry and Brady, and Susan, while very nice, is one of those people that you can talk about one of three things with: her children, the women at the club, and the weather. In that order. The fact that Lucas had gone and complained to Lance and Julie about his issues seemed abnormal. I thought only siblings on TV did that. I mean, I have known people who liked their siblings. I was not so naïve to think that my family was the norm in this world or even in this town. For instance, Jennifer and her sister, Sarah, are pretty good friends. Jennifer is Sarah's oldest son's godmother. That's not just a nicety. They genuinely like each other.

I thought back to the day before. I had been shocked that Mom and Dad had both come to the hospital to see me—one of whom had no ulterior motive of humiliating me as incentive to be there—but for Diana to come was kind of bizarre. We never talked. She was three years older than me, and we'd never been close. Even when we were little, she and Leslie had each other and I played by myself or with neighbor kids.

I had never in my life felt sorry for myself because of my family life. I have loathed certain members of my family at times, and I had for sure been angry that I was cursed with siblings and parents that were so…aggravating, I guess. But I have never felt sorry for myself. But sitting there in that four-hundred-dollar antique oak chair at a birthday party for a five-year-old, surrounded by a typical dysfunctional American family, I felt like I had been cheated out of something wonderful. Like maybe all this time, when I had been around other siblings and observing them at a distance, I had been shielding myself from what I was missing. Before, my friends were my family. Who needed a mom or a big sister to help you get ready for a date when you had two college roommates that could lecture on fashion and etiquette at Vassar? Who needed a dad or a brother to play games with you when you had good guy friends that loved sports and laughing until your abs hurt?

Clearly, I never realized what I didn't have.

It suddenly felt very warm in the dining room. And oddly like everything was spinning. I excused myself and left the room, feeling like I couldn't spend more than twenty minutes in there without feeling…wrong. I ran up the stairs again and out onto my balcony. I just needed a minute, only a minute, of fresh air and enough time to hear myself think before going back in there. I figured the party was about done anyway and prayed everyone would go home soon. I really needed to talk to Lauren.

I had just opened my balcony doors and was about to take a step out when I heard talking. I hovered in the doorway, trying to figure out where it was coming from. I finally realized it was George and Alexis, standing on their balcony. I turned to leave, ticked that I couldn't stand out on my balcony, because they would see me and feel like they had to make some sort of small talk, when I heard Alexis say, "Just tell them. See what they say."

# CHAPTER 17

I hesitated. I didn't feel that eavesdropping is right, but sometimes my baser instincts got the better of me. And I felt the need to stretch my moral code.

"Honey, I know. But after what happened last time," George said, sounding very tired, and I leaned against the door, which was now just open enough for me to be able to see and hear them through the crack made by the slightly jarred door.

"You've been divorced for twenty years, George. She has no claim on you anymore," Alexis said, dropping her voice, and despite the harshness of her words she sounded gentle.

George chuckled. "Wouldn't that be a fun conversation to have with her," he said, and I saw him shake his head. "To Maureen, I will always be the father of her children; thus, I am the man in her life. I don't like it any more than you do. There were reasons for a divorce, after all. While having her in my life was a necessity when the boys were younger, I feel it would be cruel to cut her out now. Especially because we have a grandchild."

"I understand that," Alexis said, sounding incredibly patient. "And I am by no means advocating that we never see her. I just feel like she sucks the fun out of every family event we have by insisting we raise these children together, as if you were still married. Every Christmas, every Easter, every birthday…I feel like crying every time I see an event coming up on the calendar because I know I will have to spend time with her, letting her attack me, doing nothing in return."

I almost snorted. Even if it weren't her husband's ex-wife, Alexis still wouldn't have said anything back to her. She's the nicest, sweetest person alive.

"Lex," George said in a soothing voice, "I know she can be incredibly tiresome. I was married to her for eleven years, remember? I understand perfectly how trying it can be to remain pleasant. Divorce is an ugly thing regardless of who is involved, but that had to be the hardest one in the history of time. I never knew if I was going to get a weepy, clingy, victimized woman; a mad-as-all-get-out woman; or a let's-make-this-work, stiff-upper-lip single mom. I went through this with Dani too, and Maureen was rotten to Dani for years. That doesn't mean it's okay. I just want you to see that it's not necessarily personal."

Alexis laughed. "Honey, it's very personal. If I were married to anyone else in the world and I were to meet her, she'd be perfectly lovely to me."

"That's not about you, then; that's about me."

"Do you think it's easy for me to see her look at you like you're *her* husband?" Alexis blurted out, and my mouth dropped open. That was gutsy. I pressed closer to the door to try and see George's face. "Do you think I enjoy hearing her talk about when you were married and all the fun times you had raising your children? How they are her children, first and foremost, and no amount of time or effort will ever make them so unequivocally mine? She looks at you, and I see the love there, the possession there, and I get jealous. I hate that she was married to you, that she was married to you first, that no matter who comes and goes in your life, she gets to be a constant because of Lucas and Lance, and she knows that. She knows it, and she sits there and smiles that smug smile because she knows, no matter what she says, she won't get in trouble for it!"

"I don't know what to do, Lex. I can't cut her out. I won't put my boys in the position to choose between their parents, as they inevitably would have to at some point, knowing Maureen. I can't add to what she puts on them already," George said, sounding upset by now.

"All the more reason to do something about this. You know that I'm not a confrontational person. I don't relish asking you to do this. But I can't do it anymore, George. I can't. I sit there and listen helplessly as she berates every decision I make, mocks my attempts to cater to her, and she attacks Julie, favors Lance over Lucas in a way that you know he notices, and acts like she's the queen of everything."

I frowned. Not that I expected Alexis to be so mature or whatever, but that sounded remarkably young. I agreed with everything she said, but Alexis seems like the suffer-in-silence type, not the drag her husband off and plead him to kick someone out of the house type.

"I will do something. I promise. I don't know what yet, but I promise there will be changes," George said, and I saw him move closer to her, wrapping his arms around her tiny waist. He pulled her close to him and smiled down at her. "I promise I can make all the bad stuff go away."

I watched in awkward silence, completely unable to look away (the deer in a headlight syndrome) as Alexis giggled and slid her arms around his neck. She lifted up onto her toes—a difficult feat in kitten heels—and kissed him. I whirled away from where I stood when I realized they were going to make out and pulled the door shut silently. *Ew! So didn't need to see that.*

I sat down at the foot of my bed. *Poor Alexis.* For this to happen every time her family got together for the last three years, I'd have reached the end of my rope a long time ago.

I pushed myself off of my bed and resigned myself to finish the evening with a smile on my face. No amount of grouchy, bitter ex-wives, giddy couples still in the newlywed stage of their marriage, bent out of shape friends, ridiculously cute high school teens with crushes, inquisitive older brothers, or self-pity would pick away at the tremendously well-trained fake smile that would be plastered on my face.

I spent the rest of the evening smiling, laughing loudly, and acting as though this were the most fun I had ever had. Lauren walked Connor out and came back with a glow, promising stories when everyone else had gone home. From that moment on, I glued myself to her side and never left it.

Julie announced at nine that they had to leave to get Isobel in bed, and Lance and Lucas carried all of the birthday stuff out to the car. George and Alexis rejoined the party, looking noticeably happier than when they had left it, something I tried hard not to think about.

"Well, it's about time," Maureen said, frowning. "I thought we were going to have to see ourselves out."

Alexis looked at her for a minute, then smiled. "I'm terribly sorry, Maureen," Alexis said, sounding anything but, especially with a big smile on her face, "that was very rude of us. We'll walk you out to your car."

Maureen turned up her nose and stormed out with George and Alexis following, glancing at each other in amusement. Isobel demanded that Lauren be the one that took her to the car, so Lauren picked her up and pranced out, prattling on to Julie about what Connor said and how he said it.

Left alone, I began to take the tablecloth off the table. Despite Maureen's abhorrence to the idea that a silk tablecloth be used at the child's birthday party, there wasn't a spot on it. I wondered briefly if Eliza Scotch guards.

"Eliza will be mad if you try to do her job for her," a voice said behind me, and I looked over my shoulder at Lucas.

"Really?" I asked, straightening up.

"Yeah. She thinks we're babying her if we clear the table before she gets to it. It makes her feel like we don't need her, or that she is inadequate in some way."

I laughed. "My mother would have killed for a maid like Eliza."

Lucas slid his hands into his pockets and looked at me pointedly. "So. Tonight was weird."

"Very," I agreed, crossing my arms. I leaned against the back of one of the chairs. "Your family is tiring."

Lucas nodded, his eyes not leaving mine. "That's…not what I meant."

I rolled my eyes. "Are you going to start round two? Because I'm exhausted, and this can wait until tomorrow. I advise waiting until I have the patience to deal with this."

Lucas sighed. "You are a very hard person to apologize to. You know that, right?"

I blinked, frowning. "Apologize?"

"Yeah, apologize. I overreacted tonight, and I put you on the spot about something that I didn't have the right to grill you about. And I shouldn't have said something to Lance and Julie about it. I apologize for that," he said, shrugging his shoulders a little.

My mouth was open slightly, and I couldn't make words come out. I swallowed and said, "Lucas, I wasn't mad at you. I was a little blindsided, but I wasn't mad at you. You just have to realize that I had twenty-three years before I met you, and I'm not going to be able to tell you about each second of that. Life would be boring if we knew everything about each other. That's what being friends is, right? Learning new stuff and liking the old?"

Lucas laughed. "You sound like a Barney episode."

I shook my head, trying not to smile. "You are a very hard person to accept an apology from. You know that, right?"

He grinned and ran a hand through his hair. It fell naturally back into the perfect coif, as if nothing had happened. I did not understand that. There must be something he did to his hair to make it behave so well.

It was on the tip of my tongue to ask him what, if any, product he used in his hair, when he said, "Heidi, I feel like I should be honest to you about something. I was upset because I didn't like the idea of someone asking you to marry them."

I raised my eyebrows. "Um, to coin a phrase, no duh."

He continued as if I hadn't spoken. "I realize it would be impractical to think that you would have never had boyfriends and relationships in the past. But I guess I kind of hoped…I don't know. I guess what I'm trying to say is that I like you, and, one day, I hope you'll like me too. And I hope I'm not just another Charlie in your life."

I didn't know what to say. I felt like I should, once again, let him down gently, but that didn't seem to be working. I couldn't be rude to this man, not on something like this, when he was being so sincere and open.

I was spared a response—at least for the time being—when Lauren poked her head into the dining room and said, in tones of utter delight, "Heidi! I need you upstairs. We have a lot to talk about!"

I pushed away from the chair and tried to walk past Lucas, but he grabbed my upper arm and said softly, "I just wanted you to know, without a doubt, one hundred percent for sure, how I felt. I just needed you to know."

He released my arm, and I hurried out of the room, trying not to freak out. If this were anyone else, or more specifically, anyone I had a crush on, I would have swooned on the spot like a secondary Austen character (because none of the heroines would have ever swooned—I mean, could you picture Elizabeth Bennett freaking out over Mr. Darcy saying something like that? Or Emma? Maybe Marianne Dashwood, but we all know how that kind of thing worked out for her). But since it was Lucas—handsome, smart, funny, charming Lucas—I just felt guilty for being the center of a case of unrequited…something or other. Like? Not love, but something along those lines.

I ran up the stairs to Lauren's room and flopped onto her bed, burying my face in a pillow. I braced myself for the onslaught of teenage happiness headed my way, but instead I felt a hand brush back the hair that had spread out across the pillow.

"Are you okay?" Lauren asked, sounding sympathetic without pitying me.

I lifted my head long enough to rub my eye, nod, and shoot her a half-hearted grin. "Oh, just swell."

"Do you want to talk about it?" she pressed, clearly unsure.

Sure I did. I just had no idea what to say. "Not really," I lied, rolling over and hugging the pillow to my chest. "I want to listen to how tonight went for you. Spill it, sister."

Lauren worked to keep a grin from spreading across her face. "Seriously, if you need to talk…"

"Seriously. Start squealing before I change my mind," I said, grinning.

Lauren wiggled a little where she sat, her legs "criss-cross, apple sauce," as we called it in preschool. She reminded me of a puppy when presented with a treat, completely unable to stay still. "He said he was glad he came and that he couldn't wait until the cotillion. And he even mentioned going on a date soon."

I raised my eyebrows. "So Lance, Lucas, and George didn't scare him away?"

"I guess not," she said, and she looked positively smug with pride over that fact.

Well, I guess the boy had a backbone, after all. Then again, Lauren happened to be an incredibly good-looking girl, and there were a lot of things teenage boys would endure to date an incredibly good-looking girl.

"He's really cute, isn't he?"

I nodded. "I agree…in the legal, he's a minor and I'm not and won't go into detail kind of way," I joked, and she laughed. "No, seriously, he's a doll. And he seems really nice. He would make a perfectly acceptable first boyfriend."

Lauren nodded enthusiastically. "I know!"

I laughed at that. It had been forever since I'd been giddy over a guy—I hadn't been giddy with Charlie, that was for sure—and it was kind of making me jealous. Of a fifteen-year-old. *Any moment, the guys at Webster's Dictionary will be calling for a picture and correct spelling of my name to include it next to the definition of* lame.

I turned my head to look at her better. "Did he kiss you?"

She shook her head. "No. I think he was thinking about it, but I wouldn't have wanted him to kiss me *here*. Not in the entryway, and especially not in the lobby when I walked him out. That would have been embarrassing."

True. And if any of three certain gentlemen had seen him try, he would have needed medical attention.

I played with the purple fringe on one of Lauren's throw pillows. "So do you like him like a boyfriend or what?"

Her smile softened a bit. "Yeah, I think I do," she said, smiling so hard this time that her dimples were the most pronounced I had ever seen them. "I really think I do."

"Good. He better not hurt you. I will beat him to death with a stiletto," I said, grinning up at her.

Lauren laughed. "I'll remember that. But Connor is a nice, honest guy. I can't see him hurting me. I think if it didn't work out, it would hurt, but it wouldn't be his fault."

I nodded, pretending I agreed, when in reality, I was just hoping she would be right. The first time your heart is broken, it never gets put back together just right, and I couldn't bear to watch Lauren go through that. To know that you aren't the same person from before That Boy came into your life is a hard thing to deal with, and I just hoped that Lauren wouldn't be burned too badly, not only with Connor but with any of the guys she might happen to date in the future. She was such a big-hearted girl, I could easily see her giving her whole heart to the first person she fell for; it physically hurt me to think about her getting hurt.

I told her good night soon after that and went to my room. I slipped my wrap dress off and, in the process of putting my pajamas on, noticed the large purple bruise forming from shoulder to ribs on my back. My arm was no more attractive. Believe me. I doctored my elbow where the skin had been scraped nearly all the way off and put a new band-aid on. I slipped a T-shirt and sweatpants on and climbed gingerly into bed, suddenly more aware of my aches and pains than I had been all day. The doctor had warned me that they would hurt fiercely before they would get better, but I had kind of blocked that out, hoping maybe that I would have enough medicine pumped into me that it wouldn't hurt. So much for the miracles of Western medicine.

I set my alarm for six. I had to be out of the house before Lucas came. I knew he would be there, he never made an empty promise, and I didn't want him to know that I was meeting Amanda Honey. Somehow I didn't think he would be amused by that. And I for sure wasn't ready to share with him my theory about Daniella being pregnant.

# CHAPTER 18

The next morning, when I woke up, I felt like the car actually had hit me. Despite the fact that my entire body ached, it was pitch black outside, the sun having not come up yet, and it felt like the middle of the night. I dragged myself out of bed and got in the shower, trying to let the water wake me up. I towel dried my hair, rubbing in some mousse, and put some makeup on. I somehow managed to line my eyes without stabbing myself in the pupil.

I opened my closet doors and tried to find something appropriate to wear. I didn't want to look like a slob or overly casual, considering how beautiful this woman was. I slid on my favorite black skirt with a swishy hemline, slipped on and buttoned up a white Banana Republic oxford and tucked it into the skirt, and added a black blazer. I pulled on black Pucci calf boots and, for a splash of color, added a chunky wine colored beaded necklace and a ruby cocktail ring.

I checked on Lauren. She was up, humming to herself as she straightened her hair. "Heidi, I didn't know you knew there were two six thirties during the day," Lauren teased, smiling at me.

I tried smiling back and found it difficult. I needed coffee. "I've got a ton of stuff to do today, and the earlier the start, the better," I semi-lied, widening my eyes to keep them open. I had never fallen asleep standing up before, but there was a first time for everything.

"Okay. Well, have fun. When I get home from school, we have a lot to talk about," she said, turning back toward the mirror.

"Like what?" I asked, since I was currently unable to think coherent thoughts.

"Um, last night, Lucas, Connor's reaction to me at school today, which will hopefully be quite positive, and Thanksgiving," she said in one breath.

"Huh. Okay, I can't process that right now, but, yeah, we'll talk when you get home," I said, and she laughed at me.

"Go get some coffee, Heidi," she advised, picking up her straightener again.

Somehow, I made it down the stairs without falling to my death. Between the throbbing pain in my arm, back, hip, and head, I was so tired my vision was blurring.

I stumbled into the kitchen and groped for a cup, pouring myself a cup of the coffee that was warming in the pot.

"Okay, even I'm impressed by this," I heard a voice say from behind me, and I jumped, a feat not easy to do in Pucci boots.

I whirled around and saw Lucas sitting at the counter on a bar stool, nursing a cup of something himself.

"No," I moaned, looking at him in despair. "I got up at this forsaken hour, and I didn't even beat you out of the house?"

Lucas shrugged. "I hedged my bets."

I pouted, stomping my feet over to the coffee cup and picking it up, sipping it black, and shuddering. I added some milk and sugar and sat down next to him. "Fine. You win. But I have to have some alone time today. Just an hour. Okay?"

"Uh, no. Whatever is on sale today, I'll buy you full price tomorrow. It's not worth your life," he said calmly, taking a drink from his cup. He wasn't even drinking coffee! He had tea! He was this awake without the addition of coffee into his system! Not fair!

I pursed my lips. "You are not my bodyguard. You are not my boss. You can't follow me around all day."

Lucas rested his palms against the edge of the counter and pushed back, glaring at me. "What are you doing today that you don't want me to know about?"

I fought it, but I felt myself blush anyway. "Nothing."

"Liar."

"I'm not lying!"

"Your pants are practically on fire."

I burst out laughing at that, and Lucas grinned at me, that frustrating grin that meant he thought he was winning. I decided to level with him. "Look, I am doing something private today, but it's nothing dangerous, I promise. I'll go there, and then come straight back. I swear."

"Can I at least go with you to the place, and let you go in by yourself? Just for my peace of mind?" Lucas asked, and I realized that he was afraid for me. Truly afraid for me.

I sighed. "You aren't going to like where I'm going."

Lucas's eyes narrowed slightly. "Where?"

I bit my lip. "I'm meeting Amanda Honey to get a box of photographs from her for Lauren."

Okay, so I left out the thousands of questions that I was planning on springing on her, not the least of which was whether or not Daniella was pregnant at the time she died, and when you left that part out, it really didn't sound so bad. Which is why Lucas gave me a blank look and said, "Okay. Where are you meeting her?"

"Her house, sometime between nine and one," I replied, checking my watch. It was seven-thirty. I could have been asleep if I'd known Lucas would be downstairs no matter what time I came down. That alone made me feel less than friendly toward him. The fact that he was apparently finding his new job as my shadow was just gravy.

"Since I'm here and I'm not going to leave you alone for the day, why don't you eat something while we wait?" Lucas suggested. He slid a basket of scones and muffins to me.

Resigned to my fate, I picked up a raspberry scone and nibbled off the three corners. I sat down next to him, despite the fact that I didn't really want to talk to him, but I guess he took that as an all-clear sign.

"Are you mad at me?" he asked in a voice that said he wouldn't believe me no matter what I said.

I shook my head, and when I did so, something suddenly occurred to me. I cleared my throat and said, "So I guess since you're free enough to baby sit the babysitter all day, you haven't moved on in the professional world yet."

He grinned and sipped his tea, looking at me out of the corner of his eyes. "That depends on how you look at it," he said vaguely, and I motioned for him to continue. He took another leisurely sip of his tea and said, "I'm not working, but I'm working on something. I'm in no hurry; I have plenty of savings and a trust fund I haven't touched, so I could technically be unemployed for the rest of my life and live off of that if I wanted."

I smiled. "But you aren't a hotel heiress, and I know you won't do that. So why don't you tell me what you're working on?"

"I will," he said with maddening calm, "when I'm ready."

I rolled my eyes. "Can you give me a hint?"

Lucas thought for a moment, staring into space, and then said, "You inspired me to do this. If I have any success in this particular venture, it's because you made me feel like I could do it."

I looked at him, speechless. I didn't think I had ever inspired anyone to do anything, except maybe to think I was an idiot. I felt my face turn red and I said, "You won't tell me anything more than that? Because that would be mean."

Lucas laughed. "I am mean."

"Can we play twenty questions until I figure it out?"

"Absolutely not. That would be miserable."

I felt like stomping my foot, but I was sitting down (not to mention twenty-three years old), so I didn't. "You are so frustrating! You can't tell me I inspired you to do something and then not tell me what it was!"

"Yes, I can. That's my prerogative."

I looked up at him with what my grandmother calls "cow eyes" and tried a different approach. "Please, Lucas?" I said in my sweetest voice, trying to become very appealing.

He shook his head. "Your Jedi mind tricks don't work on me. Just be patient. One day I'll show you what I'm talking about."

I frowned at him, contemplating pouting. He checked his watch, sighed, and said, "Come on. In morning traffic, it'll take us forever to get there. Let's go ahead and go."

I hopped up and adjusted my blazer, and he said, "Wow. You look nice. Great shoes."

I laughed at him and said, "Thanks. Sometimes I can clean up pretty well, huh?"

"See, you yell at me for flirting with you and complimenting you, and then you hand me something like that on a silver platter. I think you're asking for my attention, Miss Hart," Lucas said, draining his tea and putting the cup in the sink.

I did the same with my coffee. "Get over yourself. Not everything I say goes through a Lucas filter."

We walked out of the house right after Lauren left for school. Greg took her, so in lieu of calling another car for us Lucas just hailed a cab. It took forever to get to Amanda Honey's house, and I was starting to get nervous. I mean, what if Amanda didn't know anything about Daniella's prenatal stuff, and I was opening up a can of worms that I would never be able to close? Worse—what if I was right? Would I ever be able to look George or Lauren in the face again without thinking about whether they knew about the baby or not?

I tried to take some deep, inconspicuous breaths to calm myself down. When we pulled to the building that Amanda lived in, Lucas pulled out his Blackberry and started to text someone. "I'll be here. Take your time," he said, giving me a small grin.

I took another deep breath and got out of the cab. I rang the bell and Amanda opened the door a minute or two later. She had her beautiful hair pulled into a sloppy bun and a white puffy blouse tucked into a pair of high-waisted jeans.

"Heidi, right?" she said, and I breathed a sigh of relief. I was afraid she wasn't going to be nice to me since I didn't have a buffer with me.

"Yes," I said, adjusting my jacket a little. I was freezing, but trying not to look it.

"Come in. The box is in my office."

I followed her in and cleared my throat. "Amanda," I said, remembering that last time she had instructed us not to call her Ms. Honey, "I need to ask you something about Daniella."

Amanda glanced over her shoulder at me, and I don't think I imagined her look of uneasiness. "Okay," she said slowly, reaching her office.

I followed her in and watched as she got a box out from under a large chocolate brown oak desk. I took a deep breath and asked, "Did Daniella ever mention anyone named Claude Keller to you?"

Amanda straightened and looked thoughtful. "Not that I can think of," she said, placing a lid onto the box and pressing it down tightly. "It doesn't sound familiar."

I wet my lips and said, "I found…I thought…I…" I didn't know how to say this, so I blurted out, "Was Daniella pregnant when she died?"

Amanda's face drained of color, and her eyes widened. Her mouth dropped open, and she asked in a heart-wrenching tone, "Who are you? Why are you asking these questions?"

I brought my hand up to my mouth almost instinctually, not at all sure what to say. "I'm Lauren's best friend. She asked me two months ago to help her find out information about her mother at the time she died. Between people's stories and the police report and Daniella's day planner some things just added up. And so here I am, talking to the person everyone else has said was the closest friend Daniella ever had, hoping to find some answers for a fifteen-year-old girl who desperately needs some closure."

I took a deep breath. That had been quite a mouthful. Amanda stared at me as if she were staring right through me, and, finally, after the longest pause I have ever endured in my entire life, she said lightly, as if she weren't sure if her voice would work properly, "She never told me she was."

I read between the lines on that statement and decided to press further. "But you thought…"

Amanda swallowed, and she looked like she was holding back tears. "I thought. I assumed. But I don't know for sure."

I nodded, feeling a major letdown. I had so hoped that Amanda would, upon hearing this question, laugh in my face and deny any remote possibility that Daniella could have been pregnant.

How was I ever going to look Lauren in the face again?

I bit my lip and closed my eyes, and Amanda surprised me by going on, "I never asked George. I never told him what I suspected. If it weren't true…or worse, if it was…I couldn't do that to him. He had already lost so much, and he was so broken after hearing the news that I figured it was best if he never knew for sure. I saw him not long after Dani's death, with Lauren in a department store. I could barely face him. I couldn't stand there and look at him, knowing—assuming—what I couldn't get out of my head. I purposefully never saw him or Lauren again, though it hurt me to leave Lauren. She was"—Here Amanda gasped out some tears, clearly ready to lose her composure—"like Dani all over again. Lauren laughed like Dani, talked like Dani, smiled like Dani. I don't know how George lived with it. It would have broken my heart to see her every day. I know that sounds horrible, but there it is. I cut them out of my life. I tried to make Dani my old best friend, someone I only remembered fondly, and I tried to forget that she—"

I held up my hand to stop her. "I understand. Actually, that's a complete lie, because I have no idea how I would act if that happened to me, but I think I understand why you would want to keep something like that from George and Lauren. I don't know how I'm going to do it."

"There really isn't proof," Amanda said, resting her arms on the box she had prepared for Lauren. "I don't know what good it would do to torment them by telling them a what if."

I took a deep breath. "I know what doctor she was going to see."

Amanda straightened, her face completely shocked. "You're thorough," she said, appreciatively. "Wow. Do you think you can give me a call when you find out...for sure? I've been living with this for a while now, and it would be nice to know one way or the other."

I nodded and said, "I promise. It was really nice of you to put this box together for Lauren. I'll make sure she knows it was from you."

Amanda smiled. "Thank you. She...she seems like a great kid."

"I think so," I said, smiling back at her. After all, it wasn't her fault that I was right and that I now knew a potential secret that would devastate my employers.

Nope, that was entirely the fault of my nosy nose.

Amanda walked me to the door and exhaled deeply. "Do you like working there? I've known George for years, and I've worked with his new wife before, so I know they're nice people."

I paused, grappling with the response that ricocheted around my brain. "I love it there," I said lightly, smiling. "I've never been happier."

And sadly, or maybe not so sadly, that was 100 percent truth.

I told Amanda good-bye and skipped down the steps of her building, sliding into the waiting cab.

"Did you get everything you needed?" Lucas asked, glancing at the box curiously.

"And more," I said, buckling in.

# CHAPTER 19

I probably should have realized that I looked suspicious sitting on Lauren's bed next to a big cardboard box, eagerly awaiting her arrival home from school. So when she walked in and jumped, not expecting to see me there, I felt a little guilty.

"Jeez, what are you doing in here?" she asked, her hand over her heart. She shrugged off her navy blazer and tossed it over the arm of her chair. She kicked off her shoes and plopped down on the bed next to me.

"Amanda Honey sent this to you," I said, choosing to leave out the part where I went and picked it up from her. If Lauren knew that, she would ask questions, and I would crack like an egg.

She raised her eyebrows and pulled the lid off. Her lips pulled into a small smile as she reached in and pulled out a photo album. Inside were dozens of pictures, ranging from between fifteen and ten years ago. Most were Amanda and Daniella, smiling and posing for the camera. Some included a tiny Lauren; others featured more of their friend set. There were pictures from costume parties, holiday parties, luncheons, weddings, everything imaginable. A slim envelope held the pictures we were most interested in, though: the pictures from the night of Ashley's engagement party.

There were several shots of the six women, arms laced together, most of them giggling. There was a picture of Daniella and Amanda posing goofily next to the boat and another with them re-enacting the scene from Titanic where Leo DiCaprio announces he's the king of the world.

Only one held my interest. It was a candid, obviously taken when the people in the picture weren't paying attention, and it was of Daniella laughing hysterically at something with Tonia and Joyce. She had her hand in her hair, pulling the long blonde locks away from her face. Her sapphire earrings blinked in the sunlight.

Those earrings. I couldn't understand my fascination with them. I'm not a big jewelry person, and I have little time for diamonds, though they are stunning on other people; but those sapphires held my attention in the oddest way.

I put the picture down and glanced at Lauren. She had a big stack in her hands, a small smile on her face, and she looked like she was content to look at those pictures for hours. I looked over her shoulder to see what she saw and smiled at the pictures of Daniella, Amanda, and Lauren at the zoo. Lauren looked about three, and both women had a hand on her stroller. I wondered if they asked someone to take that or if they had someone like George with them.

"I do not remember this," Lauren mused, tilting her head to one side. "What's your earliest memory?"

I thought for a minute and then said, "The beach when I was like three or four, I think. I remember Max chased Leslie with a crab, and I laughed. I remember Dad yelling at him for it, and Mom griping at Dad for yelling at Max. But other than that, I can't remember that trip at all, so I don't know how accurate that memory is and how much of it is home video."

Lauren nodded. "I have a couple of memories of Mom, but I'm the same way. I'm not sure what's real and what's been told to me. The only one I know is real is when we used to go for walks in Central Park. And that's mostly leaves and big sweaters. I don't really remember anything we did."

I didn't say anything. For anyone to lose their parent at a young age is tragic, but it seemed much, much worse that it happened to Lauren so young, when she didn't even have a solid bank of memories to fuel her for the rest of her life. Everything was stuff other people told her, stuff she saw in pictures and home videos; and no matter how real those are, they aren't vivid.

I saw the sadness start to creep across Lauren's face, and I stood up. "I'm going to go get something to drink," I lied, shifting from one foot to the next. "Do you want anything?"

She shook her head and said, "Could I be alone for a few minutes?"

I nodded, putting my stack of pictures down and backing out of the room. I closed her door, and before I heard the doorknob click as it slid back into place, I heard Lauren let out a smothered sob. I leaned back against the wall next to her door, waiting to see if she called for me. When she didn't, I retreated to my room.

The following week, I noticed Lauren was a lot quieter than usual. She was going to bed a little earlier, and she didn't want to talk about Connor much. At my prompting, she reluctantly told me that he had been texting her, but she wasn't really in the mood to talk to him. She just said that she was feeling introspective and needed some alone time. I let that go, despite the fact that I really wanted to be in there comforting her as best I could.

Lucas was a no-show for the whole week. I had to admit, it was kind of a nice break from the mental warfare he had been conducting on me. Without the constant comments and questions, I actually had a chance to miss him and even appreciate him. Not that I would ever tell him that, because let's face it, it would go straight to his already inflated ego.

November in New York was kind of depressing to me. I didn't get into the whole Christmas shopping thing (that's what gift cards were invented for), and the constant reminders of the upcoming holiday season were putting me in an irritable mood. I hadn't heard from any of my family of their holiday plans, and I was hoping I wouldn't. Lauren mentioned Thanksgiving to me again, but I was reluctant to commit to another Dayton social event. The last one had been straining, and a full-blown family gathering would probably age me ten years.

When the day actually arrived and Leslie called me to inform me that I was to bring yams (that no one would eat except maybe Brady and I, because everyone else was entirely too concerned about their diets, incessant Blackberry updates, and heart problems), I surprised even myself by telling her I had a prior engagement. Leslie got really huffy and asked me if I really wanted to miss my new nephews' first holiday, and I replied that I was okay with that. I would look at pictures. If anyone thought to take any.

I surprised myself even further by telling Lauren I couldn't make the Dayton Thanksgiving. She looked so upset that I quickly amended, "I have to be somewhere first, but I can make it back here for the last half of the party."

She seemed to be appeased by that, and I snuck out of the house that Thursday morning before anyone arrived so no one could ask me where I was going. Because I didn't know what to tell them, believe me.

I wandered around Central Park, looking at all the people who had gathered to watch the parade at various points on the route. I bought a cup of coffee from a street vendor and people watched, playing a game trying to figure out if someone was a tourist or a New Yorker. I pulled my black pea coat closer around me, adjusting my scarf to cover more of my neck, and clutched my warm drink. It was frigid outside, and I was pretty sure a rogue snowflake or two could be spotted.

I brought the coffee cup up to my lips, poised to take a sip, when someone shoved against my shoulder, flying by me. I glared after them—I mean, that coffee was hot, and he got a little on me—until I noticed who it was.

No lie, Claude Keller, also known as the Crazy Car Guy of Doom and General Creeper, was looking over his shoulder at me as he ran away.

My mouth fell open. I threw my cup into a nearby trashcan and took off after him. The pursuit was an epic failure, however; between all the hundreds of thousands of people milling around the park and my four-inch Jimmy Choo boots, Claude disappeared into a much larger crowd without the chance of ever being found by me.

I pursed my lips and almost said a bad word in my frustration, but I was standing by—or so the sign said—Girl Scout Troop #487, and that didn't seem to be the best example to set for those little girls.

Instead, I hobbled away, my feet throbbing in their leather encasings, and grumbled under my breath. When I got far enough away from the parade madness, I hailed a cab and headed back to the house. My feet hurt too badly to delay it any longer. Besides, it was nearing noon, and by the time I got to the Daytons, it would easily be one or two, what with traffic like this.

Make that two forty-five. Traffic was so bad that I honestly thought at one time my cab driver just turned off the engine. I was so hungry at that point I was ready to eat my own hand, so when I finally got to the Dayton house, I threw a few bills at the driver and dashed up the stairs, my stomach protesting so loudly that it banished my aching feet to a solid second place in importance.

I walked into the apartment quietly, contemplating making a break for the kitchen so I didn't have to see anybody, but by some act of horridness against me (apparently even mental swearing in front of children counted against karma), the whole family was gathered in the entryway, looking at me in varying degrees of welcome and surprise.

I smiled sheepishly. "Hi, everybody," I said lightly, unwrapping my scarf.

Julie walked toward me. "Heidi, it's so good to see you. Happy Thanksgiving," she said, leaning in to give me a hug. So only I could hear her, she whispered, "Where were you? I'm dying here!"

I tried to keep my face straight so no one else would know she said anything, but it was hard. I sighed and said, "I just had to do a few…Thanksgiving errands."

*So lame,* I thought as Lucas narrowed his eyes at me suspiciously.

Maureen, resplendent in a cashmere crimson shirt and deep purple scarf paired with a pair of jeans and brown suede boots, gave me a tight smile and said, "Have you been with your family today, Heidi? I know you said you don't do much with them, but this is a family holiday, after all."

I shrugged out of my pea coat and handed them off to Tom, the butler. I tried to keep that smile on my face. "No, I didn't. We, um, my family isn't really in to Thanksgiving."

That was only a half lie. We all liked Thanksgiving; we just didn't like it with each other.

Lauren was looking at me with a hurt expression on her face, and I couldn't think why. She crossed her arms and raised her eyebrows, and I suddenly remembered that I had kind of let her assume I was going home for Thanksgiving, which was the reason I declined her invitation for a family dinner.

I felt like a jerk.

"I wanted to check up on a few of my friends," I said spontaneously, trying to wipe the look of disappointment off Lauren's face. "Two of my closest friends are expecting, and I wanted to see how they were."

Okay, clearly, my holiday karma was going to suck, but wasn't it better to tell one little white lie to protect someone's feelings than tell the truth and hurt a bunch of people? Although, to be completely honest, I may have reached my quota for white lies this year, especially considering all the things I was keeping to myself until I found out the truth.

Lucas shook his head, his eyes glinting with unexpressed laughter. I quickly shifted my eyes to Julie, who seemed the safest person to look at for the time being. I cast around for something to say, came up with absolutely nothing, and settled for, "How was your meal?"

She gave me a look that clearly read, "Just wait," but seeing as how we were surrounded by the entire family and she couldn't really say what she wanted to say, she simply smiled and said, "Wonderful. Eliza outdid herself. I ate more than I've ever eaten in my life."

Maureen laughed lightly and said, "Oh, come now, let's not exaggerate."

There was an awkward moment of silence as everyone in the room tried to discern whether the exaggeration was how good the cooking was or whether Julie had eaten more than she had today on several occasions. Lance cleared his throat and said, "Yes, er, lunch was great. You should make yourself a plate."

My stomach rumbled in unanimous validation of that statement, but I managed to play off a, "Sure, that would be great," with the utmost nonchalance.

"I'll help you," Lucas offered, tilting his head to the kitchen. I figured he must have had something to say to me to be offering to help me find food in the most efficiently organized kitchen in the state of New York, so I nodded and led the way.

I went straight to the cabinet with the plates and got out a large square white plate. I opened the fridge, and Lucas pulled out a bowl of mashed potatoes and a bowl of yams. He knew me and my love of complex carbohydrates well. I pulled the turkey out and asked, "Doesn't Alexis send all the leftovers to homeless shelters?"

Lucas smiled. "Not on holidays. She sends twenty turkeys and four dozen pies to the shelters downtown. Besides, she told Eliza she wanted to make sure you ate something, so Eliza wrapped everything up for you."

I was touched that Alexis had thought of putting aside food for me, just in case I didn't eat Thanksgiving dinner with anyone. My own mother wouldn't have thought of that in a million years. I was a little curious to see if she would even call to see why I wasn't at Thanksgiving dinner this year.

I spooned mashed potatoes on my plate as Lucas brought out the asparagus and a green salad. As I was arranging some turkey on my plate, he was shoveling yams into a corner across from the potatoes. He was quietly efficient, which was mildly troubling, considering I knew—I just knew—he had something to say.

"What did you think of dinner?" I asked, more to break the lengthy quiet than out of true curiosity.

He shrugged. "Nobody threw any food, if that's what you want to know."

I grinned with the sudden visual of seeing Alexis haul off and cream Maureen with a plateful of pistachio pudding. "That's good, I guess. What have you been doing lately? I haven't seen you in over a week. Did you suddenly get a life?" I teased, elbowing him.

He gave me a half-hearted smile and shrugged. "Didn't want to overstay my welcome, I guess."

I rolled my eyes. "Oh, please. George and Alexis love having you here. They spoil you horribly when you stay over."

Lucas looked at me incredulously before bursting out laughing. "Heidi, you are probably the most naïve person I have ever met."

I frowned, putting my hands on my hips. "I resent that. I may not have been around this family for that long, but I think I know enough about them to know when George and Alexis are happy to see someone. Their faces light up when you come for dinner or stay the night. Don't you try and convince me otherwise."

He surprised the heck out of me by shaking his head, smiling affectionately down at me, and saying, "You're great. You really are."

I shifted uncomfortably. "Sure," I said cautiously, not knowing where this was going. "But what makes you say it?"

Lucas's smile lessened a smidge, and he said, "I meant with you."

"With me what?" I was getting completely lost in this conversation. I carried my overflowing plate to the microwave and pressed some buttons. The whirring sound of the appliance filled the air as I turned back around to face him.

"I didn't want to wear out my welcome with you," he explained, enunciating as if I were very small and very slow.

That earned him a second eye roll. "Don't start," I warned, turning to watch my plate circle slowly in the microwave instead of having to meet his gaze.

He sighed. "See? This is what I mean. I can't help that I like you. And it's just second nature for me to flirt a little if I like someone. But all I'm getting is hostility back, which would be all right except I really like having you as a friend too."

I glanced over my shoulder at him and said curtly, "So you want me to flirt back and give you false hope? I'm not that kind of girl."

"Good. I never thought you were. I just don't want to let my feelings for you affect you in such a way that you wouldn't want me around at all anymore."

He had a point, actually. I did like having him around, as much as it frustrated me to admit it. He was fun to talk to, and he had a great sense of humor and was smart enough to stay interesting. The main reason I didn't want him around was that he made me feel guilty for not liking him back.

I blinked at that realization and tried to control the blush I felt spreading across my cheeks. I exhaled loudly and said, "Okay, here's the deal. I like spending time with you, and you've become a real friend in the past few months. If you could just curb your enthusiasm about me down to maybe junior officer of my fan club instead of president and founding member, I would find you a little more endearing."

He nodded, looking at the floor and scratching the back of his neck. "Dinner was bad," he said, and I had to work to get my mind back to our original conversation.

"Oh?" I managed to retort. My brilliance astounded me sometimes.

He nodded, sliding to his left to sit down on one of the bar stools. "Holidays are always bad, but this just sucked. Mom was on tonight; let me tell you. She should have had a microphone and the *Tonight Show* band backing her up."

I smiled, took my food out of the microwave, and sat next to him. I speared an asparagus with my fork and asked, "What triggered it?"

Lucas rolled his head, and I heard comically audible cracks in his neck. "Who knows? She was in fine form, though. I think Alexis and Julie shrunk three inches each."

My heart went out to them. That kind of constant nitpicking could really take its toll on someone. I also felt bad for Lucas, Lance, and George, who had to sit there and listen to it without being able to stand up for Alexis and Julie without appearing to take sides. That couldn't have been much easier than actually being verbally abused.

I swallowed a piece of turkey and said, "In my experience, just sitting back and smiling is the best thing to do. It's kind of like saying that all that trash talk and rudeness is amusing and doesn't even break the skin. That's what I did for twenty-three years."

Lucas snagged a sip of my water, which made me cringe. I tried not to think about that—I'm not a germ-a-phobe, but I had a bad bout of mono in high school that cured me of communal anything—and listened intently as he admitted, "That was pretty much what Daniella did. Mom was much more subtle with her, though. You never knew if she was being sarcastic or mean. Most of it went way over my head. Unfortunately, with adulthood comes awareness, and it's completely unpleasant."

I laughed at that, and he managed a happier smile. "At least we have a whole month until Christmas. I don't have to put up with it for four weeks."

I winced. "Actually…" I said, scooting away from him in case his attraction to me didn't cover killing the messenger, "Lauren sent her an invitation to the cotillion, and she's coming. So you'll have to see her in two weeks. You are coming, aren't you?"

"Yeah. Lauren made Lance and I swear up and down that we would be there. I have to go pick up my tux," he added thoughtfully.

"You had a new tux made for a high school cotillion?" I asked, raising my eyebrows.

Lucas shrugged. "I haven't worn a tux since Dad and Alexis's wedding almost three years ago. I needed a new one."

I was impressed. Most of my guy friends in college just rented one, and the ones who had a lot of money just didn't care if the one they already had was still in style or not, they just cared if it fit (and some didn't even acknowledge that stipulation).

Clearly, this was just another way that Lucas was like no one I had ever met before.

*I did not just think that.*

I turned my full attention to my plate and began to eat with a speed that would have made Emily Post crack her knuckles and go for the jugular. I didn't even care if I looked like a stray dog that suddenly found a hamburger in a trashcan; I just wanted to finish eating fast enough that I could excuse myself, go find Lauren, and do some mental flagellations.

I could not believe I almost let myself have one of "those thoughts" about Lucas Dayton; one of those passing whims that turns into a crush, that turns into a relationship, that turns into awkward meetings at social events after the relationship inevitably goes void. Lucas was a friend, and I intended to keep him in that singular capacity.

He stretched and stood up, scooting his bar stool in with his foot. "I'm going home to do stereotypical Thanksgiving stuff."

"Nap and watch football?" I guessed, smiling. Even in my resolve, he was hard not to smile at.

"Pretty much," he laughed, moving to walk around me. "I'll see you later. Be careful if you…well, just call me if you need me."

The likelihood of that happening was slim, but I appreciated the offer, so I said, "Sure. See you."

After he left, I washed my dishes and stuck them in the always-empty dishwasher. I was not sure Eliza ever ran that thing; I don't think she trusted it to get dishes as clean as she could. I made my way to Lauren's room quickly in case there were any lingering guests, and when I got there, she was laying spread eagle on her bed, eyes closed.

"Did someone have too much to eat?" I laughed, nudging her foot.

"I think I ate enough for three meals in one sitting. I am so going to have to work out every day until the cotillion to fit into that dress," she moaned, flopping over to one side so I had room to sit down, which I did.

"You'll be fine. One splurge on one meal isn't going to do much."

Unless you're me, in which case you can convince yourself that any number of meals isn't going to do much, and, before you know it, you've gained your freshman fifteen the summer *after* you graduate college. Admittedly, about five of those pounds had come off since I had been at the Daytons, mainly due to the fact that everything Eliza made tastes amazing and yet still manages to be somewhat healthy.

"So what are we going to do with the rest of your break from school?" I asked, peering down at her.

"Go Christmas shopping," she said immediately, and I laughed.

"It's November," I said, feeling as though I needed to remind her that she still had a full four and a half weeks until Christmas.

"I know. I like to take my time and get things done early. Besides, the sales are tomorrow."

My blood ran cold. Okay, so maybe it wasn't my blood, but I suddenly felt like someone had presented me with a snake and a tarantula and asked, "Which would you rather hold?" I hated Black Friday. I never left the house. Those shoppers get insane looking to find Barbie for half-price or cashmere 30 percent off. I would rather pay full price and avoid the lines and not get my toes squashed a hundred times, thank you very much.

"I, um, I don't think I can go to the sales with you tomorrow. I have some…things to do," I said lamely, trying to think of something—anything—I could go do that would be a good enough excuse for her.

Apparently nothing, considering she sat up on her elbows and said, "I didn't say a word when you skipped out on my invite to lunch. I didn't say a word about your lame Thanksgiving errands. So you owe me shopping."

She was totally right, of course, but I wasn't quite ready to accept defeat. "Couldn't I just get you that pony you've always wanted?" I asked meekly.

She smiled and said, "Nope. This is a debt payable by quality time only. Besides, I had a pony, and I rarely got to ride her. So we gave her to a little girl who would."

I nodded mutely, ensconced in misery, wallowing in self-pity. This feeling didn't get any better when Lauren suggested we leave the house at seven thirty the following morning, to make it "Worth our while," she said.

*I have got to learn how to say "no" to her.*

# CHAPTER 20

The next day wasn't as bad as I thought it was going to be. A little traumatic, yes, especially when we ventured into a toy store, but Lauren and I managed to go the whole day without getting jumped on. Hit on, yes, but jumped on, no. I even bought a couple of presents. I got each of my nephews something, plus a scarf for Alexis and Jennifer and a book that Lauren was convinced George would like. All in all, when it came time to treat ourselves at the end of our day, I felt I had totally earned the large quantity of caffeinated calories headed my way, with extra whipped cream too.

Nursing our mochas, we walked slowly down Fifth, admiring the store windows and watching two very clumsy employees trying to make a fake Santa Claus sit upright. It was nice; I felt like I was in a romantic comedy, and at any moment I was going to meet my perfect guy who would appear out of nowhere and sweep me off my feet.

This being real life and not a romance novel, that of course didn't happen. However, Lauren did get a text from Connor, and we spent about ten minutes composing an appropriate—yet totally cool and casual—response to him. We were feeling pretty giggly when we got back to the house.

We immediately lost that feeling when we found a police officer waiting in the entrance with George and Alexis.

"What's going on, Dad?" Lauren asked, looking concerned.

George looked very mad, and Alexis looked upset. The police officer looked irritated.

"Alexis received another very threatening letter, and I thought it was time to involve the police in this business," George said stiffly, literally shaking with the effort not to shout. I reached out and patted Alexis on the shoulder, and she sent me a small smile.

I agreed with George. I thought it was time to call the police about the blackmail letters. I just wished I had enough evidence to say, "Yes, and while you're at it, why don't you open up a decade-old murder investigation?"

Since I had no proof, just suspicions, I kept my mouth shut. There was no need to get myself fired and kicked out of my current living situation, especially since I was more alienated from my family than normal and couldn't exactly ask them for help were that to happen.

I started to tell the police officer that Lucas and I had both gotten letters too, but I stopped myself just in time. If I had told them about the letters, I would have had to produce the letters, then explain the letters, and that would pretty much be like telling them what Lauren, Lucas, and I had been working on secretly for the last two months or so. This secret keeping was really starting to catch up to me.

Instead, I asked if I could see the note. Alexis told me that the police had already taken it into evidence, but it was basically a threat to Alexis's life if she didn't leave George—and the country—post haste.

For some reason, I thought of Maureen. I felt guilty as soon as I did, but once the thought occurred to me, it wouldn't go away. I couldn't think of anyone that didn't like Alexis or that stood to gain anything if she weren't here—except Maureen. I had no reason to believe that Maureen would ever threaten anyone, except of course that she was rather cantankerous. But it stayed with me, a little nagging feeling that wouldn't go away.

George paid the building's day security guards to take night shifts too, to insure that no one would get into the building without first having been checked out. Personally, I didn't think this would do much good, considering how long this person had been getting away with it already, but it wasn't my place to say anything.

Lauren and I took our treasures upstairs and sat in her room for a while, talking animatedly about everything except what we both really wanted to talk about. I wasn't sure if I should start talking about the notes because that, in my mind, was connected to Daniella's death, and I wasn't sure I trusted myself to keep my mouth shut. Finally, Lauren asked me if I thought someone would really try to hurt Alexis. I noticed she said *hurt* instead of *kill*, and I knew she had made the connection between her mother's and Alexis's situations too.

"Your dad is doing everything he can to take these threats seriously, and I fully believe that Alexis will be cautious until they catch the person doing this," I said diplomatically. I did believe both of those things. I also believed they wouldn't do a lot of difference if someone really wanted Alexis out of the picture.

Lauren seemed comforted by this, and, before we could launch into another conversation, her phone rang. She checked the caller ID and squealed with delight. "He's calling me! He's calling me!" she yelped, jumping up and down.

"So answer him! Answer him!" I insisted, and she smiled.

"Hello?" she answered, managing to sound cool, calm, and collected, despite the fact that she was now pacing up and down her purple rug. "Oh, hey, Connor."

I gave her a big grin and then slipped out of her room, shutting the door behind me. I carried my sacks to my room and hid them under my bed. On a whim, I opened my closet door and pulled out my dress for the cotillion. It was an off-the-shoulder, drape-y kind of dress that came down a little above my knees, and it was pale pink. The best part was the back. It wasn't drape-y at all; it was fitted and dropped into a graceful V. I hung it back up and pulled out my pumps that I was going to wear with it. Lauren had raided my closet to ensure that I didn't, in fact, need a new pair, and she had come up with a pair of smoky, dark gray pumps that worked well with the paleness of the dress. I literally couldn't wait to wear them.

I put the shoes back and lay down on the bed. Any minute, Lauren would come bursting into my room to tell me, word for word, what Connor had said, how he had said it, and then we would have to closely read the conversation for underlying meaning. I needed to rest before I could be at full deconstructing power.

I forced my mind to stop racing about Daniella, Alexis's letters, and pesky Maureen, who kept popping up, just to be annoying. I had just about given up when Lauren flew in and threw herself onto my bed, her eyes shining with the irritating glow of people with crushes.

But I smiled. I squealed. I acted surprised that he was considerate enough to call without being prompted to do so. That was something I loved about Lauren; no matter how weird or bad my day was, she could make me smile and be fifteen again.

We spent a while like that, not caring about what was going on outside my door, just being giggly, giddy girls with a new thing to celebrate.

I'll give Connor credit. He was a pretty good sixteen-year-old boy, at least as far as I could tell. He continued to call fairly regularly over the next week and a half, always having a perfectly legitimate reason to call, and never calling too often or talking too long. He kept Lauren in such a good mood that I didn't have to answer questions about any updates on my search for answers or soothe away frazzled nerves about the doubled security downstairs.

Two days before the cotillion, I picked up Lauren from school, and Greg drove us to a spa-type thing. We both got manicures and pedicures, and Lauren had her eyebrows plucked. I would rather do it myself than pay someone else to inflict pain on me, though, so I declined that treatment. She talked non-stop about her dress, her shoes, her hair, and Connor. I thought about keeping a tally to see how many times she would say his name in an hour, but I didn't because I was fifteen once. And I remembered what it was like to have some kind of crazy crush on someone. So I smiled and listened, trying to ignore the twitch developing above my eye.

The day before the cotillion, everyone was busy getting things ready for the big day (I swear, it was more like Lauren's wedding than just a little intro into society and parade around the room, but I couldn't judge because I was excited about it too), so I slipped out and took a cab to the only Dr. Mueller I could find in New York City. I sat in his office, surrounded by pregnant women, and felt like an idiot. Everyone kept glancing at me, obviously trying to determine if I too had something growing inside me, but I stared resolutely at the floor and refused to return any of the other women's smiles. That was just tantamount for inviting them to ask me about my personal situation, and I couldn't come up with a story that was believable without pretending I was pregnant, and I had risked karma enough lately without lying about that.

When it was finally my turn, I hurried back to the exam room. The nurse came in and started arguing with me about whether or not she needed to take my vitals. I was nearing full exasperation—she wouldn't believe that I just needed to ask Dr. Mueller some questions and that I wasn't actually pregnant and just in denial—when a short, sixty-something man wearing a white coat and glasses came in. He took in the situation quickly and asked the nurse to excuse us.

Relieved, I turned to him, smiling. He sat down on the little stool next to the exam table and said, very seriously, "Would you like to talk?"

I bit back the retort that was on the tip of my tongue—there was no use antagonizing my one chance at proof—and said, "I'm actually just here to ask you a few questions about one of your old patients, Daniella Dayton."

Dr. Mueller didn't show any signs of recognition at the name, but he frowned and said, "There is such a thing as doctor-patient confidentiality, you know."

"I know," I said quickly, desperate not to let him dismiss me so easily, "but Daniella has been dead for ten years, and if you could confirm something for her family, they would all be able to get closure once and for all."

Dr. Mueller blinked in surprise and said, slowly, "Confirm what?"

"All I want to know," I said, "is whether or not Daniella Dayton was pregnant when she died."

"How would I know that?" Dr. Mueller asked skeptically.

"Because she had an appointment with you two days before she died," I said, handing him her old date book. He narrowed his eyes and read the loopy script. He heaved a sigh.

"Are you family?" he asked, sounding tired.

"Sort of. I'm her fifteen-year-old daughter's nanny," I said, hoping that would work.

He pursed his lips. "And you don't want to know about medical conditions, or anything like that? You just want a simple yes or no?"

I nodded emphatically.

Dr. Mueller sighed and left the room. I waited impatiently, drumming my fingers on the counter top until I was nearly insane from the noise. Luckily, he walked back in with a tan folder and flipped it open. I held my breath.

He skimmed through some paperwork and shook his head. "I don't know which one you were hoping for, but Daniella Dayton was pregnant the last time she visited me here, ten years ago. We did a sonogram. The baby was developed enough to have a heartbeat."

I let my breath out, feeling sick to my stomach. I had been so convinced of what I had discovered that I had never really stopped to think about the repercussions of being right. However Daniella died, accident or murder, her baby died with her. And it was possible that Dr. Mueller and I were the only ones who knew.

I put my head in my hands and silently freaked out. Should I tell George? What if he knew? How awkward would that be? And what about Lauren? Did she know that had her mother lived, she would have had a nine-year-old sibling?

Every misgiving and horrible realization that had hit me when I first thought Daniella might have been pregnant slapped me in the face all over again. I had no idea what to do, and worse, I had no one to talk to about this.

"Dr. Mueller," I asked, my voice coming out a little raw, "I don't know if anyone in her family knew she was pregnant when she died. Now that I know…if you were in my situation…what would you do? Would you tell them?"

Dr. Mueller blinked and looked pained. He was clearly sorry he had agreed to see me.

"I really don't know," he said finally. He tugged at his glasses until they came off, and then he wiped them clean with the edge of his white coat. "It's a hard position to be in. But I think if it were me, and she had been my wife, mother, or friend, I would want to know."

I nodded mutely, my fingers pressed to my mouth. I stood up and said, "Thank you so much for seeing me on such notice, and for being so helpful. I know you didn't have to be, and I appreciate it a lot."

He gave me a small smile and said, "You're welcome. I hope everything goes all right for you."

I walked out of the office with enough despair on my face that one woman asked me gently if I had received bad news. I was distracted to the point of idiocy at that point, but I knew what she was talking about. I gave her a quickly strung together negative response, hoping that I didn't sound as horrified as I felt, and left that place as soon as I could.

I rode home in deep thought. The cab driver could have taken me to Istanbul, and I probably wouldn't have noticed. My phone buzzed twice with texts—probably Lauren—but I ignored them, trying to think of some way to fix this or at least make it through the day without blurting out everything I had just found out.

That night was the longest night of my life. I tried to do things with Lauren that didn't involve talking. We watched two movies, played with our hair, trying to figure out how to fix it the next night, and took a break to con Eliza out of some cake. I feigned sleepiness to go to bed early, but I lay there for hours, trying to come up with something to make this all okay. My best bet was to talk to George. I might end up fired, but at least I could live with myself. Right now, I wasn't sure I was ever going to be able to have a normal conversation with my best friend again.

I got lucky the next day because, as a surprise for Lauren, Alexis took her to breakfast and then to get her hair done. She was gone until the early afternoon, and by that time she was so excited about putting her makeup on and getting dressed that she didn't want to talk about anything else. She hadn't asked me a single question about her mother or looking into her death since I had brought her those pictures from Amanda Honey, and I wondered if she had reached her limit for emotional trauma for a while. I made a mental note to go see Amanda Honey when the cotillion was over, and we had our normal lives back. I had a promise to keep, after all.

I set my hair in curlers and lined my eyes, trying to achieve a vintage, nineteen forties kind of look. I put on clear lip gloss and blush and touched up my mascara. I was standing over my kitchen sink, wearing my robe, taking the curlers out of my hair, when I heard a knock at the door.

I pulled out the last curler, sprayed my hair with enough hair spray that I was now highly flammable, and shook my hair out. Only then did I yell, "Come in!"

Lauren waltzed into my room, sashaying around in her floor-length purple dress, the halter-top showing off her amazing tan and her killer arms. The purple looked amazing with her blue eyes, and her smile made her whole face light up.

"What do you think?" she asked, twirling in a circle.

I smiled at her from where I stood in front of my bathroom mirror. "You look absolutely beautiful," I said, feeling oddly proud at that moment. She looked like an adult or something, all dressed up with her hair done and her makeup perfect. "Really, you belong on the red carpet next to some hot A-list actor."

Lauren giggled and played with her skirt some more. I think her favorite part about it was that it was a swishy dress.

"Let me see yours!" she urged.

I slipped the dress over my head, straightening it, smoothing the skirt of it with my hands. I adjusted the waist and carefully checked my curls to make sure none had been disturbed when the dress passed over them.

I walked out into my room, my heels making me incredibly tall, and I really felt like a forties movie star or something.

"Wow. You look amazing," Lauren said honestly, smiling widely. "Look at you! That was the perfect color for you."

I really liked it too. I wondered if I could get away with wearing this every day.

"Are you ready to go downstairs? Your dad and Alexis probably want to get a before and after picture of you."

"Before and after what?"

"Your entrance into society. Apparently upon initiation, you become a lot prettier and get a string of pearls to twirl while you select a husband from the eligible bachelors," I said, rolling my eyes.

"Heidi..." Lauren warned, her hands on her hips.

"I'm sorry! That was my first and last dig at cotillions. I will be on my very best behavior, I promise," I said, making a show out of crossing my heart.

She giggled, and we looped arms before heading downstairs.

Lauren was telling me what she was looking forward to the most about tonight as we descended the stairs. Her father and stepmother were already downstairs—George in an Armani tux, Alexis in a gray Zac Posen dress. She was affectionately fixing her husband's tie when she noticed us.

"Oh, you girls look beautiful," she said, pressing her hand to her chest as she smiled at us.

George beamed at us—a surprisingly dad-like gesture—and it made me smile. Lauren really did look like a movie star, and I made a mental note to keep an eye on Connor the entire night. Nice guy or not, he was still male.

Maureen came in from the kitchen and exclaimed, "Oh, you both look so pretty! Oh, George, make sure you get their picture together, will you?"

I nearly fell over. That was the nicest thing I had ever heard Maureen say. None of it seemed to be derogatory, and I found myself blinking in surprise. Lauren beamed at her, a la George, and said, "Thank you, Maureen. And thank you so much for coming."

She smiled at Lauren and positively purred, "Oh, it's my pleasure, sweetheart."

I was starting to think that perhaps I should pinch myself when Lucas opened the front door, his tux slung over one shoulder, and he broke into a grin when he saw Lauren.

"Hey, this isn't my little sister, is it?" he asked, moving to hug her. I smiled at the nice picture of sibling affection, and he met my gaze.

Well, at first he met my gaze. His eyes dropped down to follow the line of my dress and then my legs, and then back up again. He looked, if anything, perturbed for some reason. I couldn't think of anything confusing about my outfit, but he continued to stare at me over Lauren's shoulder in a highly embarrassing way even after they stopped hugging. She followed his gaze, and when she realized he was staring at me so hard, she poked him.

He started and tore his eyes from mine. He blinked down at Lauren, who was laughing at him.

"Have you never seen someone dressed up before, Lucas?" she teased, and he colored slightly.

"Ha, ha," Lucas said, rather lamely, and Alexis took pity on him.

"You should probably get dressed if you're going to leave with us," she said, checking the clock hanging over the staircase.

Lauren and George went into the den so he could take her picture by the fireplace, and Maureen excused herself to the kitchen so she could get something to drink. Alexis cleared her throat and smiled at me before hurrying after her husband.

I suddenly found myself a little thirsty too or at least ready to be in a room where someone wasn't staring at me, so I turned on my heel and started walking toward the kitchen.

"Good grief!" I heard Lucas exclaim, and when I turned around, he had lowered his tux to hang limply by his side and was looking after me with his mouth slightly open. Very charming.

"What?" I asked, self-conscious. Had I sat on something?

"The back of that dress," he said, gesturing a bit. He shook his head. "I'm sorry. I'm going to have to remind myself I am twenty-six years old. I suddenly seem to have forgotten that. What I'm trying to say is that…you look wonderful. You really do."

I smiled and said, "Go put your suit on, Lucas."

He saluted me and backed out of the room, down the east wing to where his "room" was. I walked into the kitchen and was about to get a drink when I saw Maureen and remembered that she had gone in there first. I didn't really know what to do, so I stood awkwardly for a moment. I took a deep breath and said, "Hi."

She smiled at me and said, "Hi," as if I were acting very peculiar, which, to be fair, I totally was. I looked at her for another moment, taking in her black silk pants and silver wrap top. I noticed her jewelry and decided that was the safest thing to comment on. Every woman likes to talk about her jewelry.

I smiled at Maureen, ready to fake liking her for the sake of my best friend and her family.

"That's an interesting broach," I said, more to make conversation than because I actually liked it. It was really weird actually. I totally wouldn't wear it. It was a gold snake glaring maniacally at me with sapphire blue eyes. Ew, the eyes were really lifelike. They even had dark points in the centers of them to look like irises and pupils.

"I had this made some time ago to remind myself that no one is as harmless and innocent as they look," Maureen said, fingering the snake's tail, which curled under its head like a hand resting under a chin. "Even the beautiful things have flaws."

I nodded, wondering why she would need reminding of that, but let it go. All through elementary school, I swear I wore day-of-the-week underwear so I wouldn't wake up on a Saturday thinking it was Friday and go rushing off to school at seven forty-five in the morning (a very real fear to my childhood self). So I totally couldn't judge.

"Well, it's really lifelike," I told her, trying desperately hard to make nice with her, why, I'm not sure. "The eyes look real. They're perfect circles, though, that's kind of weird."

"Why?" Maureen asked, looking at me curiously.

"Aren't snake eyes supposed to be slits or something?" I said, laughing uneasily. "I mean, those look like actual eyes, human eyes..."

I trailed off as realization hit me.

# CHAPTER 21

I felt myself go very, very cold.

Maureen's lips thinned into a straight line, and she looked at me suspiciously.

"Heidi?" she asked, stepping toward me.

I involuntarily took a step back, bumping into the counter as I went. "Uh, I just forgot, I have Lucas's…watch. He needs his watch. He'll be late to stuff if I don't get it to him. I'd hate for him to, uh…to, um…"

"Be late for stuff?" Maureen supplied, still not smiling normally.

I swallowed. "Exactly," I said lightly, walking backwards toward the door. "So I better…go."

She watched me leave, her eyes narrowed as I left the kitchen, and I ran, my heart pounding, to Lucas's room. I threw the door open, not bothering to knock, and slammed it shut, locking it.

I leaned against it, panting, my eyes wide open but unseeing. Those sapphires in Maureen's snake broach were identical to the ones Daniella was wearing in the pictures taken from the boat. What Maureen had said about innocence and appearances fit her feelings for Daniella perfectly.

Maureen killed Daniella.

I took a deep breath.

*Be rational,* I reminded myself. *Get the facts. You can't prove anything. You just suspect. Nancy Drew didn't get her name by Red Herring every suspect that came along.*

I could not believe I just thought that.

"Um, Heidi?"

I turned around and flushed. I had temporarily forgotten that I had run into Lucas's room (or really the guest room that Lucas always stayed in when he visited his dad and stepmom) without knocking. He stood by the bed, dressed in black slacks and a white wife beater (what a stupid name for a tank top), holding a white oxford shirt in one hand and a black bowtie in the other—all of it Prada, all of it gorgeous.

I blinked, unable to think of a way to tell him that I thought his mother might be a murderer.

"Are you okay?" he asked, moving toward me. He deposited the things in his hands on the bed and put his hands on his hips. "Heidi?"

"I think your mom knows something about Daniella's death," I blurted out, completely unable to stop myself. I slapped my hand over my mouth to keep anything else from flying out.

Lucas shook his head, looking at me as if he thought he had misheard me (and who could blame him).

"I'm sorry, what?"

"I think…your mom might know who killed Daniella," I said, wringing my hands. I watched him anxiously, waiting for a reaction.

Lucas gave me a small smile. "I hope you're kidding. Because there is no way that my mom would do anything like that. True, she didn't like Daniella, but if she knew something about her death, she would have said something."

"Not if she were…the one who killed her," I said in a rush, trying to get the worst over with. I started to babble at that point. "It all fits, Lucas. I mean, Daniella's earrings were never seen again, and just now your mom had a broach with matching sapphires in it. And she hated Daniella, and maybe she thought your dad would get back together with her or something if Daniella was out of the picture. I don't know…"

"So you're accusing my mother of murder based on jewelry?" Lucas said in an even, flat voice.

"Well, not just jewelry, but that's what made me realize…"

"Heidi," Lucas shouted, looking really mad. I took a step back. I'd never seen that look on his face before. "I get that you're trying to do a good thing here, but you're way off. My mother wouldn't hurt anyone. You've taken this too far. Stop trying to be Nancy Drew, and just leave my family alone."

"Lucas," I said, shocked. "I'm serious about this. Everything fits. We just need to go ask your mom—"

"Ask her what, if she murdered someone? If she's blackmailing people? If she would ever do a thing to hurt anyone in this family? Heidi, you are talking about something that could rip my family apart! What part of *butt out* are you having trouble with?" Lucas shouted, his face red.

I stood mutely. For once in my life, I had nothing to say. Finally, I shook my head and said, "I don't want to be right, Lucas, but if I am, I'm not going to just sit on my hands."

Lucas threw his hands up in the air. "It's like talking to a freakin' brick wall! I don't know why I bother! You only hear what you want to hear, why try to reason with you? Heidi, you listen to me. You leave my mother alone. I mean it. She stays out of this. She's been through enough without the babysitter accusing her of murdering her husband's wife."

I flinched. I felt my lower lip tremble. "The babysitter?" I asked quietly, fiddling with the small ring on my index finger. I looked away from him so he wouldn't see the tears threatening to come out. "Is that how you think of me? As the babysitter? I thought we were friends. I thought...I thought you liked me."

Lucas crossed the room in two strides and grabbed my arms, holding on tightly. "Don't you pull that with me. Do you think I'm an idiot? You know exactly how I feel about you, and if you have to question it, you're the idiot."

I jerked free from him and glared at him. "I owe it to Lauren to find out the truth."

"You owe it to this family to butt out," Lucas spat, matching my glare.

"Are you asking me to choose?"

"Looks like it."

I turned, gripped the door handle, and said evenly, "Lauren. I choose Lauren."

"Then get out of here. Because I'm not going to plead your case when Dad fires you," Lucas said angrily, looking down at me ominously.

I looked up at him for a minute, sadness mingling with my fury. Lucas was my friend. I hated—*hated*—to do this to him, but I had to.

For Lauren.

I walked out of the room in a huff, and I heard a crash from behind the door I had just slammed closed. Sounded like Lucas was just as mad as I was. *Good.*

I told Lauren to go on to the cotillion without me. I was going to stay behind and take my own cab. I had a stack of stuff that could be possible evidence to give to the police, and hopefully it would be enough for a warrant of some kind, or even just enough to spark the curiosity of someone to reopen the case. I just knew that I was right about this, and if I could prove it to the police, maybe Lucas would believe me.

After I was pretty sure everyone had left for the cotillion, I ran downstairs, a folder in my hand with all the stuff that I had gathered that could point the finger at Maureen.

"Didn't go with the others?" I heard a cold voice say behind me as I reached the door, and it froze me in my tracks.

I turned around slowly to face Maureen, who was looking at me in keen interest.

"Uh…no," I said, my tongue like lead. I was home alone with someone I was about to accuse of murder. *Holy. Crap.*

"Why not?" she asked, her eyes lighting on the file in my hand.

"I wasn't ready," I said, inching toward the door. If I lost my shoes somewhere in the process, I could make a run for it. I was pretty sure I could outrun a middle-aged woman.

"Oh, well, would you like to go with me? I wasn't quite ready, either," Maureen said, sounding so innocent, when in reality, the look in her eyes could have broken glass.

I swallowed. She knew I knew something. At that moment, I knew she had done something to Daniella, even if it wasn't killing her with her own two hands, she had a piece in it. An involuntary smile spread across my face before I could stifle it. I had figured it out.

"Proud of yourself, aren't you?" she asked when she noticed the smile. She was no longer trying to look peaceful and innocent. In fact, she looked downright scary. Her red hair framed her face like flames, and her eyes fairly sparked with intensity.

"I don't know what you're talking about," I said stiffly, trying to remember to breathe.

"Don't play dumb with me. We both know you aren't as stupid as you pretend to be," Maureen said harshly.

*Um. Ouch.*

"I don't know what you want me to say, Maureen," I said, shifting so that the file was behind my back and I was angled toward the door. "We're going to be late if we don't head out soon."

"Taking some reading along for the ride?" Maureen asked, her eyes flickering to the file before resting on mine again.

"Paperwork. I'm changing my cell phone plan," I lied. *Where had that come from?*

Maureen took two slow, even steps toward me, closing the distance, and managed to get between me and the door. She smiled at me again, with no emotion behind the empty gesture, and said, "I think I need to see that file, Heidi."

I tried not to panic. "Why don't we look at it in the cab?" I suggested, near breathlessness. Being in a cab would mean there would be a cab driver, which meant a witness if she tried to kill me.

In a swift, sudden movement that was closer to a ninja move of some sort than that of a middle-aged grandmother, Maureen reached out and ripped the file from my hands, leaving me a pretty powerful paper cut running across the center of my palm. I yelped and looked down to see the split skin turn white, then red, then start to ooze blood.

I held my hand away from me, aware even at the textbook definition of a bad time that I was wearing Chanel and blood is freaking hard to get out of chiffon. I started to back away, ready to run for some place to lock myself inside or climb out a window (though since we were on the top floor, I'm not sure what that would have done, except given me a change of scenery when I died), but she reached out and grabbed my hair, yanking so that I had to bend my knees to avoid her ripping out a significant section of my hair.

"You should have left well enough alone, little girl," she said, sounding like a mafia member and looking like a crazy person. "I tried to warn you, but you just wouldn't listen, would you?"

"Maureen, this is a big mistake," I said, wincing when she tightened her grip on my hair and crying out in pain when she pulled me toward the kitchen. I stumbled after her, trying to keep up with her so the pain she was inflicted would lessen, and she pushed me into the cabinets. Because of how I was bending my knees, I went down immediately and with a loud crash. I felt the raised edges on the tile scrape across my kneecap, and my head connected hard with the cabinet door.

"This was a mistake, Heidi, but don't worry. I'm very good at fixing other people's mistakes," she said, pulling a drawer open and selecting the grand daddy of all knives.

My blood started pumping in my veins, and I felt the color drain from my face. I looked at Maureen in horror. She had crazy eyes, glaring at me as if I had irrevocably wronged her, and that knife was no joke.

"You killed her, didn't you?" I asked, my voice squeaking with fear. "You killed Daniella!"

Maureen shuddered, and, for a second, I thought it was with remorse. "A horrible tragedy," she smirked, gripping that knife tightly enough that her knuckles were turning white. "Such a great loss…another dumb blonde who died too soon."

Her coldness, her utter lack of emotion, was almost scarier than that knife. Because had she been guilty or upset, I probably could have talked my way out of this. Or at least talked long enough for someone to come home and see her. But she looked almost delighted at the prospect of skewering me.

I moved to stand up again. My head was throbbing where it had collided with the cabinet, and my knee was now bleeding a little. My paper cut was tender but no longer bleeding, so I put my hands up in front of me and said, "Maureen, just hold on a second, okay? Let's not do anything we're going to regret."

She tilted her head and looked at me as though I had said something very strange. "I'm not going to regret this."

"Murder and blackmail aren't just felony charges, Maureen. It's serious jail time. It could be the death penalty. If you stop now, I'll testify…"

She didn't let me finish. She slapped me across the face, the sound echoing around the kitchen. "Don't do me any favors," she snapped, her eyes crackling like firecrackers.

I touched my cheek and moved my jaw around tentatively. That stung. "So you did send those blackmail letters, then?" I clarified.

"Of course I did. Don't ask me things you already know the answer to. I do not appreciate being patronized, young lady."

I cleared my throat, trying to keep calm. Going into hysterics seemed like the wrong idea. "If I found out, other people could too. Killing me will only delay the inevitable."

"A delay is a delay. And now that I have this," she brandished the file that was sitting precariously on the countertop, "I know what needs to be destroyed so no one else can find out. You've been very helpful, really, because now I know how to avoid a similar paper trail with you."

I hated to take my eyes off of her, but I quickly glanced around, trying to find something to defend myself. That was the only hesitation she needed, apparently. She swung her knife in the direction of my stomach and I jumped back, banging my elbow against the countertop. Her bent position let me slide past her, and I started to make a break for it. But she grabbed a chunk of my hair—this whole chick fight thing was highly annoying—and stepped down hard on my ankle. I felt a rip go through my leg and fell sideways, hitting the refrigerator and knocking off a few of Eliza's magnets. I gasped at the pain. I knew my ankle had to be sprained; it could have even been a torn muscle, but what kept screaming in my head was that it would be a whole lot harder to outrun her.

I held myself up with the handle on the fridge, and when I noticed her approaching me, murder quite realistically shining in her eyes, I turned and tried to limp out of the kitchen, feeling pathetic. I heard her laugh, but when nothing happened I figured maybe, just maybe…

I stopped thinking altogether when I heard a hollow crashing sound, and an instant later I saw black spots. I fell to the ground, holding my head in my hands, staring unseeingly up at Maureen, who was smugly holding a cutting board in her hands. I felt my head spinning. My eyes closed briefly, but I wrenched them back open. Now was not the time to succumb to a concussion.

She put the cutting board down and picked up the knife again. "I can't have you running away from me," she said, stepping over to me and resting one hand on the bar. "That would make this take entirely too long."

"You…hit me?" I asked, my voice coming out cracked and indignant. "I can barely run, and you…hit me?"

Even I was aware enough to realize the stupidity in this statement. I was upset that she had coldcocked me from behind with a cutting board, and yet she was standing over me with a knife that was meant for torturing and killing me. Apparently even in life or death situations, I have messed up priorities.

I licked my lips, opening my eyes wider to try and reassure myself that the black circles crowding my vision would not win, and said, "You're crazy."

That was one of the worst things I could have said in that moment. Her eyes lit with a new higher-burning fire, and her nostrils flared. She reached down and punched me, hitting my temple, and her ring cut my forehead in a gash deep enough to draw blood.

"And to think," Maureen said, tears shimmering in her green eyes as she moved over to me slowly, the knife held tightly in her shaking hand, "I actually liked you. I thought maybe—maybe—you might be good enough for him."

I sniffed, trying hard to ignore the blood trickling from my forehead, mingling with what I hoped was sweat but suspected were tears.

"For who?" I asked, hoping that if I kept her talking—or at least distracted—she might not kill me horribly right away.

Maureen looked at me like I was an idiot, which was pretty demoralizing considering the source.

"For who?" she repeated, and she tipped her head back and cackled. "Who do you think? Lucas. You know he loves you, and now it looks like you were just playing with him, you little tramp. As if you'd ever find anyone better than my boy."

*Okay, she's crazy. Don't tell her that. Lucas doesn't love me, and I haven't led him on,* I thought, trying to think rationally, because if I let my mind swerve to where it was heading—in a nutshell: *Oh, please help me, Lord, she's going to shove that knife through my head like she's serving a ham*—I would fall to pieces and have no chance at surviving this.

"I didn't mean to mislead anyone," I said feebly, trying to get her to talk to me again, giving someone some time to come home and find us.

Maureen gripped the knife and shrugged her shoulders. "Well, you won't be hurting him anymore. I'm sure he'll forget you soon. That's the thing about all of you cute young things. You're so utterly replaceable."

"Is that what you told Daniella?" I said, in a fit of courage.

I winced as she kicked me in the side. This woman had a lot of rage, and I had a lot of pain. There was no way I could fight her off, and, because of my ankle, I couldn't out run her. I looked around desperately for some sort of weapon to use against her, but everything I saw wouldn't do much against a great big mother of a butcher knife.

"We didn't talk much," Maureen said cryptically, grinning smugly.

"Did you hit her from behind too?" I asked rudely, and she kicked me again. My ribs were burning with the repeated kicks, but my ankle hurt too much to try and move away.

"You think you know so much, why don't you tell me how it happened?" Maureen taunted, raising an eyebrow.

I licked my lips and said simply, "You called her, got her to come to the deck by herself, and you fought. You scraped her stomach with your nails, and then you hit her with something that cut her forehead and I'm guessing knocked her out. Then you tied her ankles together..."

She was looking at me incredulously. "How do you know that?"

I smiled for the first time since I realized Maureen was really the killer. "I'm very thorough. What I want to know is who Claude Keller is."

Maureen rolled her eyes. "Claude is the idiot that helped me. He was a retired model that I met at the club, and he was hopelessly gullible. He was supposed to get rid of you by now, but he failed miserably at that. He was the one who drove me out to the boat to meet..."

Maureen suddenly glared at me, realizing that she had been sharing too much. She gripped that knife again and said, "Stop this. Stop distracting me. You don't want me to prolong it."

"You don't have to do this," I said desperately, inching away from her by pulling myself with my elbows.

Maureen rolled her eyes. "Oh, yeah, I'm sure you can keep a secret. Someone like you could never understand the things I've had to do to protect my family."

"Is that why you killed Daniella? You were protecting someone?" I asked, and she stopped moving to look at me seriously.

"If you think we're going to bond because you tell me some sob story about protecting people, you've got another thought coming, sugar," Maureen drawled, putting her hands on her hips. "She was going to ruin everything, and I had to stop it."

I licked my lower lip, trying to ease the sting from where she had hit me. "Because she was pregnant?" I asked, taking a big risk and hoping it paid off.

Maureen froze where she stood over me, her eyes narrowing and her mouth trembling. "How did you know about that?" she asked, breathing hard out her nose. I wouldn't have been a bit surprised if flames or smoke had come out.

"I found her date book. She had lunch with you the week she died, but she also had an appointment with an obstetrician. I'm guessing she told you her news that day, and you flipped out," I said slowly, my heart beating so hard that I was pretty sure it echoed throughout the kitchen.

Maureen laughed, an empty, hollow sound that filled the room. "She had the audacity to name her daughter Lauren," she said, hatred dripping from her words. "She thought it went well with Lance and Lucas. My children. I named them. She always treated them like they were her boys. No, no. They were my boys. She made this big front of acting like we were all one big happy family, and all she was thinking of was herself. She said she hoped it would be a girl because then she would have two boys and two girls. But they weren't her children. Those were my boys, and she was trying to take them from me."

Not that I was trying to explain away her actions, but I kind of understood how that would have hurt. Still not enough to kill for, let alone forever silence the nanny-companion over, but I could see how that would sting.

"She wanted to name her Lillian, she said," Maureen went on, and I could tell this had been building up for about a decade or so. Maureen was literally shaking with rage. "Another 'L' name for George. She went on and on about how happy George would be, how he always wanted to have a big family, how she wanted him to move to the country with her. She wanted him to take Lucas with them. My son, my baby; she wanted to take that from me too. It wasn't enough that she stole my husband—she had to take my son too!"

"I thought you and George were divorced by the time he met Daniella?" I asked, enthralled in finally hearing everything explained fully, and immediately regretted it because she stepped on my hand and ground her heel into the back of it. I cried out, fresh tears wetting my eyes, and bit my lip.

"You think just because you found out that I killed her, you know everything about us now?" she hissed, leaning down to get right in my face. "You think just because I haven't killed you yet means I won't? I had to kill her fast, because of her stupid, drunken little bimbo friends, but you…no one is around to hear you scream."

I took a deep breath, braced myself for the coming pain, and lunged forward, headbutting her. Stars lit up my vision, my head swimming from the contact, but it was enough to make her stumble away from me, clutching her head. I kicked my good foot out hard, connecting with her stomach, and heard a very satisfactory grunt of pain. I tried to pull myself up on the bar stool next to my head, but my leg wouldn't support me. I was pretty sure she had broken a bone or two in my hand when she had stepped on it. My head was throbbing, and as I was looking around for some way to knock her out, she tripped me. I hit my head hard against the tile floor.

My vision swam again, and I could feel blood drip from my hairline. I fought to keep my eyes open—they were suddenly very heavy—and I heard her stomp toward me.

"How dare you," she said through clenched teeth. "I was going to make this painless for you, but now let's see how tough you really are." She ended that phrase by pulling her arm back, the knife catching the light and glinting like a neon sign. I felt like I should be feeling something about now—fear, anger, the desperate need to use the bathroom—but all I felt was numb. My body had taken over, and my brain felt like it was wrapped in gauze. I couldn't fight her anymore. I couldn't get my arms to lift and try to stop her from shoving that knife into me. I swallowed hard and tried one last time, but my arms felt like they were made out of lead. I resigned myself to the pain that was coming to me and decided that this was probably at least better than getting hit by a car. At least this way, Lauren and Lucas wouldn't have to see me die.

Before my eyes closed and the pounding in my head started beating out my will to think, I caught a glimpse of red and heard a scream.

# CHAPTER 22

Eliza! I heard another scream and a powerful crash as Eliza yanked the silverware drawer out and used it to coldcock Maureen in the back of the head. Maureen went down hard, the knife slid across the floor, spinning, and skidded to a stop under the bar stools. Eliza bent down in front of me, and I think she was still screaming. I saw her grab the phone and dial, and I felt relief wash over me. *Oh, God bless Eliza for coming into the kitchen in time to see Maureen trying to kill me.* My last conscious thought was that I was going to campaign hard for Eliza to get a raise…if I lived through the marching band leading a parade in my brain.

I woke up in a hospital bed several hours later, my foot propped up on several pillows and my hand sporting a cast. I could feel bandages on my face, and I groaned.

I hated hospitals. This was the first time I had been in one for what I assumed was going to be an extended visit, and I was already feeling claustrophobic.

A nurse who was writing something on a clipboard noticed I was awake and went to stand beside me. She stuck a thermometer in my mouth and said, "That was some night you had, huh?"

I looked at her from under the gauze and raised my eyebrows, trying to ignore the pain in my head. I couldn't speak because of the thermometer, and let's just say she was lucky of that.

When she took it out and wrote what it said on her clipboard, I asked, "So when can I go home?"

The nurse looked at me over her glasses and shook her head. "A comedian. Lovely."

I took that as a bad sign. I groaned again and said, "No release date? I can totally lie flat on my back in the comfort of my own bed. I even have stackable pillows for my foot."

"Do you have a morphine drip for your bruised ribs and broken hand?" the nurse asked, not looking up.

"I could probably get one on eBay," I said thoughtfully.

She smiled at that and said, "Just relax. Try to sleep. It passes the time. When you're ready, you've got some people here waiting to talk to you."

I tried to sit up, but that hurt too badly. So she took pity on me and pressed the button to raise my bed a little.

"I'll see them now," I said eagerly. I had a lot of questions.

"Rest first. You can see people when you wake up," she insisted, and then she gave me a shot of something that helped make that a possibility.

I woke up the next evening, and I felt pretty blurry. The night nurse took my vitals and a policeman came in and took my statement. When I was done, he told me Maureen had confessed to killing Daniella and trying to kill me. When he left, I asked the nurse if there was anyone in the waiting room for me. She said there were several people, so I asked her if I could talk to someone, anyone.

She shrugged and walked out, and, a few minutes later, she brought George into my room. I straightened the gown they had dressed me in and tried not to look quite as beaten up. I didn't want to make him feel worse than he looked like he felt.

He stood in the doorway for a moment, looking at me with concern and dismay. His hands were in the pockets of his tuxedo pants, and I realized he must have come straight from the cotillion to the hospital. The cotillion made me think of Lauren and of Lucas, and I felt horrible all over again.

George sat down in the armchair at the foot of my hospital bed. He looked sad, tired, and like he was dreading this conversation. I wasn't much better. I mean, I was in a gown made out of material so thin it felt like paper, I had a bandage wrapped around my head, a cast on my hand, and my foot was propped up on a stack of pillows. I didn't even let myself think about the very real possibility that because of said propped up foot, George—and everyone else in the hospital—could see up my gown. I did not look my best, to say the least.

"Hi," I said, mostly to break the silence.

He smiled. "Hi," he said, running his hand over his chin. "How are you feeling?"

"Well," I said, adjusting my gown, "I'm not woozy anymore. I know my own name. I can count all ten fingers and toes. I'm good to go. I'm just counting down the minutes until they let me out."

"Already?" he laughed, but then he was serious again. "Good. I mean, good that you're feeling better. I'm sorry that they haven't let you out yet. They told us that you needed to stay for observation because of your concussion."

I pursed my lips and nodded.

An awkward silence permeated the room. I could hear the alarm clock ticking next to the bed.

"I wanted to give you an update on the situation," George said, touching his eye as if he had developed a twitch. "Maureen will be charged with murder one and attempted murder, not to mention conspiracy to commit murder. Claude Keller fled the country, but, when he is caught, he will be charged with aiding and abetting a criminal, attempted murder, and being an accessory after the fact. Eliza has volunteered to testify against Maureen, but the DA says that probably won't be necessary. Maureen has been quite vocal about certain events ever since they locked her up."

George looked out my window, and I truly felt for him. I mean, this had to rate among the suckiest days a person could have. To find out that your first wife murdered your second wife, threatened your third wife, and then tried to off the nanny? That's a lot for someone to take.

"How is Lauren doing?" I asked, hoping for the best.

George smiled. "She's worried about you. She thinks you'll quit when you get out of the hospital. That's the main concern she's vocalized anyway."

So that shoe hadn't fallen yet.

I took a deep breath and asked the question I so didn't think I wanted the answer to. "How are Lance and Lucas?"

George sighed. "Dealing," he said simply, cupping his hand around his cheek and looking miserable. "They're not sure what to think of all this. They loved Daniella like a second mother, and they adore Lauren. I think right now they're just dealing with how to be around Lauren again. Their mother killed her mother, after all. I think they feel guilty."

"They shouldn't," I said, avoiding eye contact. "I'm the one who feels guilty."

"Why on earth should you feel guilty?" George asked, looking confused.

"Because I outed their mother as a murderer, sent her to prison, and in doing so let the whole world know what their mom did. I may as well have bricked the wall between them, Lauren, and myself," I blurted out.

I had been thinking that ever since I realized Maureen was the killer, and I knew I would have to deal with the consequences of that, it was a huge relief to have it off my chest even though I was confessing to the wrong person.

George blinked and said, "Well. I don't know what to say to that. You will have to talk to them, but I don't think any of my children blame you for anything that happened. You're Lauren's best friend, Lance thinks you're charming, and Lucas…well, everyone knows how that boy feels."

I rolled my eyes and let my head fall back against the pillows—a mistake, if the throb of pain in my forehead was any indication. And here I thought George was clueless about things like that. It was painfully and unfairly embarrassing that my boss knew his son was infatuated with me—I refused to use the "L" word, even if Maureen had said it, because hello, she's a crazy person—and even worse that I was finding this out while laying in a hospital bed with my foot propped up, my gown cut so that the whole world could see up my skirt if they angled their head correctly. As if the last few days hadn't been bad enough, I now had to endure hits to my pride, too?

"I told them not to visit you until I spoke to you. I wanted to make sure you were…all right. We all feel just horrible, and I wanted you to know that if you wanted out of your contract, I would understand."

I sat in silence for a moment. The last few months had been the oddest of my life. And yet…I was really happy. I wanted to get out of the hospital, not so I could go find a new job or place to live but so I could go back to hanging out with Lauren and, even though I was loathe to admit it, Lucas. More than I wanted to have my own corner office with a Park view, I wanted to go have lattes with Lauren and drill her over whether or not Connor asked her on a real date after the cotillion. More than I wanted to be a powerful, respected part of some company, I wanted to have friends and, for all intents and purposes, a family.

So I sat up as straight as I could, looked George Dayton in the eye, and said, "Absolutely not. You're going to have to try a lot harder to get rid of me."

He blinked. "Um, okay," he said, obviously wondering if I was truly okay or if the trauma to my head had done lasting damage.

He stood, but I cleared my throat and said, "I have to tell you something."

George looked at me, blinked, and sat back down. "Yes?" he asked, and I could tell he was trying to think of what else I could possibly have to say after everything Maureen had apparently admitted to.

I wet my lips, took a deep breath, and asked cautiously, "Did Maureen tell you why she killed Daniella?"

George's face blanched, and he leaned forward. "No. She wouldn't say anything more than that she did it. Did you...did she tell you?"

I nodded. I could tell I was going to cry, so I said as evenly as I could, "I'm so sorry, George, that I have to be the one to tell you this, but Daniella was pregnant. She was going to leave the engagement party early to tell you, and..."

George's face fell, and I saw his jaw tighten against the tears forming in his eyes. I always thought seeing a man cry would be embarrassing or possibly even comical in some way, but my heart broke for him. He buried his face in his hands, and I wished there was something I could do other than just sit here.

I said softly, "She thought it was going to be a girl. She had the name Lillian picked out."

George looked up at me, his eyes red, and asked, "How did you…know that?"

I took a deep breath and said, "I think it's time I told you how all of this really happened."

He sat up straighter, and I crossed my fingers on my non-broken hand that he wouldn't fire me after hearing the whole story.

When I was finished, he sat quietly for several minutes, and then he got up and sat on the edge of my bed. He took my hand that wasn't in a cast and said, "Thank you."

I looked at him in confusion. "For what?"

"For doing what I hired you for. You were there for Lauren when no one else could be, and you helped her do something that no one else could have done. You gave her peace of mind."

I shook my head. "All I found out were bad things."

George shrugged. "I don't know. I mean, yes, these things hurt, but I can't help but feel that Dani can finally rest in peace. I can let her go. I never thought she died accidentally, and I'm glad that I can finally think about her and know that she didn't want to leave us. She fought. She was happy with her life and wanted to stay here with us."

I sniffed. I tried to control the tears that were threatening to spill, and George released my hand to hand me a Kleenex.

I wiped my eyes and said, "I feel like I know her a little bit. Is that weird?"

He shook his head. "No. I think she would have liked you. You're spunky. She appreciated spunk. You remind me of her, a little bit. That's one of the reasons I hired you. I thought you would be good for Lauren. And look at that…" he trailed off, smiling down at me, "I was right."

I smiled at him, and, for the first time since I realized what I had to do to this family, I felt good about my choice.

# CHAPTER 23

A few days later, I was seriously irked that they weren't letting me go home. I mean, hospitals weren't my favorite place in the world, and that was when I wasn't stuck in one. However, the doctor informed me when he checked me out that morning that he wanted me to get stronger before he let me go home. I felt pretty strong, but when I told the doctors and nurses that they just smiled at me like they were being incredibly compassionate to the crazy person. I felt I should take offense.

Lauren came to see me every day. I think she felt guilty that I was in the hospital for doing something she had asked me to do. I told her a million times that it wasn't her fault, that no one was to blame, but she still showed up every day to bring me the paper or a magazine or sometimes just some candy canes or the like. She had decorated the all-beige room with flowers and pictures and garlands, and it was easily the liveliest place in the hospital.

I was pretty sore still. I mean, even though I felt fine most of the time, I still found things that hurt unexpectedly. It hurt to turn my head from side to side because of the nasty cut Maureen had given me. My ankle had healed up nicely, and the swelling was almost completely gone. My concussion was gone, but I still got a little light headed when I stood up too fast. That was the kicker for me. Of all my injuries sustained in my fight with Maureen, the concussion just rubbed me the wrong way. I mean, I had a sprained ankle, for crying out loud. I was doing an extremely unproductive job of running away, and yet she felt it necessary to knock me across the back of the head with a cutting board? That just seemed unsportsmanlike.

On my sixth day in the hospital—the doctor promised that a week was all I was required to stay, hallelujah—Lauren was busily arranging her pedicure set on the side table of my bed. She had brought a way pretty plum color—very holiday hip—and was going to give me a pedicure. I took a deep breath and asked her what I'd been dying to know since I figured out who the killer was: "Are you mad at me?"

Lauren looked up, blinking in confusion. "What? Why would I be mad at you?"

I looked at her helplessly, because if I started giving her reasons she might be mad at me, odds were, she would end up realizing that she was—or at least should be—mad.

She suddenly nodded, looking down at my feet as she applied a layer of base coat. "Oh, I see. No, I'm not mad at you. You only did what I asked you to do. And now we all know the truth, and that's better, even if it…isn't."

"I feel so guilty," I admitted, playing with the hem of the thin blanket laying over me.

"You shouldn't. None of it was your fault. No one blames you, Heidi. Lance and Lucas took me to lunch yesterday, and we talked. Things aren't going to be the same, but that's not reason enough to pout and cry. It's sad, and it's a bitter pill to swallow, but we will live. We will go on. They are my brothers, no matter who our mothers are, and I love them unconditionally. Nothing can ever change that," Lauren said, smiling suddenly. "Just like you. You're my best friend, and I appreciate what you did for my family and me more than you will ever know. You risked your own life to give me closure, and I could never hate you or be mad at you for that."

My eyes filled with tears, even though for the life of me I tried to stop them. "You're pretty much amazing, you know that, right?"

Lauren grinned and unscrewed the top of the plum polish. "I try."

I watched as she painted my toenails, silent for a few minutes, but something else was bugging me to the point of distraction. "Lauren?"

"Yes?"

"Are Lance and Lucas…do they…"

She looked up at me sternly, her eyebrows lowered, and her mouth twisted into a frown. "Lance and Lucas aren't mad at you either. Lance has been by twice, but you've been asleep both times. He said he might stop by and see you tonight. Julie has been worried sick about you."

I blinked at the noticeable lack of Lucas in that answer. "What about Lucas?" I asked in a very small voice.

She shrugged. "He's been pretty quiet. I don't think he wants to see you in here like this. He told me he wasn't sure he could ever forgive his mother for killing Mom, but he didn't hate her for it. He kind of hates her for trying to kill you."

My mouth went dry. I couldn't think of anything to say to that. I cleared my throat. "I'd like to talk to him."

Lauren raised her eyebrows in interest. "What are you going to say?"

"No idea," I said honestly, biting my thumbnail. I smiled angelically at her. "What would you say if you were me?"

Lauren smiled and screwed the top of the nail polish closed. "No idea."

I closed my eyes briefly and shook my head. I reclined against the pillows and stared up at the *Charlie's Angels* rerun that was playing on the TV suspended from the ceiling. Why let myself be upset when Farrah, Jaclyn, and Kate were totally kicking butt? Lauren and I spent some time arguing about who made the better Angel, one of the originals or one of the new, revamped ones (Cameron, Drew, or Lucy). Lauren was insisting that Jaclyn Smith was the best, while I was torn between Cameron Diaz and Lucy Liu. We were talking about who wore better disguises when Lance and Julie poked their heads into my room.

"Knock, knock," Julie said, in that half-whisper I'd noticed people used in hospitals. "Can we come in?"

"Yes," I said, smiling and trying to act like an adult and not someone who had just been arguing quite adamantly about a seventies TV show and its remake.

They walked in carrying a bouquet of tulips and daffodils, a bright, colorful arrangement that Screamed, "Be happy." I smiled and thanked them for the flowers, ignoring with some difficulty that I already had seven bouquets in my room. Lauren and I were going to take them to the cancer ward when I was released.

Julie came over to stand beside me and asked, "How are you feeling?"

"I'm feeling much better," I said, plastering my "Don't feel sorry for me, check out how happy I am" smile on my face. "My ankle feels almost normal"—Total lie, it hurt every time I put weight on it—"and my concussion is pretty much gone. I just have to watch the headaches."

"And your hand?" Julie pressed, looking down at the cast with caution.

I raised the cast and waved it gently. "I've never actually broken anything before, so I'm not so bummed about the cast. I always wanted one when I was little, to be honest. I know that's weird, but all my friends had broken some sort of bone, and I never had. I always thought it would be cool to have a cast. It's a little cumbersome, but I don't mind it."

Julie nodded, and I noticed she looked questioningly at the wrapping around my ribs and the massive bruise on my forehead. I shook my head slightly and said, "I'm much better. Really."

Lance cleared his throat, and Julie immediately said, "Lauren, will you show me where the bathroom is?"

Lauren frowned. "Heidi has one in her room. It's that door right there."

Julie paused, but recovered by saying, "Right, well, where are the vending machines? I suddenly have the worst craving for Reese's."

Lauren looked confused, but she stood and motioned for Julie to follow her. When they had left the room, I turned to Lance.

He was smiling wryly after them, shaking his head. "She's really something, isn't she?"

I assumed he meant Julie, but it would have fit Lauren too, so I just nodded and said, "Yeah, she is."

He sat down where Lauren had been sitting and looked at me, his lips pursed, clearly not knowing where to start.

I started for him. "How are you?" I asked, feeling self-conscious. I just kept repeating that I had sent his mother to prison, for the rest of her life, and I had no idea how to talk to him anymore. He hadn't been easy to talk to before this mess, and now things were irrevocably different.

He didn't smile as I thought he would. Instead, he sighed and said, "Not great. Things have been hard. But I wanted to come and say this to you in person. Julie and I talked about it for a long time, and, when I finally reached a conclusion about how I felt, she told me to talk to you."

*That Julie. Little Miss Fix-It.*

"Okay," I said slowly, adjusting in my upright position uncomfortably.

Lance took a deep breath and said, "First of all, I would like to thank you for giving my father and my sister closure. Dad always believed that Daniella couldn't have drowned, but he had no way of proving it. And Lauren has a right to know about how her mother died, so thank you for finding the truth for her."

I nodded, trying to work around the knot forming in my throat. I could not let myself cry in front of him.

"Secondly," he continued, "I would like to commend you for having the courage to say something about what you found out. I know you were in a difficult position. Lucas told me about your conversation that night, and I want to applaud you for your tenacity."

I fought the urge to narrow my eyes suspiciously. This sounded like a rehearsed speech. Although to be honest, I didn't blame him. I couldn't think of anything to say to him that didn't sound completely stupid.

"Thirdly, I would like to apologize profusely for all of your injuries. I am deeply sorry that you were hurt, and I want you to know that Dad has taken care of all of your medical bills."

I knew this, and I was about to protest that he had no need to apologize—the injuries were certainly not his fault—when he started talking again:

"Lastly, I just wanted to tell you that while this time will undoubtedly be difficult for all of us, none of us hold any kind of grudge against you. We appreciate and respect all the work you put into finding out what really happened, and we are grateful that you're okay and willing to come back to work. Lauren thinks of you as a sister. We all really like you, so we're thrilled to know that you want to stay."

I was dying to know if George had told his kids about Daniella's pregnancy, but that wasn't my place to ask. Besides, what if he said "no" or "What pregnancy?" Then I would be knee deep in it. And what if he had told them? What did I expect to hear

Lance say that would make any of that tragedy easier to live with? Nothing. It would only force him to talk about something that would cause nothing but pain.

"I really appreciate you saying all this," I said, smoothing my palms along my thighs in a subtle effort to wipe the sweat off of them without letting him know how nervous I was. "And I'm glad you don't resent me for what happened. I just want to tell you that…I'm sorry, I guess. I'm sorry that…that…"

Before I could dig myself neck deep in a rambling grave and throw up the shovel, Lance nodded. "I know," he said, and I relaxed a little, because even if I couldn't say it, he seemed to know what I meant. "I know you are. And so does Lucas."

I clenched my jaw at the sound of Lucas's name. The last words I had spoken to him before the incident were bitter, mean, and rang in my memory with crushing finality. The fact that he hadn't come to see me or sent any kind of stupid note or card—despite what Lauren said about not wanting to see me this way—made me think that maybe, no matter what Lauren, Lance, and George assured me, he really did resent me for sending his mother to prison.

"How is he…doing?" I asked casually, not meeting Lance's eyes.

Lance shrugged. "He's dealing the best he can. He feels terrible for not believing you. He blames himself for what happened to you because he thinks if he'd just listened to you, you wouldn't have been by yourself in the house with her, and she couldn't have hurt you like this."

I frowned and furrowed my eyebrows. "But it's not his fault at all. He shouldn't blame himself."

Lance cast me an amused look. "Yes, I know. We all know. He even knows, but it's easier to be mad at himself than deal with who he's really mad at."

I nodded miserably. "Me."

"No. Jeez, I never realized just how alike you two are until just now. You're both such throw-yourself-upon-the-fire kind of people. He's mad at Mom, and he knows this is her fault. But he hasn't quite been able to cope with both her murdering Daniella and her attacking you. She could have killed you, you know," Lance said softly, more to himself than me, but I responded anyway.

"Yes, I know. I was there," I said dryly.

He nodded. "So you were," he mused, and I noticed he was now turning his wedding ring nervously.

I took pity on his uncomfortable state and said, "I'm fine, Lance. Nothing a little time won't heal. Don't feel sorry for me or guilty about it. And I know it's going to take some time to get through this, but everything will be fine. If you are handed it, you can handle it," I said, quoting a little magnet that Lauren had in her room.

Lance looked at me skeptically. "You really missed your calling as a motivational speaker, didn't you?"

I laughed and then remembered a time when Lucas had said the same thing to me and instantly sobered. "You have a lot of people who care about you and want to see you happy. Take comfort in that rather than dwell on the bad stuff, okay?"

Lance smiled, and, suddenly, he didn't seem skeptical or sad anymore. In fact, he looked like the textbook definition of ornery. "Do you want me to tell Lucas to come visit you? It sounds like you really want to talk to him."

I fought that stupid blush and said, a little stiffly, "I don't want him to do something he doesn't want to do. If he has something to say to me, he can visit. If not, I will see him…eventually."

Even as I was saying it, I knew I sounded like a petulant child, or worse, a jilted teenager. I desperately wanted to wipe that smug, knowing smile right off of Lance's face, but I figured he had been through enough in the last week without that.

Besides, I knew the truth about how I felt, so why should it bother me that other people had their own opinions?

"Okay. I'll pass that along. It will make him feel better to know you're thinking of him," Lance said, obviously trying to bait me.

Maybe I did care what other people think.

"Lance, don't you dare—" I started, sitting up and shaking my finger at him as though he were four, but at that moment, Julie and Lauren walked back in, and I had to stop off what I was saying in fear that an audience would make it worse.

"It was nice to talk to you, Heidi," Lance said, smiling that annoyingly knowing grin as he picked up his coat and went to his wife's side. "We'll see you at Christmas, won't we?"

I nodded mutely, a tight smile on my face. Anything I said at this point would have definitely made it worse.

Julie told me to call her when I was better so we could have lunch, and amid waves and good-byes, they left.

I turned to Lauren and said, "Your brothers are going to drive me insane."

Lauren smiled at me and said, "You'll learn to live with it."

# CHAPTER 24

I was finally back at the Daytons. It seemed like an eternity had passed since the last time I was there. I had a hard time standing in the living room or the kitchen because I found myself reliving it at the weirdest times. As much as I told everybody I was fine, it still terrified me to be alone in that house. I avoided it at all costs.

I didn't have to work that hard to stay with people because Lauren was nearly always by my side. She even slept in the armchair in my room one night because we stayed up late talking, and she fell asleep. I don't know why exactly she felt like she needed to watch me every second, but I wasn't complaining.

Jennifer and Rachel stopped by one day to see me, which was a pleasant, if not rather astounding, surprise. They were both about six months pregnant, and while Jennifer had a cute, round little belly, Rachel was already huge and lamenting the daunting task of getting her figure back before they went to the Hamptons for the summer. They were both having boys, which was fine. And neither of their sons were going to be named after their fathers, which I applauded. In fact, Jennifer was already referring to her baby as Spencer, whereas Rachel was more interested in setting up a nursery than settling on one of the several names she and Donald liked.

Their visit was great, though. I didn't realize how much I missed them. I mean, I had way more in common with Lauren, and she was way easier to talk to than Jen and Rachel, but they were part of my old life. They were shallow and sophisticated and fashion-conscious and completely, totally dear. I made myself a promise to spend more time with them and to try and get over my fear of babies so I could be fun Aunt Heidi to their boys.

I knew my parents knew what had happened—George called them—but I didn't hear from either of them until two weeks after the incident when Mom called to ask me what I wanted for Christmas. I didn't even bring up the fact that I most likely wouldn't be there (or if I did guilt myself into going, I would stay for exactly two hours and then extricate myself with a speed that would make Superman blink in surprise) or the tiny matter of my week-long stay in the hospital. I just told her to get me some jeans or something. Then I remembered who I was talking to and amended that list to include the amazing Christian Louboutin heels I saw on Fifth a few weeks ago and some Alexander McQueen sunglasses. I told her Dad could buy me a Thomas Wylde bag.

When I hung up, I felt pretty good. I mean, we hadn't had some heart to heart about our relationship or our feelings or anything, but when I mentioned the Thomas Wylde bag, Mom started in on how badly she wanted a Birkin, and we had a five-minute discussion on handbags that was borderline friendly. It was probably the closest I had felt to my mother since I was five.

The one thing that marred my triumphant return from the hospital was that I still hadn't seen Lucas. Part of me wasn't surprised, and a small piece of me wasn't disappointed—I was dreading that meeting more than anything—but I still felt a little betrayed. I mean, for three months, the guy hung on to my every word and showed up at every little thing. Then, suddenly, he's—*poof!*—nowhere to be found?

Okay, so I knew I was totally over-simplifying the matter, but come on. He was my friend. Shouldn't that come first? Shouldn't that be more important than his stupid male pride or some sort of guilt trip he's put himself on?

I held onto this bah-humbug feeling for several days, letting its bitterness make me feel oddly better about the world. I now had a new obsession to think about twenty-four/seven. Because of this, I was more than surprised when, after ten minutes of Lauren helping me down the stairs, I showed up to dinner quite out of breath and a little sweaty, only to find him sitting silently at the table.

Dinner was filled with Alexis, George, and Lauren discussing Christmas plans. Lucas and I were both silent unless our opinions were requested. It was one of the longest meals of my life, and I had been to Spain on holiday, so I had a bar on which to measure it.

It wasn't until after dinner, when George had gone to his study and Alexis and Lauren were arguing about which fireplace to put the milk and cookies out for Santa next week (nope, not kidding, and, yes, I refrained from commenting) that Lucas approached me with the air of one approaching a baby tiger; he looked like he wasn't sure whether I would purr or bite.

I tried to smile at him, but I was so panicked about what to say to him that I'm pretty sure I just grimaced or managed some other facial contortion that was anything but pretty. He somehow overlooked that and simply asked, "Do you have anything going on tomorrow? I would like to take you to breakfast. To talk."

Bluntness may not be a trait universally admired, but right then, I was so relieved he wasn't mad or trying to be subtle and act like nothing had happened that it was officially my favorite thing about him. I nodded, and before I could form words to actually respond to his request, he said, "We can leave at nine. We'll talk then."

He abruptly left the room, and I nodded my head. *That went well. Probably because I wasn't allowed to speak.*

I knew Lauren and Alexis had noticed this interchange, but they were nice enough—or perhaps had the highly intuitive preservation skills—to refrain from asking about it. Instead, Lauren helped me upstairs and into a bubble bath. I tried to relax for a while, but that backfired. I flipped through a magazine and nearly ruined it when I heard a door slam, because I dropped it into the bubbles. Luckily, Lauren had poured so much bubble bath into the tub before leaving me to try to figure out how to get in using only one leg that the bubbles caught the magazine before it could get to the water.

I finally gave up relaxing and got out of the tub. I dried off and put on some floral boxer shorts and a green T-shirt. I pulled my hair into a ponytail and climbed into bed early, trying to think of things to concentrate on so I could go to sleep and morning would hurry up and get there. I wanted to know what Lucas had to say to me, but, more than that, I wanted this all over.

Several hours later, I admitted to myself that I just couldn't sleep. My hand hurt, my foot hurt, and my head hurt, but, more than that, I was dreading the morning so badly that my whole body seemed to ache. I knew I would see Lucas at breakfast, not my best time of day by any means, and I had no idea what to say to him. I sighed, threw back the covers with my good hand, slid my feet carefully into a pair of old tan Ugg slippers, and shuffled toward the door, favoring my left foot. I managed to make it down the stairs, even though it hurt more than I thought it would. I limped to the kitchen and paused in the doorway, shocked. Lucas was standing in the middle of the kitchen, his back to me. He was in faded, soft-looking navy plaid pajama pants and a T-shirt that looked like it had once been blue but had since succumbed to being a washed out gray.

I saw him putting up a package of crackers and cleared my throat awkwardly. "You're still awake?" I asked, and he jumped, shutting the cabinet harder than he probably would have.

"Do you want me to have a heart attack, or do you sneak up on everybody late at night?" he asked, looking at me with unreadable eyes before dropping his gaze to the floor.

"We need to talk. About…what's been going on," I said before I realized what I was saying. Once it was out, I knew I couldn't take it back, so I just took a deep breath and walked forward, placing my hands palm down on the counter to keep them from shaking; I was that nervous. I winced when my cast made a loud clinking noise with the countertop, and Lucas looked pained at the reminder of my…incident.

"I'm going to get coffee. Coffee always makes these things less uncomfortable," he said, pouring two cups.

"I thought you didn't drink coffee," I said suspiciously, narrowing my eyes.

"Since you've come into my life, it has become a necessity," Lucas said over his shoulder, grinning. It was the first time I'd seen him grin since before all the drama started.

"Thanks for that," I said sarcastically.

"What are friends for?" he asked, adding some cream and sugar. I cringed. Any second, rambling madness was going to come bursting out, and he was calmly making a caffeinated beverage that wouldn't make the blabbering any easier to understand.

"What's on your mind?" he asked mildly enough as he stirred both cups. It was an innocent enough question, but the uncertainty in his eyes made my throat clench and my stomach feel all jumbly.

"I just don't know what to do, you know? I feel weird around you and Lance. I feel like I should be apologizing all the time, but I know you don't want that. All I can think about is how I don't want to lose your friendship," I blurted out as he handed me my cup of coffee.

He flinched at my words, although I didn't think they had been that significant. He took a long sip from his coffee and said, "You know, neither Lance nor I hold you responsible in any way. He said he talked to you. And I don't want anything to happen to our…friendship either. Although, Heidi, you know I want more than a friendship with you."

I nearly choked on my coffee. I decided that this wasn't the kind of conversation to be had with steaming hot liquid there for the spilling. I slid my cup across the counter, and he took it and rinsed it out. Even though it was certainly not a new sentiment, it still managed to take me by surprise. "Lucas…" I said, not sure what to say. I didn't want to hurt him.

"So what are you doing this weekend? Do you want to, I don't know, grab a cup of coffee or maybe do dinner and a movie?" Lucas asked, looking at me from where he stood at the sink, rinsing out his coffee cup. Eliza had long ago gone to bed, but Lucas seemed fine with washing his own dishes, upping my estimation of him in my mind. He had a teasing smile on his face, but I could tell his offer was genuine.

"I can't believe that after everything that happened in the last two months, in the last two weeks, you still want to date me," I said, utterly disbelieving his staying power.

"It's hard, what happened to my mother. But she did something wrong, something horrible, and she's paying for it. I can't overlook what she did to our family. Or to you, for that matter. She gave me life and love, and she will always be my mother. I love her, but she has to pay for what she did. Justice will out," Lucas said, his voice sad.

I lowered my head. "And you don't kind of resent me for sending your mother to prison?"

"I love my mother. But I love my little sister too, and someone hurt her beyond words ten years ago. Now that person has been brought to light. Like I said, it's hard. But I'm grateful that Lauren knows the truth now."

My eyes were starting to hurt with the effort I was making not to cry. "You guys are amazing. I can't believe you're…you're being so wonderful about all of this. I don't…I don't know what to say."

Lucas leaned over and smoothed down one of the highly unattractive bumps in my ponytail. The warmth of his hand was more reassuring than any series of empty words, more affectionate than any hug could ever dream of being. I moved away from him casually, trying to remind myself that this was not the time to be weak, and that I couldn't let him believe something that wasn't true. I cleared my throat, and that seemed to break whatever spell the soft light of the kitchen counter lamp and the late hour had cast over the room. Suddenly, the smell of coffee became clearer, and the ticking of the clock over the stove seemed louder.

Lucas gave me a small smile and said, "In some ways, even through all that's happened, nothing's changed, Heidi. We all still want you here."

I leaned against the counter, crossing my legs at the ankles (carefully, to avoid putting too much weight on my still sore sprain) and narrowing my eyes. "I'm glad and relieved that you're still my friend." I emphasized the word *friend* and raised my eyebrows.

"Why won't you let me take you out sometime?" Lucas asked, leaning forward on his folded arms and grinning at me. It was a genuine smile, and, suddenly, the horribleness of the last few weeks was gone. It was Lucas again, the Lucas that I had brained at Starbucks, the Lucas that had called in a favor to the police station so I didn't get arrested for stealing documents, the Lucas that had saved me from being mowed down by an SUV.

I smiled, imitating him. "Because I'm not going to date my boss's son. Or my charge's brother, for that matter."

"You know that Lauren thinks we like each other."

"I've heard," I responded dryly. I was going to kill Lauren for saying something to him. "However, Lauren also thinks there's still hope for Brad and Jen, so don't judge me for not taking her word as testament."

Lucas grinned even wider and said, "You want to make a bet? I bet by the time Lauren graduates in three years and your services are no longer needed, you and I will have gone out. I would raise the bet that you and I will be together, but I don't want to jinx that."

I shook my head. "Why would you bet on something you'll never win?"

Lucas shrugged, the glint in his eyes gleaming under the dim kitchen light. "I'm an optimist."